SURROUNDED BY DARKNESS

RACHEL DYLAN

COPYRIGHT

This book is licensed to you for your personal enjoyment only.

NYLA Publishing
121 W 27th St., Suite 1201, New York, NY 10001
http://www.nyliterary.com

SURROUNDED BY DARKNESS

"Submit yourselves therefore to God. Resist the devil, and he will flee from you."
James 4:7

ACKNOWLEDGMENTS

Leslie L. McKee—thank you for your exceptional editing. You are a joy to work with on these books.

Thank you to all the wonderful members of Rachel's Justice League. Your continued support means so much to me.

As always, many thanks to my agent Sarah Younger and the Nancy Yost Literary Agency. Sarah—you let me spread my wings, and it's so amazing to continue this writing journey with you.

Mama—I love you. You're the biggest fan of this series, and I can't thank you enough for your love and support.

CHAPTER ONE

"Is the defense ready to call your next witness?" Judge Gonzalez asked.

"Yes, Your Honor." The high-priced defense counsel rose from his chair and buttoned his navy suit jacket. Layton Alito had hired one of the best criminal lawyers in the state of Illinois.

Olivia Murray sucked in a breath as she sat in the courtroom clenching her fists. She wasn't used to this spectator role, and it wasn't one she liked. It had been over six months since Nina Marie had been brutally attacked and left for dead by Layton Alito. And now it was time for Layton to be held accountable by the justice system, but things weren't going as planned.

As Olivia looked over at Nina Marie's pale cheeks, she wondered if her friend would be strong enough to get through the rest of the trial. She couldn't even imagine the psychological toll this was taking on her, but Nina Marie refused to back down, even if she was much weaker than ever before.

"The defense calls the Honorable Louise Martinique to the stand."

Murmurs sounded throughout the courtroom at the mention of calling a sitting judge to the witness stand. Given how discovery worked in criminal cases, the prosecution didn't have the benefit of knowing what Louise would testify to. But Olivia had a sick feeling in the pit of her stomach and knew it wasn't going to be anything that could help the prosecution.

While it wasn't public knowledge, Louise was aligned with Layton and his New Age group called Optimism.

Looking at Louise, though, you'd never think that. Her long gray hair was pulled back in a low bun. Of course, she didn't have on her judge's robe, but her occupation was going to be presented very clearly to the jury. She was playing the role of a friendly grandmother perfectly today, and that concerned Olivia greatly.

Louise was sworn in and took her seat in the witness box.

"Ms. Martinique," the defense lawyer started, "for the purposes of today's trial, I'll refer to you as Ms. Martinique, is that all right with you?"

Louise gave him a warm smile. "Of course."

The lawyer took a step toward the jury. "But just to be clear so the jury understands a bit about you, you are a sitting judge. That's your job, correct?"

Louise nodded. "Yes, sir, I am, but today I'm here purely in my personal capacity, not as a judge."

The lawyer glanced back at his notes and then continued. "Thank you again for your time, and I'll do my best to get through this quickly, but as you can imagine the allegations against my client here are quite serious. Let's get right to it. How do you know Mr. Layton Alito?"

"Mr. Alito and I have known each other for years—probably around ten or so. I met him because of my charity work in the community and service on various boards."

"What type of boards?" the lawyer asked.

"The one I work with him the most on is for Optimism's nonprofit division."

Defense counsel nodded. "In all the years that you've known him, what can you say about his reputation?"

"Objection, Your Honor," the prosecutor said. "I'm not sure how general reputational testimony is relevant at this point."

The defense lawyer turned and looked at the jury. "It's actually highly relevant. We have an esteemed member of the community here to talk about her relationship and knowledge of Mr. Alito and what type of man he is. Given the nature of the charges against him, the jury should be permitted to hear that."

"I tend to agree," the judge said. "Objection overruled."

Olivia wasn't shocked in the least about the judge's ruling. She was actually surprised the prosecutor made the objection, but she knew second-guessing and playing armchair quarterback wasn't the best thing for her to do at this point, even though it was incredibly difficult for her to stay quiet. She tried to settle in and figure out what the defense lawyer's play was. Louise's testimony about Layton's character may have some weight, but it wouldn't determine the entire case.

The attorney turned his attention back to Louise. "You may go ahead and answer the question."

Louise took a breath. "I've known Mr. Alito to be a man of great integrity. He is highly generous with his time and financial contributions to the community. The nonprofit we work on together has been instrumental in preparing people to go back into the workplace after periods of unemployment. We've been able to make a positive and tangible impact on people's lives."

"And in the time that you have known Mr. Alito, have you ever had any concerns about him being a violent person?"

Louise shook her head. "Absolutely not. Just the opposite. I've known him to be a kind and gentle man, slow to anger, with a very good head on his shoulders."

Hearing those words almost made Olivia sick because she knew the true Layton Alito. The man was ruthless, conniving, and extremely violent. But even more important than all those things, he was directly tied to evil. He sold his soul a long time ago and was proud of it. Olivia knew all too well what he was capable of. She was certain his supernatural activities would not be on display today in courtroom. Very few people knew what his company really stood for.

Olivia took a moment and surveyed the courtroom. It was such a shame Stacey Malone was sitting there on the defense side rooting for Layton. She'd been seduced by everything Layton could provide her, including what she believed was her freedom but was actually her captivity. The college student had probably just started to learn what Layton was all about, and Olivia could only hope and pray that one day Stacey would change her mind and leave that type of life. Pushing those thoughts aside, Olivia focused back on the issue at hand and Louise's testimony.

"I don't want to waste anyone's time, so I'll get right to the bottom line. Ms. Martinique, do you know where you were on the night of February the twentieth?"

Louise nodded. "Why yes, I do."

"And can you please tell the jury your whereabouts that night?" the lawyer asked.

"I was having dinner at my home with Mr. Alito."

"And when did Mr. Alito leave your house that evening?"

Louise glanced over at the jury. "It was probably around 11 p.m. We had a late dinner because we were working on various budget issues for the annual board meeting."

The defense lawyer took a step forward. "And do you recall what time Mr. Alito arrived at your home that night?"

"I believe it was around six p.m. We had quite a bit of work to do so we got to it. We took a break for dinner before finishing up."

"And you're sure about the date of this dinner meeting you had with Mr. Alito?"

"Yes, and we don't have to just rely on my memory. It's in my calendar."

"Your Honor, I'd like to enter that page from Ms. Martinique's desk calendar into evidence." The defense attorney walked over and provided a copy to the prosecutor and then approached the bench after asking for permission.

"Any objection?" the judge asked.

"No, Your Honor," the prosecutor responded.

Olivia figured the judge was almost certainly going to let in anything Louise said was in her calendar. They spent a minute authenticating the document, and it was introduced into evidence. The defense wrapped up his questions, and the prosecutor would now get his chance.

Olivia so wished she could be the one conducting the cross-examination. She'd tried her best to convince the prosecutor that there were forces of evil at work in the midst of this seemingly regular case, but the prosecutor had given her the brush off. He didn't believe in any of this and thought Olivia was a bit crazy— well, more than a bit crazy. Absolutely crazy and he had said as much. The cross-examination wasn't going to be as effective as it could've been.

She glanced over and saw Nina Marie's boyfriend Abe Perez squeeze her hand. Not only had Nina Marie almost been killed by Layton, now she had to live in fear that he would come back and try to finish the job. Thankfully, Abe was sticking close to make sure that didn't happen.

Olivia took a deep, steadying breath before the prosecutor jumped into his questioning.

He cleared his throat and approached the witness. It occurred to Olivia this prosecutor most likely knew Louise. That couldn't be a good thing because he wouldn't want to rock the boat with a judge he would have to be in front of again in his career. This was all going downhill quickly.

"Ms. Martinique, I appreciate your time today."

Already highly deferential.

"You're more than welcome," Louise responded.

"I looked closely at your calendar, and it appears you do keep a very meticulous record. But what would you say about the eyewitness testimony from the victim in this case? She did identify Mr. Alito as the man who attacked and tried to kill her."

Louise didn't look at the prosecutor. No, she was far too seasoned for that. She put on her best grandma face and looked directly at the jurors. "I know all too well about false identifications in my line of work. Eyewitness testimony, especially after a terrible trauma, is notoriously unreliable."

That question had opened the door to a harmful response and let Louise set up the stage perfectly to make her point.

"So, you aren't calling Ms. Crane a liar?"

Louise's eyes widened in feigned disbelief. "Of course not. My heart goes out to her for what she suffered, but I also don't want an innocent man to go to jail over this."

"And it's still your contention that Mr. Alito was with you that night?"

"Absolutely."

Olivia shifted in her seat. This was beginning to sound like a second direct exam instead of a cross-examination. The prosecutor wasn't getting anywhere and was just solidifying her already strong testimony. If things kept going like this, there was no doubt in her mind Layton would walk out of the courtroom a free man.

A sense of powerlessness washed over her. *Lord, is this really your plan? That Layton would go free?* Olivia had learned the hard way that things in Windy Ridge weren't always surface level. There was so much spiritual activity in the town with the two big New Age groups that had thriving front companies. She had to remember there was a larger picture here, and Layton was only one piece of it —albeit a very evil one.

A chill shot down her arms as she looked at Nina Marie who turned even more pale. Olivia couldn't help but glance over at Stacey and her friend Morena. There was something sinister happening in the courtroom, and Olivia couldn't get out of there fast enough.

––––––

GRANT BAXTER STOOD outside the courtroom door waiting for them to recess. He could've slipped in, but he'd had a crummy day

—one of the worst he'd had in a while. He needed a few moments to lick his wounds.

He just had a settlement blow up that he'd been working on for months. No one was happy about it, but that was the nature of the business. As a plaintiff's lawyer, he liked to think he was fighting the good fight, but some days there were no winners, just losers. And today felt like one of those days.

Grant hoped things were going better for his girlfriend Olivia, who was a spectator in Layton's trial. It was hard for him to even fathom that only a year ago he had actually represented Layton's company, Optimism. He'd been a career-driven, single skeptic with no plans to settle down or alter his lifestyle. It had all been about him and what he wanted.

Once he met Olivia, all of that changed. Now he was a different man, but he still had struggles, including how he could ever be a good enough man for the woman he truly loved. As those thoughts flitted through his mind, a young guy came up to him with an envelope in hand.

"Are you Grant Baxter?" the man asked.

"Yeah, that's me," Grant responded.

The guy handed him the manila envelope. "You've been served."

Grant assumed this had to do with one of his cases. He tore open the envelope and had to hold back language that used to flow freely from his mouth. This was about one of his cases, but not in the way he thought.

I'm being sued for malpractice.

Before he could fully soak in the reality of the situation, the courtroom doors opened and people started milling out. It wasn't long before he saw Olivia, Nina Marie, and Abe making their way toward him. He couldn't deal with the reality of the malpractice suit right now. Especially not in front of all of them. He'd wait until he was alone with Olivia.

"What's going on?" Grant asked them.

Olivia's pretty brown eyes locked in on him. "We're done. It's in the hands of the jury now."

"I take it from the frowns all around that it didn't go well." Just what he needed. More negativity.

Abe shook his head, and Nina Marie looked off into the distance. She didn't look good. She was already a thin woman before the attack, and she'd lost even more weight over the past few months. Her auburn hair no longer had its luster and fell limply past her shoulders. He felt sorry for everything she had gone through. Yeah, she used to be on the wrong side of the fence, but so had he. He only felt empathy for her right now.

"The prosecutor wasn't good," Olivia added. "He basically let Louise tell her story a second time. I don't have high hopes for a conviction. I think he'll walk."

"No one believes me," Nina Marie said quietly.

Olivia reached out and wrapped her arm around Nina Marie. "It's not like that. We've got a sitting judge who took the stand and lied, but the jury doesn't know what we all know, and the prosecutor didn't have the guts to try to go toe to toe with her."

"I know you wished it could've been you up there." Grant had no doubt Olivia would've done an amazing job. She was one of the most talented attorneys he knew, and he didn't just think that because he had fallen for her. He'd been on the opposing side of her when they had first met and seen firsthand what a worthy adversary she was.

"Layton always wins. That's the moral to this story," Nina Marie said.

"Remember, this isn't the final battle. He will be defeated. If not now, eventually," Olivia said.

Grant wasn't as optimistic as Olivia, but he admired her tenacity. The events in Windy Ridge had taken a great toll on his life over the past year. He was trying to take it one day at a time.

Since it was almost the end of the day, the jury would probably get their deliberations fully going in the morning. They told Abe and Nina Marie goodbye, and then he and Olivia headed out of the courthouse.

"Something's wrong with you," Olivia said. "I can tell."

They walked through the turnstiles out the front door into the warm, summer air. He dreaded telling her this on top of everything else that was on her shoulders, but they were a team and made a promise to each other not to have secrets. "You're right."

"Is it your settlement?" Olivia asked.

"Well, yes, that blew up too, but there's more. Let's get to the car."

They made their way to the parking garage and into his Jeep. He started the Wrangler and then looked over at her before he put it in reverse. "While waiting for you to finish up in court, I got served with a malpractice suit."

"What?" Olivia's voice was uncharacteristically loud. "For what?"

He started to drive and told her what he knew, which wasn't much. "It's for a case where the jury found against my client and for the company. The complaint was sparse, but they're basically saying I was negligent."

She reached over and placed her hand on his arm. "I know you, Grant. You're a very diligent lawyer. There's no way you were negligent."

He only wished he were as confident as her, but he didn't want to show weakness right now. "I don't think so either. I've got insurance, but this is going to be a big thorn in my side."

"You know I'll do anything to help you. I'd offer to represent you myself, but I know your insurance carrier would flip over that."

"And you can't be objective."

Olivia smiled. "Probably not, but I'd fight to the end to defend your good name."

"I know you would and then some. Let's take it one step at a time. I'll call my insurance company and go from there."

"All right, but if the lawyer they assign isn't up to snuff, I'll be there in a heartbeat."

He gripped the steering wheel. "This has been a completely rotten day. Maybe I should drop you off at your place. I know we'd talked about dinner, but I think I'd be lousy company."

She didn't immediately respond.

"I can practically hear you thinking, Olivia."

"Don't try to push me away, Grant."

"I'm not, but I want to wallow a little bit and don't want to subject you to that."

"I'm in for all sides of you, not just the good days."

Now it was his turn to smile. Leave it to Olivia to know the exact right thing to say. "I don't deserve you."

"We'll tackle this like we do everything else. Together."

———

BEN AND MICAH exchanged glances as they hovered over the white Wrangler as it pulled into Olivia's driveway. The angels kept close tabs on Olivia and Grant because the spiritual battle that had started when Olivia stepped foot into Windy Ridge still raged on as strong as ever. The levels of occult activity had only increased in the past year.

Yes, they'd had some victories, but the forces of darkness were bound and determined to go after this power couple. It was up to Ben and Micah to help protect them.

"Grant's struggling," Ben said. "And this latest blow isn't helping."

"It's because Othan and his demon cohorts are sticking way too close and nagging him to death. This lawsuit is probably their doing too. They have their ways of putting ideas into people's heads."

Ben nodded. "Don't I know it."

"We have to be prepared for Layton to be released, and then he'll be on a warpath too."

"Yes, he will," a loud booming voice interrupted them.

They had an unwelcome visitor—Othan, the lead demon in Windy Ridge.

Micah floated forward. "Othan, you have no place at Olivia's house. Get out of here."

Othan laughed, his eyes sparkling brightly. "I can go anywhere I want on this earth, and you and I both know that. Those tactics won't work with me."

"Where's your minion? Did he not make the cut?" Ben asked.

"I'm working solo tonight but don't worry. There's plenty of us around, and all I have to do is say the word and I'll have reinforcements."

"What, are you afraid of two angels?" Micah asked.

"Hardly," Othan responded. "With Layton soon to be back in business with his name cleared, the tide is definitely turning our way."

"That still doesn't explain why you're here at Olivia's tonight," Ben said.

Othan turned toward Ben. "Because Grant's doubts are letting me in. He's opened a door, and the two of you are too blind to see the truth."

Before they could respond, Othan vanished.

"I don't like the sound of that," Micah said.

"Me either. They both need our prayers, but we must be extra vigilant with Grant. We can't lose him."

That would be a disaster.

CHAPTER TWO

Nina Marie took a deep breath as she walked into Windy Ridge Community Church. She was there today to meet with Pastor Dan Light. After being wrongly accused of embezzling, it would've been easy and understandable for Pastor Dan to pack up and leave. Since his wife died there was nothing tying him to this community, but Nina Marie had learned that wasn't the type of man Pastor Dan was. He wouldn't tuck his tail and run.

Nina Marie stopped for a moment and thought about how her life had changed so much over the past year. She had once been the CEO and spiritual leader of Astral Tech—a thriving New Age tech company. A woman who had actively and openly practiced witchcraft and the dark arts.

But the Lord had worked as only He could, and now she was a believer. Even with the changes in her life, she still needed a lot of help. She'd had multiple counseling sessions with Pastor Dan, but her pain ran deep. It was to be expected that someone who had lived in the darkness for so long would have many struggles in trying to live her new life. She had a solid net of people around her to help, and Dan wanted to make sure he did his part—not just as her pastor, but also as a friend.

Nina Marie walked into his office a few minutes later. Today she'd chosen to wear a simple ivory blouse and black pants with a strand of pearls. She adjusted her horn-rimmed glasses before she gave Pastor Dan a quick embrace. Then she sat in one of the chairs.

"I heard about the trial." Dan's light blue eyes focused in on her.

Nina Marie nodded. "Yeah. I think I've come to terms with the fact that Layton will walk. I don't know what that means for me. Will I always be looking over my shoulder? I don't think he's going to let it go. To let me go. He's a vindictive man with a very long memory."

"You've already been spared once, Nina Marie, against all the odds. I believe with all my heart that God has a bigger plan for you. You didn't die that night for a reason. I think you should pour your energy into getting completely well and then see where the Lord wants to take you."

She clasped her hands together in her lap. "I've thought about it and wondered why God would've allowed me to live after all the heinous things I've done in my life. The pain I've caused others and intentionally inflicted..."

"That's the beauty of your testimony, Nina Marie. The power of God can transcend even the darkest of hearts."

Nina Marie stood and walked over to the window. "I'm not the same person. Not even close." She paused. "There's something else we haven't talked about that's been weighing on me."

"Please, whatever it is, you can tell me." He urged her to continue.

When they'd first started their counseling sessions, it was tough for Nina Marie to open up to him given their rocky history and her previous spiritual activities, but over the past few weeks, she'd gotten more comfortable. Still standing by the window, she turned to face him. "You may think I'm crazy."

Dan shook his head. "No, don't say that. I'm here to listen to whatever is on your mind."

She took a breath. How could she try to explain this to him? "After Layton stabbed me and I was lying there in my house, certain I was going to die, I started going in and out of consciousness."

He tilted his head. "That's completely normal given the circumstances."

She nodded. "Yes, and while I was in and out, I saw things."

"Like a dream?" he asked.

"Yes, but it was even clearer than a regular dream. It was like I was seeing it and experiencing it at the same time."

"What happened?"

"It was a battle. Right here in Windy Ridge. I don't think I survived." She paused. "I don't think anyone did. It was just death all around." Her voice shook as she spoke.

Dan rose from his chair and walked over to her. "Nina Marie, that type of dream would be awful for anyone. I'm not discounting it at all, but we have to consider that it really was a dream or hallucination as you lost consciousness."

"And what if it wasn't? What if it was a vision of things to come?" Her voice trembled.

He reached out and placed his hand on her shoulder. "God will protect us. Do you believe that?"

She took a step back and turned toward the window. "I hope so, but I know I can't get it out of my head."

"Has it occurred to you this is just one of the evil schemes Satan is using to try to bring you down and get you on a detour? He plants those seeds of fear and anguish and tries to get them to grow."

Nina Marie faced him again. "That's a good point, and it's completely rational. I used to think I was a logical person, but reason doesn't work for me anymore. I'm having these visceral experiences, and I can't deny them."

Dan nodded. "Then we'll both pray about it. I'll make sure I'm specifically praying for you. God can give you peace, Nina Marie, even in the midst of the darkness."

She didn't feel entirely convinced, but she gave him a slight nod.

"How's Abe doing?" he asked.

She smiled. "Abe is my rock. Out of this awful mess has come something good. He's different than all the other men I've ever had in my life. I literally wouldn't be alive if he hadn't found me, and I'm still alive because he's in my life. Each day he supports me and pushes me to move forward and not dwell in the past."

"God has a way of bringing people into our lives at the exact right time." Dan took a breath. "I do think it might be helpful for you to attend services a bit more regularly. I see Abe here all the time, but he's alone."

Nina Marie blew out a breath. "I figured you were going to mention that at some point."

"What's your hesitation? I can sense it. What's holding you back?"

She bit her bottom lip. "People in this town know me. They know what I've done. I can't help feeling like right when I walk into service, people will start chattering about the witch who was almost killed and then found Jesus." Nina Marie paused. "I don't like the attention and people talking about me and being put under a microscope."

"Here's the thing, we all have a past. Every single person in this church has made mistakes, has sinned, has done things they are ashamed of—myself included. You shouldn't feel like you're any different. Yes, you are a bit more high profile, but my experience is that people tire of the chatter quickly and will move onto some-thing else or someone else. Don't deprive yourself because you're worried about what others will say. There's only one opinion that matters in the end."

She looked up at him feeling the tears coming on. "I can only hope that's true, because if it's not, there's still a place in Hell for me."

Dan placed both his hands on her shoulders. "No. There is no longer a place there for you. You're a child of God, now, Nina Marie, and nothing can change that. Do you understand me?"

"You really believe that God's grace goes that far?" she asked expectantly.

"Absolutely. You may have your doubts, but God doesn't."

She gave him a small smile. "If you think that it would be okay, then I'll be here on Sunday."

"We'll be waiting with open arms."

———

STACEY MALONE STARED at her calculus notebook, but her mind wasn't on her college homework. It was on the fact that Layton had been found not guilty by the jury. It didn't come as a surprise to her as she had sat in the courtroom for most of the trial and had been able to get a good feel for the jurors and their reactions to the testimony.

Stacey knew Layton didn't have to resort to witchcraft to be able to get the verdict they wanted. She wasn't naïve anymore—her eyes were wide open. Layton had tried to kill Nina Marie, and the woman had deserved it. She had turned her back on everything they had fought for in Windy Ridge.

In her mind, Nina Marie was the worst kind of traitor. It was inconceivable to Stacey to think that a woman with so much power and promise could have gone over to the church. Now Nina Marie called herself a so-called believer.

Stacey had been there once herself, a prisoner of the church, and it only brought her pain and confusion. They were always putting constraints on her and telling her how to live. But now with her newfound freedom, she was stronger and more determined than ever to make her mark on this world. Life was too short to live with regrets.

When there was a knock at her apartment door, she set down her notebook and went to answer it. She looked through the peephole and saw her friend and mentor Morena Isley on the other side. She opened the door and Morena stepped inside. The pretty, curly haired blonde didn't look like a practitioner of the dark arts, but she definitely was. Morena had not only been a teacher but a great friend to Stacey, but Stacey realized she was advancing so quickly that she had overtaken Morena in the spiritual arena.

"Isn't the news about Layton wonderful?" Morena's light blue eyes sparkled.

Stacey nodded. "Yeah, but I wasn't that concerned. I didn't think the jury would find him guilty because there were way too many holes in the prosecution's story. Of course, it helped that we had Louise on our side. She had the jurors eating out of the palm of her hand." The move to bring in Louise had been absolutely brilliant, and probably orchestrated by Layton. He had such a strategic mind, especially when it came to legal entanglements.

"I thought we might go out and celebrate," Morena said.

"Aww. I would love to, but I'm trying to get through some calculus homework. Although it's days like these that I regret taking this one summer course." Yes, Stacey might have a lot of interest in partying, but at the end of the day, she still wanted to be a strong businesswoman in her own right. And that meant not having to rely on Layton or Morena for anything.

Stacey appreciated the internship she currently had, and the offer for full-time employment, but she needed to keep her options open. Layton had taught her a lot—and he was the best. But his self-interested model was something she was trying to imitate for her own benefit. She also had a call scheduled later that night with a New Age practitioner in California who was going to share some of her teachings. Stacey hadn't told anyone, but she had started to go out on her own to learn more areas of the dark arts. She had a bigger plan at work.

Morena punched her arm playfully. "You're always diligent. You know there is such a thing as trying to have fun. Especially at this point in your life before you get too old."

Stacey laughed loudly. "I think I can do it all."

"Spoken like a true millennial." Morena smiled widely. "So, on another topic, what do you think is going to happen to Nina Marie?"

Stacey had given that a bit of thought. "I don't know. Layton isn't one to let things go, but he might be over it at this point and ready to move on to bigger and better things. I would not want to be Nina Marie. I'd be sleeping with one eye open."

"If she hadn't sold out on us, I'd almost feel sorry for her."

Stacey had once admired the woman. "She looks awful. Not anything like the person I used to know, but I will tell you that her boyfriend is one hottie."

Morena raised an eyebrow. "Yeah, I noticed that too. I guess he's a private investigator. What he sees in her at this point, I'm not sure. Nina Marie has fallen so far, and I don't even know what she's going to do with her life from here on out." Morena paused. "But she isn't our problem anymore."

Stacey fully agreed with that. "I'm ready for the next step and to see where Layton is going to take Optimism. I know he said he had some new ideas before trial started, but we haven't had a chance to discuss anything. Now that it'll all be over, we'll be able to decide the direction of the group, especially now that Nina Marie will almost certainly be completely out of the picture. Astral Tech as a company will struggle and probably collapse. Although we could probably recruit people from there who we want to cherry-pick and bring into our fold."

"Stacey, you are wise beyond your years. Are you sure I can't convince you to come out?"

Stacey shook her head. "As much as I'd like to, I really should hit the books."

"Understood. I won't pressure you. We can catch up later. I'll let myself out."

Stacey heard the door shut, and she couldn't help but wonder what her future would hold. She was going to be a new type of practitioner of the dark arts—not old school like Layton. She would make her own way and use her skills and gifts in the way she wanted. If one day she would take on Layton himself, then so be it. And that meant she had a lot of work to do.

———

Layton Alito sat in his dining room waiting on the arrival of his guests. He was hosting a dinner party not only to celebrate the verdict and exoneration, but the plan for what was next for Optimism. His company was a thriving business that focused on a broad range of New Age products and activities, but the other side of Optimism wasn't just a business—it was a spiritual lifestyle. He was selling not only products but a way of life, and people in Windy Ridge were buying and buying big.

He had built the company over the past eleven years. He'd taken over once the original founder passed, but he'd made it *his* company and was bound and determined to see it thrive. But even more than the financial statements, he measured his success by how many people he could bring over to his way of life.

Optimism, the company, had products that were bestsellers—crystals, meditation devices, divination tools, incense, oils, and herbs all under his brand. Optimism products were in New Age stores, yoga studies, and wellness retreats throughout the country. The Optimism brand was strong and well-known in the New Age community.

Their products helped open the door to the masses to be exposed to New Age principles and lifestyle. It was the perfect gateway to his real endgame—which was a lot more than incense and meditation. Those were the stereotypes, but it went far beyond that for him.

The entire murder investigation and trial had thrown him for a loop. He never should have left Nina Marie's house without making sure she was dead. It was his own pride and his disdain for her, wanting her to die slowly and painfully, that had him in the spot he was in now.

He had to smirk to himself, though, because it all had worked out wonderfully. He never could've predicted the end to this story. Nina Marie had been one of the most powerful and confident people he'd ever known. A vibrant and energetic woman. Seeing what she had now become, a shriveled-up prune—meek, defeated, and, best of all, no longer any threat to him—was the biggest payoff. Watching her live like that was almost worth all the headache and drama he'd been subjected to. He was once again a free man, and it was a no brainer for him that he'd come out on top with this thing.

Layton was going to take Nina Marie's former company Astral Tech apart piece by piece and handpick those he wanted and discard the others. Then he could finally get back to his original plan of the spiritual transformation of Windy Ridge, taking down Pastor Dan and, even more importantly, his nemesis Olivia Murray. The lawyer stood to thwart him at every single turn, and now that she had taken up permanent residence in his town, he was committed to action.

The doorbell rang, and he eagerly greeted his first guests. About an hour later, the formal dining area was filled with laughter, fine wine, and a five-star meal, and he was surrounded by his close circle of friends.

Later in the evening as dessert was about to be served, it was time for him to speak to his guests. He stood up from his chair and surveyed the room, making eye contact with Morena, Louise, and some other members.

"I'd like to take a moment to thank you all for the support you gave me during this difficult time. But even more than that, I don't want to look at the past, but I want us to figure out our wonderful future together. The church is definitely weakened, and with our chief competitor in shambles, this city is ours for the taking." He lifted his glass of champagne. "Cheers."

As the toast ended, he took a seat, but he still had matters to discuss with the group. "While this is a night of celebration, there are a few things to talk about. We have to be smarter though about how we handle matters. I'm talking to myself as much as I'm talking to you."

Louise nodded. "You're right, Layton. This whole fiasco was a bit too high-profile for my taste. I helped get you out of this one, but I can't play that card again. We need to focus on where our strengths are—the spiritual realm and what we have to offer. Taking physical action is not going to be the best way to get to our end result. And obviously, it's quite messy."

His protégé Stacey took a sip of wine before speaking. "On that note, I'd like to add something if I could."

Layton was proud of her. She'd come so far in such a short time. "Of course, Stacey. The floor is yours."

She tucked a long strand of strawberry blonde hair behind her ear. "I have an opportunity I found out about that I'd like to share with the group. I've been doing a lot of thinking on how I could expand my skill set and ways we all could do more learning and growing in the arts we practice. I found out about this conference that takes place in Las Vegas. It's one of the largest New Age and Wiccan-based conferences in the whole country. I think it would be great if a few of us could go as a group and then bring back the learning to the entire Optimism family." Stacey's face lit up as she spoke.

"That's a wonderful idea," Layton said. He thought to himself for a moment and was even more proud of how Stacey was taking the bull by the horns and coming up with ideas about how she could develop her skills. "When is the conference?"

"It's not until the later this year, but registration fills up quickly. I'd love for us to be able to go."

Morena cleared her throat "I agree with Stacey. I'm sure we have funding in the budget. What better place than Vegas to really explore. I'm all in."

Layton was thrilled to see their enthusiasm had not subsided while he had been preoccupied with legal matters. "Then it's settled. The ones who would like to go and are able, Optimism will cover the costs." Layton adjusted his cufflinks before continuing.

"Please, Stacey, can you take the lead on this? And have everyone coordinate with you."

"Of course."

Layton cleared his throat. "Now there's a bit of an elephant in the room." Layton surveyed the faces of his dinner guests. "At this point, my directive is not to bother with Nina Marie. That witch has taken enough of our time, energy, and effort. She's no longer a threat to any of us. We need to look forward and decide what our next initiatives are going to be for the community. I'm happy to hear any thoughts the group may have on that."

Morena took the floor. "I think we have to focus on recruitment and keeping our numbers strong. Also, we need to get deeper into our own abilities and be willing to use them. Like you said, this criminal matter was a waste of time, and our strength comes from what we can do. What powers of darkness we can bring to this place. The church hasn't fully recovered from the scandal with Pastor Dan, but it's like a dying cockroach, kicking its little scrawny legs, but it won't ever completely die."

That statement got some affirmative murmurs throughout the room.

"We also have to keep an eye out for that lawyer," Louise added. "Olivia Murray is not to be taken lightly. I have no idea what her next mission is going to be, but it appears she will be around here for the long term, and we need to figure out how to handle her. We don't need her messing around in our business."

Stacey looked up at Layton. "Do you really think Olivia is going to care that much about us right now? Doesn't she have her work and career to build? I know if I was in her position at the law firm, I'd be more focused on my career than trying to fight some spiritual battle. I think that's what we should exploit. Let's target her ego and ambition to keep her busy with legal work so she doesn't have time to bother us."

"Speaking of legal work," Louise said, "I have some news that would be of interest to all of you." A sly smile spread across Louise's thin pink lips.

"Well don't make us wait too long," Layton said. Louise wasn't one for much theatrics, so her words had piqued his interest.

"You all will remember our friend Grant Baxter. Olivia's partner in crime. Well, I heard through the grapevine that a malpractice suit has been filed against him. This could be big. A suit like that could close his firm down for good."

Layton's mind started to run wild. It wasn't long ago that Grant had been Optimism's attorney facing off against Olivia in a battle over the Astral Tech app. The case was long since settled, but this nugget did provide him with some level of delight. At first, Grant had been benign. A complete skeptic who was perfectly fine to work with, but then Olivia had gotten into his head and turned him into a believer. And now he was a threat. "This is very interesting news, Louise. We need to figure out how we can help along this lawsuit. Can someone take on the task of digging into the suit to figure out who is involved and what the story is?"

Stacey eagerly raised her hand. "I'd be happy to. Especially if Louise will lend me her expertise."

Louise nodded. "Of course. It will be a pleasure to work with you. I think it would be a good experience for both of us."

Layton felt a flood of energy rush through him. This could be what they needed as a group to provide him a kick-starter. Making Grant feel the pain would be one of the best ways to get to Olivia. Because one thing Layton had figured out was that the two of them were no longer just friends—they had become much more than that. And he was going to use that to his strategic advantage. He needed to develop a plan to bring down Olivia Murray once and for all.

CHAPTER THREE

The next day Grant sat in a large conference room at his law office across the table from Scott O'Brien—his lawyer appointed by the insurance company.

"Let's start at the beginning." Scott's hazel eyes focused in on him.

Grant would've felt much better with someone more seasoned. Scott had only been practicing law for five years, but given Grant's malpractice insurance, he didn't have much of a choice. The insurance company picked the lawyer, and he didn't have any say in it.

"The complaint alleges a few things." Scott flipped through his notes. "Why don't you give me some case background?"

"Certainly." Grant had only had sleepless nights since this case had been filed. They'd waited until the final week before the two-year statute of limitations had run. But once he saw the name on the complaint, there was an immediate fear that struck into the pit of his stomach. He hadn't told anyone about his fears, including Olivia. "This was one of my early cases I worked on after having started The Baxter Group. Obviously, I lost, or I wouldn't be sitting here with you right now."

"Tell me more." Scott leaned in with pen and legal pad in hand.

"I told Leslie Ramos that this would be a hard case, but I took it on anyway. I was looking for clients, and in plaintiff's work we operate on a contingency fee basis anyway, so it made sense."

"And the nature of the claim?" Scott asked.

"It was supposed to be a simple slip and fall case. Ms. Ramos fell in the store while shopping, but in the discovery process, I found documents from the store about a completely unrelated matter regarding the company's financial reporting. I couldn't help myself—I started going down that rabbit hole." The memories flooded back to him as he spoke. He had been so excited about the prospect of breaking a huge case wide open.

"And the complaint alleges you didn't give Ms. Ramos's case the time it deserved. That you were negligent in the discovery phase and weren't able to get certain key evidence in at trial. She's saying that cost her the case and millions in damages."

Grant blew out a breath. "I have to be honest with you because you're my attorney."

Scott leaned in. "Yes, I need to hear the good, the bad, and the ugly."

Grant figured Scott should hear the truth. That would give him the best chance at beating this thing. "I was distracted. I was trying to prove myself, grow my practice. When I found those other documents that, at the time, I believed could be the tip of the iceberg for a much larger case, I let it dominate my attention."

"And did something bigger come of it?"

Grant shook his head. "No. At the end of the day, once I got all the documents, I realized that the company was clean. There was nothing to report to the SEC or any government agency. It was basically a wild goose chase and a waste of time with no payoff."

"And did you shirk your professional duty to Ms. Ramos?"

Grant considered Scott's question. "No. I don't think I did. Was I distracted? Yes, but I still put my time in on her case. I prepared for trial."

"I don't know how familiar you are with the elements of a malpractice case." Scott looked at him.

"I think I know them generally but refresh me to make sure we're on the same page." Thankfully, this wasn't something Grant had actually dealt with before in his legal practice.

"The key elements in dispute here are whether you breached your duty to the client and whether there is proximate cause—did that breach directly cause harm to the client, that is, causing her to lose the lawsuit she should've otherwise won."

"Yeah, I get all that." It was straightforward enough.

Scott tapped his pen on the desk. "The important question is whether the mistakes you made during discovery and at trial rose to the level of malpractice. We need to go through the errors identified in the complaint."

And that's what scared him, because he knew he did make mistakes on that case. "I'm ready." Time to face the music.

Scott held up the page and started reading. "The complaint states that you failed to depose a key witness who was an employee at the store. Is that accurate?"

"I was really slammed at that point, and I missed it. I thought I had all the possible deponents covered. It was an innocent mistake." Grant could hear the uncertainty in his own voice.

Scott opened up his laptop and started typing. "So, you did conduct other depositions, just not the one for a Mr. Sanders, who was one of the store clerks at the scene, is that correct?"

"Yes." Now Grant felt like he was the one being deposed. Scott was all business.

"The next point is that you failed to enter one of the doctor's reports into evidence, is that right?"

Hearing it all come out of Scott's mouth made it seem even worse. "Yes, but there were multiple reports from various doctors. This was just one of them. One of many reports."

"They're arguing it was an important one." Scott kept typing. "Ms. Ramos suffered serious injuries—the most important being a broken neck and vertebrae."

"Yes, I recall that clearly." How could he forget that?

"She's claiming she could've been entitled to a two-million-dollar verdict. What are your thoughts on that?"

"If we would've proven liability, then yes, I agree with the damage assessment based on all of her medical bills and continuing pain and suffering. But proving the initial liability on the part of the store wasn't going to be easy under any circumstances, and I was clear with her about that. The store was really buttoned up on their safety policies and procedures. There was some type of leak that had occurred because of a very bad storm just two days before. The store's attorney argued that as soon as they found the leak, they took swift action."

Scott continued to type. "But the way they found out about it was because of Ms. Ramos's accident."

"True, but it wasn't the case of something sitting around for weeks or months and not being taken care of. They do weekly inspections, and they had the records showing the inspection from the prior week was all clear, and they were also able to provide evidence about the storm timing and comparable structural damages to other buildings in the area."

Scott nodded. "Remember, I'm on your side here. I'm just trying to gather the facts." Scott placed his pen behind his ear. "We should also talk nuts and bolts. Your policy limit is one million. She's seeking two."

"What do you suggest?" Grant was truly interested in Scott's opinion here.

"I always think settlement is preferable, so I'll reach out to her attorney and try to get that conversation started and see where their heads are at."

"I should tell you something."

Scott quirked an eyebrow. "What?"

"I don't have a good feeling about this. I think they're going to want to fight."

"What makes you say that?"

"Just a gut feeling." A very deep, dark gut feeling.

"Well, good thing for you, I don't operate on feelings, but facts. Let me see what I can do and get back with you."

Scott gathered up his stuff and walked out of the conference room.

Grant put his head in his hands. *God, what I have I gotten myself into?*

Would God even answer him? Nothing seemed right in his life, and he couldn't push aside this wave of depression that was weighing him down. He was trying to do his best to put on a brave face, but this case scared him to death. This could be the end to his legal career.

———

OLIVIA SAT in her office in the Brown, Carter, and Reed high-rise in the city. She'd talked to Grant earlier, and he didn't seem like himself. The lawsuit was taking a toll on him, but she also felt a bit helpless about what she could do to help.

The two of them had fallen into a nice rhythm in their relationship, but she knew times weren't always going to be easy. It seemed like they were headed into a rocky period. She wished he would open up more to her about his feelings, but he wasn't that type of guy. They'd been dating for a while now, but they hadn't had any discussions about moving their relationship forward, and it wasn't the time to push that. But she did eventually want to settle down, and she hoped he would be the one for her.

Right now, she couldn't fix things with Grant, so she had to shift her attention to work matters. She was about to have a firm-wide videoconference with the BCR pro bono committee and find out if her clinic proposal and business plan had been accepted. BCR's practice focus was on defending large corporations, but they did have a thriving pro bono program—where they offered legal services for free to those who needed it. And Olivia had built up enough capital at the firm that she was pushing hard to institute her new idea and start out with a pilot program in Windy Ridge.

She adjusted her gray suit jacket as she waited for the video-conference screen to populate and then she saw her colleagues from around the firm—including Julia Prince, the partner in charge of the pro bono program.

As the screen lit up and she saw the faces of the committee members, Olivia's heart raced with excitement. They went through introductions and preliminaries before getting to her issue. It seemed like it took forever, but it was only a few minutes.

Julia's dark eyes locked in on hers. "Olivia, let's talk about your proposal."

"Great," she said. She held her breath awaiting the response.

"The partners have discussed it, and good news. We think it's a great idea."

Olivia had to hold back a screech of joy. "That's amazing."

"We're giving you the green light to open your legal clinic there in the suburbs outside Chicago."

Olivia thought she might cry tears of joy, but she held it back because that wouldn't be professional. "I am so thankful for this opportunity."

Julia lifted up her hand. "There *is* a catch."

And just like that her balloon deflated. Wasn't there always a catch when it came to the firm? "And that is?"

"This is a pilot program. You've got six months to get it up and running. The clinic will be your full-time job. You'll be posted onsite at the clinic and only come into the BCR office as needed. After the six months, we'll do a full evaluation of the program and community impact. If you want to keep it going, we need to make sure the firm resources are being well spent and victims are getting the results they need."

"I completely understand. I'm willing to put the hard work into this to make the program a success." For Olivia, it wasn't about the metrics. It was about positively impacting the lives of women. This had been a dream laid on her heart for a long time, and it was hard to imagine it was actually about to be a reality.

"We would expect nothing but the best from you, Olivia. Get to work and keep me and Chet updated on your progress."

"Absolutely." Chet was the managing partner in the DC office of BCR where Olivia used to work. She'd been tasked with being one of the lawyers to start up the Chicago office, and it was a job she had fully embraced. The firm didn't do pro bono purely out of the goodness of their hearts. For BCR, it was all about the good publicity and high-profile programs the elite law firms wanted. It wasn't enough to be great lawyers on big cases. They needed to also be seen as committed to the community and giving back, and that's where Olivia came in.

Olivia listened attentively as the rest of the meeting took place. It was hard for her not to be thinking about her own project, but she wanted to be courteous and give everyone her full attention.

But the moment the meeting ended, she jumped out of her chair and did a victory lap around her office in excitement. *Lord, thank you for letting this happen. I really want to help people.*

She wanted to share her good news with Grant, so she walked over and dialed his number from her office phone. She stood because she was too excited to sit down.

He answered on the second ring. "Hey."

"Hey," she said. "I've got good news."

"I could use some of that," he said quietly.

She immediately knew something was wrong, and she deflated. "What's wrong?"

"The meeting with my lawyer didn't go that great."

Her heart broke for him as he gave her the high points. He told her he didn't want to share specific details because of attorney-client privilege. "I'm sorry, Grant, but remember this was the first meeting, and I'm sure the plaintiff will be interested in talking settlement. That's guaranteed money. The bar for winning on a legal malpractice suit in the state of Illinois is quite high."

Grant sighed. "I know all of that logically, but in my head, I'm a disaster. I'm also a selfish pig wallowing in my own mess. You called to tell me something. Please let me hear it."

She hoped she could do a little to brighten his day. "My clinic program proposal got approved for a six-month pilot."

"That's amazing news!" His voice filled with enthusiasm. "I am so proud of you, Olivia. You knew what you wanted to do, and you're making it happen."

"You're sweet, Grant. Thank you for all your support and input on my proposal. I couldn't have done it without you."

"Oh, yes, you could have. This was all you."

Grant had played a role and, even more importantly, been there for her emotionally as she poured her heart into figuring out the structure of the clinic. "Can we see each other tonight?" she asked expectantly.

"You sure you want to hang out with a downer?"

"I'm positive." She refused to let him shut her out. He was going through a rough time, and she feared he might retreat into his own little hole. "I'll come to your place after work, and I'll bring takeout with me." That way he couldn't bail on her.

"You're too good to me, Olivia."

She refused to let him go.

———

TRUE TO HER WORD, Olivia showed up at his place that night armed with some of their favorite Thai takeout. If anything could give him a boost, it would be a big plate of spicy noodles.

After Grant had devoured his food, they watched a movie. It was at moments like this he wished he could hit pause. He had the woman he loved next to him and everything seemed right. It was when he hit the play button, and was forced to go out into the big, bad world, that things started to go off the rails.

"Grant, are you actually watching the movie?" Olivia turned to him.

"Yeah. Why do you think I'm not?"

She placed her hand on his cheek. "Because you're staring off to the side of the TV."

He hadn't even realized he'd been doing that. He had been in his own world. "Maybe I got distracted for a bit."

"Is it the lawsuit?" she asked.

"No. Yes." He paused, struggling. "I mean, there's not a moment that goes by that the lawsuit isn't on my mind—even if it's just a nagging thought."

She leaned in and gave him a quick kiss. "It's natural to be concerned, but you shouldn't let it overtake your life. You have other work, important cases that need your attention."

"Is that it?"

"And me too." Olivia smiled.

"You're always on my mind." He'd thought about moving their relationship to the next phase, but that was before he'd gotten served those papers. If his entire legal career was going to go up in flames, how could he saddle her with that burden?

"You're doing it again. What's on your mind? Tell me."

"I want it to be over so I can get back to business as usual."

She leaned her head on his shoulder. "Nothing is ever going to be easy for us in this town, Grant. Ultimately, are you going to be okay with that? Knowing what we face in Windy Ridge."

He didn't immediately answer. "It would be much easier to leave and start over somewhere without the extreme negative influences we have here, but I've seen firsthand what's at stake. The hearts and minds of this town. I can't turn my eyes away and pretend like I don't see it. That I don't know what a danger Layton and Optimism are to this town. To the church. To you."

Olivia shifted and looked directly at him. "We have God on our side, Grant. He's stronger than Layton or any demonic influences in Windy Ridge. Our faith is what sustains us. What gives us hope for tomorrow. The promise the Lord has given us."

Her words flowed through him. She always had such a strong perspective on faith. He was the one that needed to get stronger. When he'd first found Christ last year, he'd been passionate about reading the Bible and learning and questioning. But if he was being honest with himself, for the past few months, he'd started coasting. It was easier to focus on work and the daily routine and not as much on growing his faith and tackling such weighty issues. "Sometimes it's a lot to deal with on a daily basis. Maybe you don't feel that way, but it is for me." There, he'd said it. Put it out on the table.

She tilted her head and a strand of dark hair fell across her shoulders. "Grant, I struggle too. I think there's this perception that I have this perpetual strength." She took a breath. "I'm weak. Without God's love and protection, I'm nothing. There are some days I'd like to get out of here. Go back to DC. But then I realize this is bigger than me."

Olivia was so much better than he was at putting others first. He was a genius at making himself number one, but once Olivia had come into his life, suddenly he'd wanted to put her above him. It was a welcome change and made him want to grow that side of himself, but it wasn't an easy task.

"You don't have to be a superhero, Grant. Just be you. The Lord will do the rest if you put your faith and trust in him."

He grabbed her hands in his. "Please pray with me, Olivia."

Her eyes widened for a second. Probably not because he was asking for prayer but because she must've sensed he really needed this.

As they held hands and prayed, he hoped he would be strong enough to get through this trial. Not for himself, but for the woman he loved.

———

ON SATURDAY AFTERNOON, Stacey walked through the Windy Ridge summer festival with Morena by her side. It was a perfect, sunny day with a light, warm breeze. She loved the festival and visiting all the various local artists and vendors.

What she liked even more was that Optimism was sponsoring a social in the park that was bound to bring in some interesting people who wanted to learn more about New Age ideas.

"Be on the lookout for people we can invite to the social." Morena was armed with lavender flyers.

There had been something Stacey wanted to ask her. "Hey, I've got a question for you."

"Shoot." The two of them kept walking down the street and looking at the booths.

"I talked to a woman in the bookstore Indigo the other day, and she said there was a growing Wiccan presence in Windy Ridge. She was a member of the group herself, but they don't have any connection to Astral Tech or Optimism. It's a completely separate coven of witches who do their own thing."

Morena turned toward her. "Are you wondering whether we should try to bring them in?"

Stacey nodded. "Yeah, I told her about Optimism, but she seemed to think she liked what her group had going. I got the feeling she might even be in charge, even though she didn't say it."

Morena picked up a shiny piece of aqua crystal and held it up to catch the sunlight. "This is a good conversation for us to have."

Stacey waited patiently for Morena to enlighten her.

"Wiccans aren't necessarily on board with all of our teachings and practices. They definitely believe in magic and witchcraft but, depending on the group, they may reject our beliefs regarding the Prince of Darkness—and God, for that matter."

Stacey found that interesting. "You're saying they operate outside of that sphere?"

"Yeah. Think of them as being more into the elements. Some of them worship the mother goddess and the horned god. It's a different belief system than ours. They like to be one with nature and everything in it. They also believe in peaceful coexistence."

Stacey wasn't familiar with any of that. "You don't think it's worth the time to talk to them?"

Morena shook her head. "No, I didn't say that. They can be powerful allies and useful when we need them, but they can also be a big thorn in our side if they get too territorial about how they want this town to be. Their god and goddess worship is not something that interests our group. But whether they want to believe it or not, their devotion to witchcraft opens the door to what we know as the true forces of power in this world—and beyond. Their members would totally discount that though."

Stacey examined another type of crystal and picked it up. "It was interesting to hear her talk about the elements and how dedicated they were to peace and all that."

"Exactly. That's the tension. They claim they want peace, and we want a battle because we *know* we are in a cosmic war. Make no mistake about it, Stace, this is a war, and you have to choose sides. If they don't get in our way, then I'm fine with them, but if they do, then they will have to come to our side or be our enemy."

"She did say that she only practiced white magic."

"What was her name?" Morena asked.

"Eliza. I didn't get a last name. She's tall with light brown wavy hair."

Morena frowned. "Doesn't sound familiar."

Stacey glanced around. "She said she would be here. Maybe you'll get to meet her and make your own assessment."

Morena grabbed onto her arm. "You aren't seriously considering becoming one of them, are you?"

Stacey felt her eyes widen. "No way. I'm interested in what they think and do, but that's not my path. I know where my allegiance lies and who my power comes from."

Morena took her hand and squeezed tightly. "I know it's tempting to want to experiment and see what's out there, but we serve a very jealous master, and he will not allow for flirting with other ways if he believes it doesn't serve his greater purpose."

She wondered why Morena had such a strong reaction to this conversation. If Morena knew about her side activities, she really would flip. But Stacey had to look out for herself. The more she learned, the more powerful she became. There were bigger things in her future. "You don't have anything to worry about." There had to be more to this story than Morena was letting on, and that only made Stacey more intrigued.

CHAPTER FOUR

Eliza Fitzpatrick took in a deep breath of the summer air and closed her eyes—in full meditation mode as she sat in the warm grass at the summer festival. She was surrounded by her friends and spiritual sisters from her coven, and it was turning out to be a great day.

She had spotted Stacey Malone, the young woman she'd met at the bookstore, walking with one of her friends. Eliza felt drawn to Stacey, but she also knew better than trying to get into a tussle with Optimism. The last thing she wanted was to create a rift. She would much prefer peaceful coexistence, and she didn't understand why Optimism members were filled with such a desire for the darkness. She thought it best not to approach Stacey and wait and see if she reached out. Stacey seemed awfully deep and well versed in the dark arts, given her age. It made Eliza wonder what all Stacey was into.

Eliza stood and picked the pieces of grass off her shorts, and that's when she noticed another woman approaching her. The petite brunette with big dark eyes locked onto her and approached with a pile of flyers in her hands. There was a lot of that at the festival. But Eliza liked to be nice to everyone, even if she didn't want to attend every single person's event or buy each person's product.

"Hi there, how are you today?" The pretty brunette gave her a bright smile.

Eliza couldn't help but smile back. "I'm doing fine. It's such a beautiful day, especially nice after a long and miserable winter. I was enjoying some meditation."

For a brief moment, something troubling flashed across the woman's face, but she quickly changed her expression. "I don't want to bother you, but I did want to share some information. I'm a lawyer, and I'm going to be opening a domestic violence clinic in Windy Ridge. I'm trying to get the word out so that people know there is a resource in town for those who need it. I think we've all known someone, even if it's not ourselves, who has been touched by this issue."

Immediately Eliza softened toward her. She was doing important and good work. "Definitely. You said you're just starting it up?"

"Yes. I work for the law firm of Brown, Carter, and Reed. We're a big firm nationally, but our Chicago office opened recently. I've taken on this project pro bono because it's close to my heart, and I want to be able to give something back. So here I am going around the festival in hopes of helping spread the word and get it out to those who may need it."

Eliza instantly liked this woman. "I'm Eliza by the way. What's your name?"

The woman stretched out her hand. "I'm Olivia Murray."

Eliza took Olivia's hand and held onto it firmly. There was something special about this woman—she radiated with positive energy. "Your name sounds familiar."

Olivia nodded. "Yeah, you might've seen it in the news at some point. I was working on the defense of Pastor Dan Light some months ago."

Now it was all starting to make sense. This woman was a believer. But unlike her Optimism counterparts, Eliza didn't see Olivia as the enemy—at least not yet. She would give her a chance because she hated when people made prejudgments about her and her Wiccan lifestyle. "Yes, I bet that's it. I did follow the case closely. I found it was very interesting."

"Dan is a dear friend of mine, and that was how I started working in the pro bono area."

Eliza laughed. "At some point isn't the firm going to make you do billable work?"

Olivia brushed a lock of dark hair out of her eyes. "I've done my fair share of billable work, but pro bono is really my passion. So, you know law firm lingo?"

"Yeah. My dad's a lawyer. I know about billable hours all too well." Growing up, Eliza rarely saw her father because he'd been chained to his office, but she also knew he was trying to do the best he could to provide for the family.

"Can I ask you something?" Olivia moved a little closer to her.

"Sure."

"You said you were out here meditating. Is that something you do often?"

Eliza weighed her answer. In the end, she decided to put it out there because that's what she felt Olivia was probably trying to get at. "Yes, it is. I'm a practicing Wiccan. I don't know how much you know about what we do and who we are, but given your experience on that case, you have to know about Optimism. And I can assure you that I'm nothing like them. I do meditate a lot because it's important. It centers me and allows me to connect with my surroundings and the earth."

Olivia cocked her head to the side. "You're right that I'm not an expert on Wicca, but I know Optimism and its beliefs all too well. I would caution anyone not to get involved with them."

Eliza placed her hands on her hips. "I'm assuming you would also caution me about my beliefs. You did defend a pastor."

"I'd be happy to talk to you about it anytime, but I find that people don't react well to having their beliefs questioned in the first five minutes of getting to know someone." Olivia's eyes warmed.

This woman was interesting. She wondered what caused Olivia to be a believer, but now wasn't the time to ask that either. Eliza wished more women would embrace the Wiccan way and not seek out a religion with such arcane beliefs.

Olivia arched an eyebrow. "I feel like you really want to say something."

"Our belief systems are very different, but what I can totally get on board with is the work you're doing for victims of domestic violence. Count me in, and I will definitely help you spread the word.

"Thank you so much."

"I have a feeling we'll be seeing more of each other."

Olivia gave her a sweet smile before turning and walking away.

———

LAYTON WATCHED as people gathered all around the park for the Optimism event. In some ways, he felt the summer festival was cheesy, but it served its purpose. It was one of their biggest recruitment events of the year because the people who tended to show up almost always had some interest in spiritual matters.

Their goal today was to show people the fun, lighter side of Optimism. They couldn't lead with the more serious stuff. Most people took time before they could handle that. Not everyone was as gifted as Stacey. He looked over at his young protégé and smiled. She was thriving like he never could have imagined. He could only hope that he'd be able to keep control of her as she grew in strength.

"Thanks to everyone for coming," Layton said. "We're going to have some music, great food, and plenty of time to chat and get to know each other. Please join us in whatever way you like. The members from Optimism here are all wearing purple so you can identify us. Please talk to any of us to learn more about joining our group. We would love to have you."

Music started up and the mood was jovial, just as he had hoped. The warm sun beat down as he walked around saying hello. The audience was largely women. It helped that he was good looking because he often got the attention of the ladies. After he'd been burned by Nina Marie, he learned he needed to keep business and pleasure separate. That was another reason why he had taken a hands-off approach to Stacey. Not only was she too young for him, the risks were way too high. He wasn't a fool.

Layton made his way through the crowd but stopped short when he heard a voice he knew all too well. He turned around and there she was, his nemesis—Olivia Murray. What in the world was she doing here? She had no business being at a summer festival like this that targeted New Age-ers.

He couldn't help himself as he strode over to where she was talking to a girl he didn't recognize. After a couple of moments, they ended their conversation, and Olivia looked up at him.

"Hello, Layton," Olivia said.

He was always amazed at the strength and poise she possessed. They had done battle before, and she didn't bat an eye. One day he was going to take her down. He had to figure out how. "Olivia, I would not have expected to see you here. What are you evangelizing these days? Trying to save those who have gone astray?" He knew the sarcasm dripped from his voice, and he didn't care. They weren't on good terms and she knew that.

Olivia smiled. "Layton, sometimes I really do pity you, but my purpose here today is about my legal work. I'm opening a clinic for domestic violence victims right here in Windy Ridge."

"Did you leave the law firm?" he asked.

Olivia shook her head. "No. I'm doing this as part of the pro bono initiative at BCR."

He lifted up his hand. "Well, aren't you just the do-good lawyer these days. First our favorite pastor and now this."

She scowled at him. "Layton, I can't imagine you have something against this type of work, do you? Not with all of your many charitable and community endeavors."

"It's not the type of work I have something against. It's *who* is doing it."

"I hate to tell you this, Layton, but I'm not going anywhere. You're not gonna get rid of me that easily. You might as well learn to accept my presence here in Windy Ridge."

He laughed loudly. "You do realize I'm winning here, right? The church still hasn't recovered from the scandal. My numbers are looking better than ever. Yours are dwindling. You might want to get down from that high horse or yours."

"My high horse? You're the one filled with pride, and it will be your downfall. I'm sure you're familiar with how that all works, right?"

"How dare you say that?"

She looked at him with determination and drive. "I'm not afraid of you. I'm not afraid of the evil spirits that are here today or those here who practice the dark arts. I am here trying to help people—women who have been abused. Women who have been abused by men like you."

He placed his hand over his heart. "Oh, now you're trying to provoke me. You have no evidence that I've ever abused any woman."

"Are we really gonna go there?" Olivia took a breath and looked up toward the sky before responding. "Just stay out of my way. This clinic is going to do good work."

"I think we can both agree we would like to stay out of each other's way. We are both in a battle for this town. Whether you want to be or not, you're the leader. That puts us at odds. We're on a war footing."

"It doesn't have to be like this. There's another way, Layton. Even for you," Olivia pled with him.

He laughed. "You leave me speechless, Olivia. You truly can't think you would ever convince me to become a believer. That is never going to happen. I am not soft and weak like Nina Marie. I was surprised she turned, given how strong she used to be at one point. And I also will admit you are very convincing, but let's set the record straight. Your words and deeds have no impact on me. Zero. Make no mistake. I am much stronger than Nina Marie ever was or will be. I am the strongest person you will ever meet." He couldn't believe she would actually have the gall to think she could open the door to preaching to him. And it was that kind of boldness on her part that made him particularly nervous about having her in his town.

Olivia took a step toward him. "I have more people to speak to here today, but you should also know something, Layton. Your hold on power isn't as strong as you think. Your group isn't as organized or unified. Look around you. How many of these women standing in this park are actually members of Optimism? I think you know the answer to that."

"But they're all potential candidates, and that's a lot more than you have." He'd had enough of her tactics for one day, so he turned around and joined the festivities. He refused to let her ruin his good mood.

A couple of minutes later, Stacey came up to him. "What were you talking to Olivia about?"

"It turns out that Olivia is here telling people about the legal clinic she's opening for domestic violence victims."

"Oh. Hard to argue with that, right?" Stacey asked.

"My dear Stacey, the fact that *she* is involved means I have to argue with it. Do you think she's going to be helping women from a legal perspective out of the goodness of her heart? No. She's going to try to influence them and feed them all of her lies. Olivia's not stupid. She'll use this as an opportunity for recruitment in the same way we use our activities. We have to keep a really close eye on this. We'll talk about it at our next meeting. I don't want to bring down the jovial mood today."

"I guess I wasn't even thinking of it like that," she responded.

Stacey heard "clinic for domestic violence victims" and thought it was a good thing, but Layton knew better. "How are your discussions going?"

She smiled. "Really well. I met some people who definitely seem interested, at least in some elements of what we practice. We also have a Wiccan element here today."

Layton did not like the Wiccans at all. He tolerated them because he didn't see them as a threat, but they didn't help him get to his greatest goal. "Their numbers have been growing steadily in Windy Ridge, and we need to understand why people would choose to join their way of life over ours. Their power is limited, and their view of the world is skewed. Our eyes have been opened. We know what the true landscape is and whose side we have to be on."

Stacey cocked her head to the side. "You sound a lot like Morena. I met a Wiccan in the bookstore last week, and I thought she was perfectly nice, but then Morena told me I didn't understand how they function."

He was a little disturbed Stacey had that contact. The last thing he needed was for her to decide their way was better. Stacey was the most spiritually gifted person he had ever dealt with. Even more than Nina Marie had been. For her to be at this place in her life was nothing short of amazing. Which was all the more reason he had to keep her on a tight leash. She didn't even realize how powerful she was. "Morena was right. We should all have a sit down and get in depth on what they believe and how it's different than us so there is no confusion amongst our members. I refuse to let those witches recruit our people. That would be unacceptable."

"I get the feeling they are actively expanding their numbers. It's something we should look at."

"It's not just the Bible thumpers who threaten us. We've got it coming from all angles." Layton had given over his life many years ago to the Prince of Darkness. That came at a price, but he also gained great rewards. His direct alignment with the evil one made him supremely confident that he'd have more power than a so-called white witch could. He was much more concerned with the likes of Olivia Murray, because there was one thing he knew: Olivia had God on her side.

CHAPTER FIVE

Olivia sat with Grant at their favorite pizza place sharing a half deluxe, half cheese and pineapple. They'd agreed to meet for lunch, and Olivia was so happy to see him. She looked into his bright, aqua eyes.

"How did it go at the summer festival?" Grant asked.

"It was a little weird to be in that element, but it was well worth it. I handed out a couple hundred flyers for the clinic, and that's the most important thing."

Grant smiled at her. "This clinic is going to be big, Olivia. I can feel it."

She took a sip of iced tea. "I hope so. Being able to use my legal skills to make a real positive impact on women's lives is amazing. I just hope I'm up for the task."

Grant grabbed her hand. "You're always up for the task. I'm the one who's the problem."

And there it was. The elephant in the room. Grant's malpractice case and his general malaise as of late. She kept pushing through trying to be upbeat, but at some point, she didn't know if that was going to cut it. "Do you want to talk about it?" She didn't want to push, but she also wanted to provide him a safe place to discuss his thoughts.

"I keep going through the facts in my mind. Replaying them like a broken record." He stared off into the distance.

"You can't beat yourself up about how you handled things. All you can do now is put up the best defense you can."

Grant nodded. "I've got a relatively young attorney and some bad facts. That doesn't bode well."

She wanted to remind him of something. "Just because you're young doesn't mean anything. Think about how much you and I were underestimated early on in our careers. If he's committed to the case, that's the thing that matters the most. Do you think he is?"

Grant dumped some parmesan cheese on top of his deluxe slice before responding. "I actually think he is. He seems like a straight shooter, and from what he tells me, malpractice cases are difficult to prove, so that weighs in our favor."

"You'll get through this, Grant. Remember you're not alone. I'll always be here for you, and God will listen to your prayers. Don't think otherwise."

"What made you say that?" he raised an eyebrow.

"I get that you're a super independent guy, and I love that about you. But sometimes you have to ask for help. God will always provide, and I'm here when you need me. Recognizing that is not a weakness."

"I tell myself that, but old habits are hard to break." He took a big bite of pizza.

Olivia stabbed a piece of lettuce. She made herself eat a side salad along with the pizza to try to offset. "Since we met each other, our lives have been one thing after the next. It's been a wild roller coaster, but we've done it together. We've fought the battles, and we'll keep doing it."

He looked up at her. "I love you, Olivia."

"I love you too." She couldn't help but sense a bit of sadness in him even as he said the words. "Whatever you need from me, just say it. Even if it's just to vent about your lawyer."

He laughed, and she was happy to lighten up the moment.

"Did you see any of our Optimism friends at the festival?" he asked.

Olivia groaned. "All of them. Layton tried to flex his muscles, but I wasn't biting." She picked up her pizza. "If he tries to mess with my clinic clients, we're going to have a big problem."

Grant ran his hand through his thick dark hair. "Maybe he'll mind his business and focus on his own issues. He's got his hands full trying to get Optimism back on track."

"According to him, he's on the top of the world."

Grant scoffed. "He's taken a few hits. He hasn't come out of this unscathed."

Olivia tended to agree with him. "But he's tenacious. I have to give him that."

"Do you think Nina Marie will be safe?"

"Abe's making sure she is. Plus, I get the sick feeling that Layton thinks he has gotten the best of her. He's already thinking of the next big thing. That's my concern. Where he plans to take Optimism. We know he will keep targeting the church."

"Dan's ready. He's more fired up than I've ever seen him."

She twirled the straw in her tea. "Dan went through a lot. He's stronger for it now." As the words came out of her mouth, she realized he could think she was trying to make a point. That hadn't actually been her intention.

Regardless, he let it go and continued to eat. They finished up in a comfortable silence. As she watched the man she loved, she prayed he would be able to face down these malpractice allegations. *Lord, please give Grant strength.*

———

STACEY HAD RUN into Eliza again at Indigo, and they'd had a great conversation. That had led Stacey to where she was now—sitting in Eliza's house with one of her friends.

Yes, Morena had told her not to get involved with Eliza, but Stacey was at the point where she wanted to make her own decisions and spread her wings, especially when it came to her own spiritual development. There were some things Eliza and her Wiccan friends could teach her if only she would open up to the possibilities, and that's why she was there tonight. To hear what Eliza had to say. Stacey didn't bring the baggage and preconceived notions with her that Morena held onto tightly. The further Stacey developed, the weaker she saw Morena—and the others, for that matter.

"Dinner was amazing. I haven't had something that tasty in a long time. My cooking skills are nonexistent." Stacey's idea of cooking was opening up a frozen meal and popping it in the microwave.

Eliza smiled warmly her. "So happy that you enjoyed it. Cooking is one of my passions. I'm glad you decided to join us tonight."

The other woman, named Randi, also smiled.

Eliza offered Stacey a homemade oatmeal cookie, and she took it. If she hung out too much with Eliza she'd need to be on diet within days.

Eliza took a bite of her cookie before speaking. "We talked at Indigo a little bit about what we're all about, but I know you had some questions, and I wanted to let you have the opportunity to talk to us, and then we can go from there."

Stacey looked at Eliza's big chocolate eyes and tried hard to read her. It was strange because it seemed like she was getting mixed messages. In one way, she felt like she could trust her, but on the other hand, there was something a little bit off that made Stacey hesitant. At the end of the day, Stacey wanted to learn more about what types of witchcraft they practiced because she thought it could help her. "Thanks for being so welcoming. My main focus is learning about what you do and how you do it."

Randi twirled her blonde hair around her finger and turned her attention to Stacey. "I'm actually pretty new at this. I've only been doing it for six months, so I think I can help with some perspective. Eliza has been at it for quite a few years and has a lot more power and knowledge. You can learn a lot from her, and she's a great and patient teacher."

Eliza blushed at Randi's compliments.

Stacey had a lot of questions. "You're the leader of the group, Eliza?"

Eliza shook her head. "Not exactly. It's not like Optimism or other groups. But from a know-how perspective, I would say I am one of the more knowledgeable ones, and from an organizational perspective, I guess I have become in charge by default. I would hate for you to think of it that way because that's not how I see it. It's a group of sisters who want to live this way of life."

"And what exactly is that way of life?" That's what Stacey had to get to the bottom to.

Eliza leaned forward. "First off, let me put this on the table. We do not practice black magic nor do we consort with a supposed devil nor do we worship him. We don't even really believe he exists in the same way that you do. In our eyes, there is no such thing as angels and demons. But we definitely *do* believe there are spiritual elements in this world and that we can connect with them, and we also believe we can connect with the other side—people who have passed on but are now spirits. We believe in good and evil spirits but not in the same way you do."

So that's why Morena was wary of them. They rejected some of the key tenets Optimism held onto. Stacey wasn't deterred. There was still some merit to cultivating this relationship. "But you do practice witchcraft, right?"

Randi jumped in. "Absolutely. We rely on many different outlets for that including each person's individual Book of Shadows, which is where each member keeps her spells. But our spells are usually for things like healing or understanding or asking for some type of wisdom. We purposely do not use our spells to hurt others or cause any type of harm. That's one of the very first things I learned when I met these women."

"Is that a tenant of Wicca in general or just your group?"

Eliza took a sip of her tea. "I'd like to tell you that it's across the board, but it's not. There are definitely those of us who use witchcraft in very damaging ways. If I'm being completely honest, I'm worried you might be in that boat. I was hoping to have some time with you to explain another path. A path that promotes peace and unification."

Stacey had wondered how long it was going to take for Eliza to try to convince her to change her ways. Stacey had no intention of doing that. This was a fact-finding mission. "I figured you'd say that, but I think I can learn things from you and would love to hear more though. Do you use crystals or other magical objects?" Stacey hoped she could keep getting them to explain and talk without having to shift back to her own worldview.

"Yes, we do. We have a variety of items we believe are enchanted and help with our process. Do you want to see some of them?"

Now they were getting somewhere. "I'd love to."

Eliza stood up. "Be right back."

"So how did you meet Eliza?" Stacey asked Randi.

"We actually met at a yoga class. We both love yoga and we started talking one day, and before you knew it, we were great friends. Then Eliza introduced me to other Wiccans in town. At first, I thought it was all a little hokey. I never grew up believing anything, and I didn't go to church. I also never really thought that the spiritual realm was real, but once I started spending time with these women, I realized I was wrong. Things I have felt in Eliza's presence are unexplainable by pure logic and rationality. She's really unique."

Stacey could relate. "I completely understand what you're saying because I've experienced things too. Things that defy all human explanation, but I'm also one of those people who doesn't want to throw out logic and rationality. I like having the mix of both worlds. I think that gives me the most likely chance to succeed in this life."

Randi leaned in toward her. "I can tell you're very ambitious, but I can't tell for what. What's your plan? Do you want to actually be a leader of Optimism? Eliza told me about your involvement with them."

"Right now, I'm still finding my footing, but who knows, one day." Stacey didn't want to reveal her hand to this woman she just met. Layton had spies everywhere and the last thing she needed was for him to think that she was ready to launch a coup.

"I'm back and I come bringing gifts." Eliza, holding a large pink box in her hands, walked over to where they were all sitting on the sofa. She sat down and opened up the box. "Here are my goodies."

Stacey took a minute and examined the contents of the box. "It's good to see you also use crystals. I've used them quite often, and I feel like I've been successful."

"Yes, we have a wide range of items here, but crystals are one of the most user-friendly. Why don't you actually sit back and watch Randi and me as we practice some of our spells."

"That would be great." Stacey thought she could learn a lot by watching them. Also, she wanted to determine whether they were playing around or actually had any real source of power. She wasn't convinced they did have any magical powers, but that they were just a nice group of women who had convinced themselves they were witches of some sort and liked tinkering with New Age stuff and hanging out at yoga studios.

What Stacey had seen and lived through was real, and she found it hard to believe these women had anything close to that, but she sat back and watched them do their thing. They turned off the lights, lit candles and incense, and started chanting. For a few minutes nothing happened, and Stacey was beginning to think this is was all a big waste of time. At least she had satisfied her curiosity.

After a good ten minutes went by, a coolness crept through the room and hit her skin. That coolness was quickly replaced by flashes of searing heat. "Hey, what are you doing?"

"A cleansing ritual," Eliza responded, her eyes still shut.

"You're hurting me." The pain only increased as it shot through Stacey's neck and down her back. She'd had enough of this. If Eliza was calling on her horned goddess or whatever it was, she'd show her what real power was. Stacey took in a breath and started chanting to the evil one. He would listen to her because she had given over her life to serve him. The forces of darkness would show Eliza who had true power on this earth.

Stacey looked over at Eliza as she continued chanting, and Eliza's eyes opened. Her face became white as a sheet, and her chanting stopped. "We should stop. Like right now."

Eliza stood up, blew out the candles, and turned on the lights. "Stacey, come on. Let's walk out on the back porch and get some fresh air."

Stacey rose from the couch feeling more powerful after the show of force. She knew what she had done. She was waiting on Eliza to tell her. The ladies all stood in silence for a moment on the porch.

"What just happened?" Stacey asked, feigning ignorance.

"You didn't see them?" Eliza asked.

"I didn't see anything," Stacey said.

"Me neither," Randi replied.

"Are you certain you didn't see them?" Eliza asked with wide eyes.

"I didn't see them," Stacey said. Which was the truth, but she knew exactly what they were. What she had conjured by going to the dark side and seeking the Prince of Darkness.

"I think we had some visitors." Eliza's voice shook.

"What type of visitors?" Stacey asked, wanting Eliza to have to admit it.

Eliza looked down and back up, her face still pale. "Demonic ones."

Stacey wanted to smile but held herself back. "That's because I invited them."

Eliza's hands shook as she spoke. "Why? Why would you do that?"

"Your little séance was only getting us so far. I wanted to expose what lies beneath. What you could be working with if you accepted our way. You said you didn't believe in demons. Now you saw them, so you know I'm telling you the truth."

"Stacey, I saw them clearly surrounding you. I can't even put into words how they looked, but I know what they were."

A powerful point had been made. "I think you found out tonight why I'm a member of Optimism. That's where the real power is."

———

On Sunday morning, Nina Marie sat in the passenger seat of Abe's truck in the parking lot of Windy Ridge Community Church. She looked over at Abe. His normally unruly jet-black hair was combed back smooth. His dark eyes held so much kindness and light—such a difference compared to what she was used to.

"Are you ready to go in?" Abe asked.

Nina Marie was afraid of the whispers and looks. It was inevitable and human nature that people would talk about her given the situation. How many reformed witches did they have in the congregation? One! She'd attended services a few times before her attack, but this was her first time back since then.

Abe reached over and squeezed her hand. "I'll be by your side the entire time."

She smiled. "I know that. You're too good to me, Abe."

Now it was his turn to smile before he got out of the truck and walked around to her side, opening the door for her. Always a complete gentleman. Unlike Layton, who would put on the gentleman act in public only, Abe was this way twenty-four seven.

"You're going to be fine. Remember the reason you're here. It's not about the people and what they will think. It's about God." Abe's voice held a firm conviction.

It was ironic that it took Nina Marie's experience to bring Abe back to his childhood faith. But now he was all in, and they were all in together.

Abe took her hand in his, and they walked toward the church. When she saw Olivia standing and talking to Grant and Pastor Dan, she let out a sigh of relief. Friendly faces.

When Olivia noticed her, she smiled broadly and motioned them over. Olivia embraced her tightly. Once her great foe, this woman was now one of her only true friends.

"Nina Marie, Abe, so glad you're here." Pastor Dan greeted them.

Nina Marie told everyone hello, but she couldn't help but notice that Grant didn't seem like his normal self. Instead of standing right beside Olivia, he was one step back. Maybe it was nothing, but she sensed something was off.

"You two should go in and have a seat," Pastor Dan said.

"Come sit by us," Olivia encouraged.

Nina Marie was most afraid of entering that sanctuary. Would the whispers start the moment she walked in there?

Abe must have sensed her hesitation because he leaned down and gave her some encouraging words and then said something in Spanish that she couldn't decipher but knew was an endearment. He often said sweet things to her in Spanish, and while she spoke zero Spanish except the few words Abe was teaching her, it warmed her heart to hear him speak to her in any language. She felt the emotion behind his words. *Thank you again, God, for sending Abe into my life.*

Nina Marie prepared herself for the worst, but as she walked down the aisle, she didn't see much response at all. Most people were engaged in their own conversations and didn't pay her much attention.

Flanked by Abe and Olivia, she felt safe. Coming today was a big step. Once she was seated, she let out a breath.

It wasn't long before the worship team hit the stage and the music was playing loudly. Not much of a singer herself, she stood and bobbed her head to the beat. She willed herself to focus on the words of each song. They weren't familiar to her, but in time, she hoped she would learn to be comfortable listening to worship music. How could she ever explain to anyone how she felt having transformed from a person of darkness to a person of light? *Jesus, I know you can help me. Open my eyes to what I need to hear today.*

By the time Dan started preaching, she felt more at ease. His message was about God's relentless love and redemptive grace. It was like he had tailored the sermon for her, but she knew that wasn't true. For the next forty minutes she allowed herself to solely focus on what Dan was saying and block out the concerns and fears about those around her.

Even though she was born again and forgiven, her decisions had consequences. And those consequences would still follow her the rest of her life. If people wanted to talk, then she had only herself to blame.

When the service was over, Nina Marie steeled herself for the aftermath.

Abe leaned over to her. "That was a great sermon."

She nodded. "Yes, it was just what I needed." She looked over at Olivia who was focused on Grant. Yes, something was definitely off with them, but Nina Marie didn't want to start poking her nose in. Olivia would tell her if she wanted to.

They stood up and began to make their way out of the row and down the aisle. When she heard someone call her name, she came up short.

Nina Marie turned around and saw a petite, black-haired woman walking toward her. The woman was probably in her fifties with red cheeks. "Are you Nina Marie Crane?" the woman asked.

Nina Marie was afraid to answer, but at least Abe was right there by her side. "Yes, I am."

"I'm Patrice. I've heard a lot about you, but I wanted to meet you in person."

Nina Marie's stomach sank as she feared the worst about where Patrice was going with this. Abe squeezed her hand, assuring her he was not going anywhere.

Patrice took a step toward her. "My daughter is Stacey Malone."

Nina Marie started to feel ill. This couldn't be good.

Patrice reached out and grabbed onto her arm. "You are my only hope right now."

"What?" Nina Marie was confused.

"If you can turn your life around, then I think there may be hope for my little girl."

A wave of emotion washed over Nina Marie. Ever since the attack, she was more emotional than she ever had been before. Her eyes welled up with tears. "Patrice, God can reach anyone. Even someone as far off as I was."

A single tear fell down Patrice's cheek. "Can I please ask you a favor?"

"Of course."

"If you ever get the chance to talk to my Stacey again, will you try to get through to her? Maybe she'd listen to you. She's completely shut me out. It breaks my heart."

Nina Marie nodded. "Yes. I can't make any promises about her reaction, but I'll do what I can. She has to want to make the change, and sometimes that is difficult."

"I know," Patrice said, "but you standing in this church right now shows me that God still does miraculous work."

"That He does," Abe added.

Patrice reached out and gave her a hug. Nina Marie was finally starting to understand what Christ's love looked like.

———

THAT EVENING, Grant looked over at Olivia as they sat together on the couch in her living room.

"You're quiet tonight," he said.

Olivia tilted her head up. "Tomorrow's a big day. I think I'm trying to get in the right frame of mind."

Olivia would officially start working at her legal clinic tomorrow. "Have I told you how proud I am of you?"

She smiled. "About a million times. What do you have going on?"

Grant groaned. "My day will be unpleasant. I'm meeting with my lawyer to prepare for the initial mediation."

"So, they agreed to mediation? Isn't that good?" Her brown eyes focused on him.

Grant's stomach had been in knots over the whole thing. "In theory, yes, but we'll also get a sense of their settlement posture and how much they want. If it's way out of bounds, then that means we could be headed for a trial collision course, and that would obviously be bad."

Olivia squeezed his hand tightly. "You are not alone, Grant. I'm not going anywhere, and God isn't going to leave you either. In tough times, you have to rely on Him, not on your own strength."

"I know what you're saying makes sense, but it's a lot harder to do for a man like me who has always fought his own battles and been independent—not needing or wanting anyone else to help."

"We both know you've changed. I've seen the changes myself in the time we've known each other."

He felt it too, but there was something else. "I agree with you that I've changed, and it's all for the better. But, Olivia, I want to be completely honest with you because I believe that's been a foundation to our relationship."

She shifted on the sofa to face him. "What is it?"

"I can't shake the negative thoughts and depressing feelings. You know I'm not the type of guy to feel beaten down or to have a pity party for myself, but right now I have that urge all the time."

"Did the malpractice suit set this off?" she asked.

He shook his head. "No. It was brewing in the weeks leading up to the suit. That just put the icing on the cake. I don't want to bring you down with me, especially since you have such an amazing opportunity you're about to jump into."

"Grant, you're not going to bring me down. We're a team. A partnership. Right?"

He loved her more than he could ever put into words, and that's why this was so hard. "I'm wondering whether we should be."

"What? Are you breaking up with me?" Her voice cracked.

"It's the last thing I want, but I really think you'd be better off with someone else."

Olivia shook her head. "That's not true, Grant. I refuse to believe that."

"I know you believe God brought us together, and I think it too. But just because it happened doesn't mean we're supposed to be together forever."

"Are you worried we're getting too serious too quickly? Is that what this is about?" The worry was evident on her beautiful face.

"Honestly, I don't know what this is about. I'm just telling you how I feel, and my gut is saying you're better off without me. A lot better off."

"Have you considered that it's not your gut at all but the negative forces we deal with all the time in this town? We're stronger together, Grant. Not apart. I love you."

"And I love you too. More than you can even imagine."

She leaned in closer to him. "Then don't cut and run. Fight for us. I'm not going to bail."

Once again, Olivia's strength was palpable. He wanted to believe her, but he still had his doubts.

"Don't overthink this, Grant. Our love is stronger than these obstacles you're facing."

"I want to believe that. I really do."

"But?"

"I'm not you, Olivia. I don't have endless faith and strength and determination. You need a man who can match you. You'd be better off with Pastor Dan."

Olivia moved back away from him. "Now you're being outright ridiculous."

He was making an even bigger mess of this than he had imagined when he had rehearsed this conversation in his head. "I'm not trying to be. I'm really not. I'm trying to help you. I've done a lot of thinking about this, and I believe you'll be much happier in the long run without me."

Olivia shook her head. "This isn't the Grant I know talking. You're under tremendous pressure from the malpractice claim. It's clouding your vision. As much as I hate to say it, maybe you need to get away for a few days. Try to clear your head and rid yourself of the influences of Windy Ridge. This town is still under attack, and you're being unduly influenced by that. You have too much on your plate right now."

Maybe she had a point. A long weekend away could be nice. "I'll think about it." Now was the really tough part, but he had to go there. "But I still think we should take a break. I need some time."

The hurt in her eyes was palpable, and it was like a punch to his gut.

"Don't do this, Grant. Please don't," she whispered.

"A break. That's it." He had to make her understand he needed this. That *she* needed this. "I love you, and I can't stand to cause you pain. It kills me that I'm disappointing you."

"Why would you think that?"

"You don't have to say it. I see it on your face. You want a man who isn't me right now. That's why I need this time to try to pull myself back together."

She sighed. "I'm scared once we take a break, you'll never come back."

Seeing the fear in her eyes slayed him. "That's not my intention."

"Even if it isn't, I'm afraid it will be the result."

He hadn't seen Olivia this hurt before, and once again, it bothered him that he was the cause of it. "See, I'm making you unhappy right now."

"Because you're not thinking straight, and I don't want to throw away everything we have. I never thought you would either."

How could he ever make her see what he was going through? "Olivia, you don't understand what's going on in my head. You can't because you're not like me."

"Try me," she pled with him. "I want to help."

"I know you do, but I wonder if I'm past the point of help."

Her eyes widened. "You can't really believe that. Not after everything we've lived through and shared in Windy Ridge. God is bigger than our problems. Bigger than our pain and doubt."

Grant shook his head. "I want to rely on God, but I feel like this is more about me. My problems. My inability to make you happy. To provide for you. All of that is in question right now. Everything." His voice started to crack. "I don't want to say something stupid to you because you're not the target of my anger." He stood up. "I think it's probably best that I go home."

Olivia followed him as he walked toward the door. Before he could open it, she grabbed onto him and pulled him into a fierce hug, but she didn't say another word.

He held onto her, wondering why he was going so crazy. Why he would ever think of leaving her. But that's exactly what he did.

CHAPTER SIX

Olivia brushed the hot tears out of her eyes. She had to find a way to compartmentalize. Last night had been awful. Grant had basically broken her heart, and she couldn't for the life of her figure out why he was trying so hard to push her away.

She'd called Dan and asked him to reach out to Grant to see if he could figure out what was really eating at him. Unlike Grant's suggestion, she would never view Dan in a romantic way, but he was one of her most trusted friends and a spiritual mentor for her.

Lord, what is going on here?

She thought she and Grant were rock solid—moving toward a proposal, even. Boy, had she been wrong. It made her question whether she'd been misreading her relationship for months. Did Grant not love her in the same way she loved him?

Taking a deep breath, she prayed she'd be able to put her own issues aside and focus on the very important work to come. She was driving to the office space that BCR had rented in Windy Ridge for her to run the clinic.

As she heard her GPS tell her that she was almost there, a sick chill went down her spine. She looked at the GPS screen and groaned loudly. BCR had been in charge of finding the office space and had handled that without her input.

The rental space was in the same sprawling complex as Optimism. There were multiple businesses on that block, but she hated being so close to Optimism. She couldn't let that deter her right now because there was legal work to take care of.

BCR had placed the signage outside. It wasn't anything fancy, but it was enough to indicate that it was a legal clinic.

A few minutes later, she was inside the office where the clinic would be housed. It wasn't that large, but it would suit her needs. There was a reception lounge area and two private offices. *Lord, please let me touch the lives of women here and do your work.*

Olivia would be working with a local law student named Jess Haven who would be completing an externship at the clinic. The pro bono committee had done the screening and interviewing, so today would be her first time meeting the student, and she was looking forward to it. The plan was to get everything ready with Jess today and then officially start seeing clients tomorrow.

It wasn't long before she heard a knock on the main door. It opened, revealing a tall, fresh-faced Jess Haven. She wore her black hair pulled back in a low ponytail. She smiled when she saw Olivia.

"You must be Olivia Murray." Jess walked over to her with outstretched hand.

"Jess, it's nice to meet you in person." They'd exchanged some emails about their game plan. "I'm glad to have you here."

Jess's dark eyes glistened with excitement. "I'm excited about this job. It's more than a job to me."

"Your application and essay were very impressive. The committee raved about you, so I'm looking forward to you being part of the team. A very small team." Olivia laughed.

"This is my heart's work. Just so we have it out on the table, I'm a victim of domestic violence. Twice in my life, actually—my father and my college boyfriend."

Olivia's heart ached for Jess. She reached out and placed her hand on Jess's shoulder. "You're in the right place."

Jess nodded vigorously. "Where do we start?"

They took a few minutes and talked about the setup of the office and some general ideas before they went into what would be Olivia's office to chat.

Olivia took a seat behind the desk and pulled a file out of her bag. "We've already got appointments set up for tomorrow. Since you're still in law school, I do have to supervise you closely, especially at first, but I want you to take an active role here. We'll do the intake interviews together, for now, since we have the time to do it."

"That makes sense to me. I realize I'm still in school, but I think I can add a lot of value because I know what it's like to have lived through it." Jess paused. "I know it's really personal and you can say you aren't comfortable answering, but is that why you're doing this too?"

"Thankfully, I have never experienced domestic violence firsthand, but I've had friends who have. Also, since we're being open here, I'm a person of faith, and for me, this type of work is important because of that."

Jess's eyes widened. "That actually surprises me."

"My faith?"

Jess straightened in her chair. "Yes. I get the impression that most highly educated women like you these days don't adhere to patriarchal religions."

Olivia smiled at Jess's comment.

Jess cocked her head to the side. "I'm sorry. I think I just insulted you, but now I'm confused because you're smiling."

"You're not the first to say something like that, and I don't take offense. I'm very comfortable in my beliefs, and I'm even comfortable when people question me about them."

"Maybe we'll have a good debate one day then. And I probably should've kept my mouth shut since you're my boss, but you'll come to find out that I speak my mind freely."

This was off to a bit of a rocky start. "I'd rather you speak your mind than be fake, so I think we'll get along fine.

Our purpose here is to provide legal assistance to these women."

"You've got that right. Should we start taking a look at the list for tomorrow?"

"Yes." As they got to work, Olivia wondered how this was going to work with Jess. Olivia wasn't one to back down from a challenge.

———

GRANT HEARD the knock on his office door and looked up to find Pastor Dan in the doorway. "Dan, is everything all right?"

Dan walked into his office and shook his hand. "Yes, I was in the neighborhood, and I thought I'd stop in."

As he heard the words come out of Dan's mouth he realized why Dan was there. "Olivia called you, didn't she?"

Dan grinned sheepishly. "She did. I have to admit it." Dan took a seat across from him.

Grant should've known, but wasn't that exactly why she would be better off with a man like Dan, or Dan himself? They were already so close. "I don't know what she told you, but it's very complicated."

"You realize I'm a pastor that does all sorts of complicated counseling every single day. I've heard it all."

It still felt strange to him. "Yeah, I know that, but it's different. You're way too close to this. You and Olivia are practically best friends."

Dan frowned. "Grant, this whole thing isn't about my friendship with Olivia, is it? Because I can guarantee you that is all it is and will ever be. Nothing more."

"Funny because she said the same thing to me."

"And you don't believe her or me?"

"I think the two of you don't think it's the right match, but from the outside it's obvious."

Dan placed his head in his hands before looking back up. "Oh,

Grant. How can I make you understand? I've already been married to the love of my life. I lost her far too soon. I'm not looking for love again right now because I'm still in love with my wife and grieving over her loss. And even if I were, Olivia isn't that woman for me. I fear that you're putting up roadblocks because you're afraid of the type of love Olivia is willing to give you and the commitment that she will rightfully expect from you."

Grant's frustration started to boil up inside of him. "I don't need to be lectured at right now. Can't you see that I'm trying to do the right thing by Olivia? This isn't about me. It's about her."

"Actually, I do think you need some tough love. I'm your friend and pastor, and I'm trying to help you through this, but you have to want to get help. Yes, you're facing some tough personal and business issues, but haven't we all?"

Grant felt a bit like an idiot given what had happened to Dan. "I know that. It's not lost on me that you were jailed for something you didn't even do. Rationally, I know you want to help, but in my own messed-up, dark place of a mind, none of that matters. I can't process everything. I barely want to get up in the morning. Nothing seems to matter anymore. Nothing," he croaked.

Dan sat silently for a moment. The sound of the box fan was the only one that filled the air. "Where are you at with God right now?"

"What do you mean by that?"

"You know what I mean."

And he did know. "I don't feel like God is paying much attention to me, so I guess I haven't been paying that much attention to him. Work has been busy, and it's one string of bad things after another."

Dan cleared his throat. "I'm not saying all your problems are the result of where you're at spiritually, but given everything that has happened ever since you represented Optimism and then you becoming a believer, you've been through a lot. And if you're not continuing to grow in your faith and putting in the time and effort it takes, I fear you're an easy target."

"You make me sound like a sitting duck."

"Don't you feel like one?" Dan asked.

And he did. That was the thing. Dan was right—again. "So, what's your suggestion?"

"I think you have to seriously go back to where you were months ago when you had that hunger to know more about God. The man I see in front of me today is depressed and defeated. God does not want you to feel that way. I'm also going to suggest that we actually do formal counseling sessions. If you're not comfortable with me, then we can find you someone else. And if that doesn't work, then I'm going to highly recommend you talk to a medical professional. Prayer solves a lot, but God doesn't turn a blind eye to medical care. Both physical and mental. You're neglecting yourself on every front, and it's beginning to show."

Dan spoke the truth. Each sentence out of his mouth was spot on, but that didn't make Grant feel better about it. "And what about Olivia? What about my relationship with her?"

"I can't give you an answer on that. My advice as a friend to both of you is that you shouldn't do anything without thinking about it—and more importantly, praying about it. You running away from her isn't going to solve your problems. That much I can promise you."

"She could do so much better. You have to see that. You won't offend me by stating the obvious because I feel it every day." Saying the words made the situation seem even more dark.

"Is that what this is about? That you don't think you deserve her?"

"I don't, Dan. She's the most amazing person I've ever known in my life, and look at me." He threw up his hands. "I'm a mess both inside and out right now. I could lose my law license. I could lose my savings. I could lose it all."

Dan shook his head. "No, because those things aren't everything. Remember that. I know you've worked hard to build up your law practice, and you are entitled to be upset about it, but Olivia isn't measuring you as a man because you have a successful law practice. Can't you see that she loves you no matter what? She's all in, man."

"And that scares me to death."

"Why?"

"Because the last thing in this world I'd ever want is to hurt her or let her down, and I feel like I'm doing both." A feeling of complete helplessness washed over him.

Dan got out of his seat and walked around to his side of the desk. "Stand up."

Grant did as he instructed.

"Let's take a walk. It's a gorgeous day."

"All right." Grant wasn't sure that a walk was going to solve anything, but it felt good to move and get some fresh air.

A few minutes later they were out of the building.

"Hear me out," Dan said.

"I'm listening."

Dan looked over at him as they continued to walk. "I honestly think you have multiple things going on right now. You are dealing with a tremendously stressful situation with your career, and that would put even the strongest man on edge."

"I agree with you so far. It's very stressful. I'm having trouble sleeping, and then I'm exhausted when I'm at work. It makes me irritable and cranky."

"Yes. I completely agree with all of that, but I'm feeling there is more at stake here with you. Have you thought about going back to your old ways?"

How could Dan possibly know what he was thinking? He blew out a breath. "Not seriously, but I'd be lying if I said I hadn't thought about it. I know you must think I'm crazy given all the things I've experienced and even seen with my own eyes. But my life before was much simpler. When I didn't believe that anything existed beyond this world and the here and now, I had it easier. Ever since my eyes were opened, things have only gotten harder. Some days, I don't know if it's worth it." There, he said it. He could've never said that to Olivia because he feared it would crush her. But he couldn't hold it in any longer, and he felt like he had a safe space in Dan.

Dan placed his hand on Grant's shoulder. "You're not telling me anything I hadn't already figured out, Grant. And your fears are leading you to an even worse place—one where you're not putting on the whole armor of God. One where you are left more vulnerable."

"You really think there's a spiritual component to my problems?" Grant asked.

"I do. I think it's compounding an already bad situation. The devil will use these cracks in our armor as opportunities, and if he senses our fear and desperation, he will pounce. Remember, the verse, 'Be sober, be vigilant; because your adversary the devil, as a roaring lion, walketh about, seeking whom he may devour.' It's real Grant. You have said so yourself. Don't turn a blind eye to it now. You need to face all of this down and fight, but to do that, you need to be better equipped."

"I guess," Grant mumbled.

"You have to want this, Grant. I can't do it for you. I can't build your faith."

"I know." He didn't know what he was doing here. He wanted to crawl into a hole.

"Why did you stop coming to men's bible study?" Dan asked.

"I've been busy." Grant knew it sounded like a lousy excuse.

"You're always busy and you used to come," Dan said.

"True."

"Okay, so let's make that a first step. Also, I think you should go see your medical doctor. Tell him how you're feeling."

Grant shook his head. "He'll think I'm crazy and send me to a shrink. I don't want that."

"You can't do this alone."

"I have you, don't I?"

Dan smiled. "Of course you do, but I'm not a medical doctor. If you truly are clinically depressed, you need to see someone. I'll do my part and then some, but we need to focus on the whole you."

"I'll think about it." Grant wasn't willing to commit right now.

"Before you go back, I want to pray with you. How does that sound?"

"That I can handle." He needed all the help he could get.

––––––––

BEN AND MICAH looked down on Grant and Dan as they walked back to the office.

Othan and two of his demon companions were lurking around the entrance to Grant's office.

Ben drew his sword. "We have to do something to keep them away. Grant may break if we allow them to have their way here."

"Do you want to pick a fight here and now?" Micah asked. "We'd be outnumbered in a matter of minutes."

"Yes, but we're stronger because we have God on our side."

"Let's wait a minute and see what happens." Micah could fight if need be and he wasn't afraid, but he wondered if this was the right time.

As Dan and Grant got closer, the demons started to twitch. Dan's presence was causing them some concern. "They don't like Dan being around," Ben said.

The closer Dan got to the office, the demons started to vanish one by one. But Othan didn't budge.

As Dan was telling Grant good-bye by the front entrance, Othan looked over his shoulder and scowled. Then he flew over to where Micah and Ben were hovering.

"I see that the two of you are a bit concerned about your little fledging pup, huh?"

"We're just paying attention to one of ours, and you should remember that, Othan. He's no longer the world's. He's a child of God."

Othan huffed. "If you say so, but he's certainly not acting like one."

"Stay away from him." Ben moved toward Othan.

"Or what? We all know you two won't touch me, so stop it with your idle threats."

Micah grabbed onto Othan, and Othan shrieked before disappearing.

"I couldn't let him linger here," Micah said.

"I agree with you. Better you than me. I wouldn't have been as lenient."

"I think there's a concerted effort to go after Grant. They sense his weakness, and they won't let this go. That means we have to redouble our efforts."

———

NINA MARIE SAT on her back porch with a large glass of lemonade. Abe sat beside her playing his guitar.

It was at moments like this Nina Marie couldn't believe the turn of events in her life, and it was all because of the love of the Lord. He had pulled her out of the jaws of death and given her a new life.

Abe strummed on the guitar. "I invited Grant and Olivia over tonight."

"That's great." Nina Marie loved spending time with them.

Abe shook his head. "Grant couldn't make it. I told him we could do it another time."

"Was he busy?"

Abe kept playing. "Yeah, that's what he said, but honestly, I get the sense it's more than that. I know he has this lawsuit that got filed against him. He didn't want to talk much about it, though."

Nina Marie frowned. "What's it about?"

"One of his former clients is suing him for malpractice."

"That's awful. No wonder he doesn't want to socialize." That seemed perfectly reasonable to her. "And I bet that's why he seemed a little preoccupied the other day at church."

Abe mumbled something in Spanish.

"What?"

"Sorry. Just saying that I think he's having a hard time. Sometimes when people tell you no, you still have to keep trying. He needs his friends and support around him right now."

"I'll do whatever I can to help." Then something else occurred to her. "I wonder how Olivia is handling things. Maybe I'll give her a call."

"I think that's a great idea. I'm going inside to start on dinner." He leaned down and kissed her.

Before Abe, a kiss wouldn't have meant anything to her. But now, every kiss he gave her seemed special. *Thank you, Jesus, that I'm alive.* She closed her eyes and took a moment to let the warm sun wash over her. Then she picked up her cell and called Olivia.

"Nina Marie, hey."

"Do you have a minute?"

"Sure. What's going on?" Olivia asked.

Nina Marie wondered the best way to go about this. "Did Grant tell you about Abe's dinner invite for tonight?"

Silence.

"No," Olivia said. "I haven't talked to Grant today."

And it was at that moment Nina Marie knew something was really wrong. "Olivia, what's going on with you two?"

"Grant told me he wants to take a break."

"Seriously?" Nina Marie couldn't believe that. Grant was making a big mistake. "I'm sorry." She figured Olivia didn't want to hear her other thoughts.

"Thanks. It's tough. He's having a rough time."

"Abe told me about the malpractice suit."

"Yeah. That's a big piece of it. It could really impact his career and his business."

"But?" Nina Marie sensed there was more.

"I think he's depressed, and nothing I seem to do helps. I only make it worse the harder I try. I'm at a loss. He has asked for space."

"Are you going to give him the space he wants?"

"Yes, but we're still bound to see each other." Olivia paused.

"It's just hard not to text and call him all the time. We'd gotten into such a routine, and now it's all gone."

Nina Marie's heart hurt for her friend. "Olivia, why don't you come over anyway?"

"I was ravenous when I got home, so I already ate, but thank you for the invite."

Nina Marie wanted to be able to help. "Is there anything else I can do?"

"Just knowing that you're there for me means a lot."

Nina Marie decided to open up a bit more. "Olivia, I'm not used to having real friends, especially girlfriends. It hurts me to see you hurting. You've done so much for me. If you need me, anytime, day or night, let me know."

"That means a lot to me," Olivia said softly.

"I can even bring over a tub of ice cream. Or two."

Oliva let out a little laugh. "I might take you up on that one day. Double fudge is my favorite."

"You've got it."

"Nina Marie, we've been through a lot together, and knowing now that you're in my life as a friend does give me great hope."

"Me too. More than you could know. And I'll be praying for you and Grant. You'll make it through this. If anyone can, it's you."

"Thank you. Call me tomorrow if you have time."

"Will do." Nina Marie ended the call. Olivia had helped her out so much. It was now time for her to step up and be the friend she'd never been before.

———

ELIZA STILL FELT shaky after what had happened at her house. She was meeting Stacey for coffee and hoped that she could calm herself down.

When Stacey arrived, instead of feeling more at ease, Eliza felt worse.

Stacey gave her a quick hug, but Eliza didn't linger. Something was terribly off with this young woman, and now she was somehow in the middle of it all.

"Thanks for meeting me," Stacey said.

"Sure. What's on your mind?" Eliza tried to act nonchalant as she sipped her chai tea latte.

Stacey tied her hair up in a quick bun. "Honestly, I wanted to check on you. Saturday night was super intense."

"Can I ask you something?" Eliza couldn't hold back.

"Sure."

"Why did you really come over to my house?" Eliza asked.

"I wanted to see what you were all about."

Recognition hit her. "You were trying to see if we were for real or not."

"I'll admit, that was one of the things I was doing, but I also sincerely wanted to use it as a learning experience. I'd like to expand my horizons and learn as much as I can about developing the gifts I have."

"And you think I can help you with that?" Eliza asked.

Stacey shrugged. "That's what I'm trying to figure out."

Stacey perplexed Eliza. She didn't know how someone in college could wield such power, but she had seen it with her own eyes—and it scared her to death. "I am still in a bit of shock over what I saw, and I was hoping you could help me."

"You're telling me you've never seen anything like that before?"

This was a completely different playing field for her. "No. I've felt various spirit presences multiple times. Especially when we reach out to the other side, use our Ouija board, or cast other spells. But the creatures I saw around you were almost unexplainable. In a way they were majestic, but they were also frightening. Does that make sense?"

"Absolutely. I've seen them before. At first, I was frightened, but then I got over it because I realized that I'm on their team. They wouldn't want to truly hurt me."

Eliza tightly gripped her cup. "But I'm not!"

"And you're worried they're going to come back?" Stacey asked.

It was even worse than that. "I don't even know if they've left. I haven't felt the same since that night."

"What do you say we make a deal?"

The hair on Eliza's neck stood up because she wasn't sure she was going to like Stacey's bargain. "Let's hear it."

"I'll get them to back off of you if you help me expand my spiritual repertoire."

Eliza couldn't believe Stacey's offer. "You want *me* to teach *you*? Just a minute ago you said you didn't even know if I was for real."

"I still don't, but I think you have skills I could use. Even if you aren't the proper vessel for them, I might be. I need to unlock my full potential, and what I'm learning from Morena and those at Optimism is only one piece. They're all cut from the same cloth. You, on the other hand, bring something fresh and unique, and I think I could capitalize on that."

"But I don't want any part of the demons or evil spirits or anything like that. Whatever they are, I want them to leave me alone. If you can assure me that will happen, then I will help you. But the moment they pop back up, we're done. That's the only way I'll do it." And Eliza meant it.

Stacey smiled. "Don't you worry about them. I'll get them in line. They'll listen to me."

Eliza wasn't so sure. "And how can you be confident that you can control them? No offense, Stacey, but you're a young woman who hasn't even been on this playing field for that long."

Stacey beamed. "Because I know for a fact I'm special. I'm destined for greatness."

Eliza feared that Stacey's ambition would prove dangerous. "I'd give you a friendly word of caution. I'm not sure exactly what those things were in my house, but I can tell you this. I'd be more careful if I were you. You may get lulled into a false sense of security, and the next thing you know, it's all over."

Stacey scoffed. "I promise you that is not going to happen. Don't worry another thought about me. I'm perfectly fine. You're the one we need to deal with."

"All right. Please come to my house and make sure that nothing is there. I haven't even been able to sleep at home. I had to go spend the night at Randi's."

"That bad?" Stacey asked.

"Yes. Which is why I need you to stop it."

Stacey nodded. "I can do that."

"And why would they keep bothering me?" Eliza asked.

"Maybe they realize that you do actually have potential too, and they want you on our side."

"Or maybe they don't want us to be friends."

"I don't think they care that much about our friendship," Stacey said.

"I'm not taking any chances. Please come back to my place and help me out." Eliza was convinced she really needed Stacey's help.

Stacey frowned. "I'm sorry. I never wanted you to be harassed like this."

"Just make it stop and we'll be all good." Eliza needed some peace of mind and hoped she'd be able to get it. But she couldn't help feeling her life had been forever changed the day she invited Stacey into her home.

CHAPTER SEVEN

On Sunday morning, Olivia walked into Windy Ridge Community Church with an unease that wasn't familiar. Usually, church was her safe space, but she knew she might see Grant for the first time since their breakup. If he even showed up. There was a part of her that wondered if he would come to the service today.

She walked into the atrium and immediately saw Pastor Dan. She went over and gave him a hug, and she could see the concern in his eyes.

"How're you holding up?" Dan asked.

"I've been better. Do you think Grant is going to show today?" she couldn't help but ask.

Dan looked away. "I'm not sure. I hope he does. I told him breaking away from the church wasn't going to solve his problems."

That was the truth. But sometimes it was easier to bail in the short term. "You've got others to talk to. I won't keep you."

He placed his hand on her shoulder. "I'm there for Grant, but I'm also here for you too, Olivia. I hope you don't think you'd be imposing. Those in this flock are never imposing when they seek help. My door is always open."

And she knew that, but it was good to hear it. "Thank you. Looking forward to your message today." She made her way into the chapel and sat in her normal seat in her regular row, wondering if Grant was going to show up.

Olivia tapped her foot as she waited for the service to start. She thought Grant had probably decided not to come today, but right when the worship team walked onto the stage, Grant came and sat down beside her in his normal seat.

She looked over at him, but he avoided eye contact. At least he was there. That said something to her. He hadn't completely shut down. Maybe Dan had gotten through to him, but she wouldn't get her hopes up. And besides, this was the Lord's time, not hers. She tried to refocus and get in the right mind-set for worship.

Olivia stood as the music began to play. She loved singing, so she had no problem pouring herself into the worship set. Then she listened attentively while Dan delivered the sermon, but she had to remind herself every few minutes not to get derailed and start thinking about Grant. It was hard with him sitting right there next to her. *Lord, please help Grant. Give him peace and strength.*

As Dan said the closing prayer, she peeked over at Grant, and her heart broke. He had his head down in his hands, clearly in pain. *Lord, what can I do?* She wanted to reach out and touch him, to provide him with a show of affection, but she held back.

When the service ended, it was the moment of truth. Was he going to speak to her? What would he say? What would she say?

One thing for sure, she couldn't let him get up and walk out of there without her saying something to him.

"Hey," she said.

Grant turned toward her. "Hey."

"Glad you made it today." As the words came out, she realized how cheesy she sounded. She hated this awkwardness between them.

"I figured it could only help."

They would normally go eat together after church, but that wasn't going to happen today. She could accept that, though. Even if she didn't like it. "Well, hopefully it did help."

Grant shrugged. "Maybe so."

This was going nowhere fast. "Anything new on your case?"

"Nothing major. We have the mediation coming up." He stared off in the distance.

It hurt her that he didn't make eye contact, but she pushed forward. "If there's anything I can do to help, just let me know."

Grant nodded. "My lawyer has things under control for now." He paused. "Well, I'm going to get out of here."

"It was good to see you," she said softly.

"Yeah." For a moment he locked eyes with her, but he didn't say anything else before turning and walking away.

———

LAYTON SAT in his office at Optimism across from Morena. She had quickly become his right-hand woman, and he relied on her. So when she'd requested a meeting, he'd immediately obliged. The curly haired blonde was beautiful, but they had a very familial relationship. He'd never considered making a move on her. He was an only child, but Morena felt like his little sister.

"What's on your mind?" he asked.

"A few things I need to update you on."

There was none of the usual lightness in her voice. That got his attention. Something must be wrong. "Give it to me straight."

"It's a mixed bag actually. The good news is I found out we have a new neighbor in our complex."

"Who?"

Morena smiled. "We got lucky this time. Olivia's legal clinic has opened right here on our turf."

"You can't be serious."

"I am," Morena responded.

"Did she do that on purpose?"

"From the digging I've been able to do, it looks like the lease was negotiated between BCR and the owner, so I have no idea if Olivia was involved or if the firm took care of the real estate angle."

"Well, this could be good, right? Keep your enemies close. We'll be able to track what she's doing and see if she's just providing legal services or something more." Layton didn't care about Olivia's legal work, per se. What he *did* care about was if Olivia was using the clinic to promote her beliefs and try to turn unsuspecting women to her ways.

"We'll be keeping close tabs and will report back."

Another idea struck him. "I'll also pop in and pay her a visit. I'm sure she'll love that."

"Good." Morena made some notes. "Next item, I spoke to Louise, and Grant's lawsuit is about to heat up."

"Do we have details on the allegations?" He would like to know that.

"A woman is suing him for malpractice over a slip and fall case. Basically saying that she lost the jury trial because of his incompetence. We're still working on getting specifics, but Louise thinks there's going to be an initial mediation. The insurance company has provided a lawyer for Grant."

"Do we know who the woman's lawyer is?"

Morena kept taking notes. "I can find out. What're you thinking?"

"Depending on how good of a lawyer they are, maybe we could assist with additional representation."

Morena smiled. "Remind me to never get on your bad side."

Layton nodded. "Grant had every opportunity to walk away from all of this and go on with his life. I would've left him alone, but when he aligned with Olivia, he gave me no choice."

"I think it's a great idea. I'll circle back with Louise and get right on it."

Layton lifted up his hand. "Wait a minute. Wasn't Stacey going to be doing the leg work on this one?"

"That's the last thing I wanted to talk to you about. I offered to take it off her plate, but I had an ulterior motive."

He didn't like the sound of where this might be heading. "Tell me."

"Something is up with her. She met Eliza Fitzpatrick at Indigo, and I think she's been seeing her even though I told her not to."

"And remind me, who is Eliza?"

"The newest head witch of the local Wiccans."

He blew out a breath. "Stacey deliberately defied you?"

Morena nodded. "Stacey is a handful. She's determined and headstrong. Plus, she has a strong craving for learning and is curious. I think she wanted to check out what the Wiccans in Windy Ridge were all about."

Layton carefully considered his options. "I need to put some thought into how to play this. Stacey is young and experimental. If we pull the reins too hard, she may cut and run—and I can't allow that to happen. Maybe we let this simmer and see how it develops before taking any action. What all do you know about this Eliza woman?"

"Thirty years old, single, lives alone. She works from home doing IT consulting. She has a degree in computer science, so she's high tech."

"Not your everyday witch, huh?" He laughed.

"Layton, I don't know if you're taking this seriously enough."

"What's your concern?" he asked.

"Stacey will end up thinking the Wiccan way is more compatible with her underlying belief system."

He disagreed. "That's where I think you have it wrong. Stacey's highly ambitious. The Wiccans are too egalitarian for her. She wants to be in charge. Their touchy-feely stuff won't be enough for her."

Morena leaned back in her chair and stared out the window. "Maybe you're right. I just have a bad feeling about it."

"Remember, she's made her decision. She's given her life to the Prince of Darkness. He won't just let her go. I'm not totally opposed to the presence of the Wiccans in Windy Ridge. They're the perfect gateway drug. People think they're practicing harmless spells, and before you know it, *bam*, they've opened the door. And once that door is open, then all bets are off."

"What we can't have is them taking our people," Morena said in defiance.

"Of course not, but why don't we turn the tables and try to recruit theirs? Maybe Stacey would even be the perfect vehicle to make that happen. Let her get ingrained and then use her in that way."

"That's if she's on board," Morena replied.

"And I'm telling you that she won't have a choice. There's no turning back for her—or for us, for that matter." Stacey wasn't going anywhere.

"I know that," Morena said flatly. "I'm telling you I have a bad feeling about all of this."

He reached out and took her hand. "I trust your instincts. Keep a close eye on her and provide me with updates. I will intervene if needed. I'm trying to find a way to turn this into a positive for us."

"I get that." Morena took a breath. "Have you seen or heard anything from Nina Marie?"

"Not a peep. She's pretty much a recluse these days. I still think she's trying to recover—not only physically but mentally."

"And you're okay with that?"

He actually was. "She's not a player anymore. Let her rot for all I care."

Morena looked at him. "I'm surprised you're able to let her go."

He chuckled. "Me too, Morena. But I'm doing it. Believe me, if I felt she were still any type of threat, I'd finish the job, but she's nothing."

Morena didn't respond.

"You seem skeptical."

Morena nodded. "Once again, just a feeling, but maybe I'm paranoid all the way around."

"A bit of paranoia is good. Keeps us focused on the mission."

"If you say so."

"Morena, I get the sense that something else is wrong with you. You know you can talk to me about anything." And he meant that. Morena was probably one of the people he was closest to in this world. He had a fondness for her and didn't want her to be troubled.

"Like I said, I keep having bad gut feelings about too many things. I don't think it's a fluke or coincidence. I think something dangerous is coming down the pike. I just don't know what or who."

"All the more reason to keep close tabs on Olivia and make sure that she won't start causing trouble for us." He still thought Morena was holding back, but he wasn't going to push her right now. They had bigger battles to fight.

———

OLIVIA SAT with a woman named Hope who had just shared her story of abuse. Olivia thought she was fully prepared for this type of legal work, but Hope's story had gotten to her.

Thankfully, Jess jumped right in and was able to connect with Hope and get even more information. The twenty-year-old, pregnant woman was in a very abusive relationship with her boyfriend. Hope was afraid for her life and the life of the baby.

"We've teamed up with the women's crisis center in town. I'm going to make a call and see if we can secure temporary housing there to get you out of your boyfriend's apartment."

Hope's pale hands shook. "He'll kill me."

Olivia believed those words. "That's why we have to get you out. Because eventually, he will kill you or the baby or both. If not in the short term, then in the long one."

"I meant he'll kill me if I leave. He'll hunt me down."

Jess took Hope's hand. "We're going to get a restraining order."

Hope sniffled. "You really think Bobby cares about the law?

He's already an ex-con. He wouldn't think twice about it. It's like when he's angry, he turns into a raging monster."

"Given that the baby will be here in the next two months, have you thought about getting out of town? Starting over. Getting a fresh start for you and the baby?" Jess asked.

Hope nodded. "Yeah, but that takes money. Money I don't have."

Olivia's heart was tied up in knots over this situation. "We'll take it one step at a time and file for the order of protection while also getting with the women's center to see if they can provide temporary housing."

"And what's the order of protection again?" Hope asked.

"It's the court order that will say he can't get near you. If he does violate it, we can take further legal action against him."

"If I'm still alive then," Hope mumbled.

Olivia needed to motivate this woman. "Hope, you have to be strong for the baby. You're a smart and brave woman. You've come this far, and the fact you came here today says a lot. We're not going to leave you high and dry."

The tears started to flow down Hope's face. "No one has ever treated me this nicely before. I don't even know how to handle it or how I could ever repay you."

"A simple thank you is all we need. Jess, why don't you get Hope something to drink and wait in the reception area while I make some phone calls?"

"Of course." Jess ushered Hope out of Olivia's office and shut the door.

Olivia spent the next twenty minutes on the phone with the women's center, but they had no vacancies at the moment. The person who worked there thought they could get Hope in next week, but that left her homeless until then. She reserved Hope a spot for a week out and ended the call.

Lord, I've got to help this woman.

She picked up the phone and called Dan.

"Hey, Olivia."

"I need the church's help." She explained the entire story and waited for him to respond.

"I'm sure one of our members could house her for the next week. Let me make some phone calls, and I'll get back to you. I have two people in mind at the top of my list. Older women who live alone but who have plenty of room for a guest."

An hour later, Olivia took a deep breath and walked back into the reception area where she found Hope and Jess.

"Okay. Here's the deal. I've got you down for temporary housing at the women's center starting next week."

Before she could finish Hope stood up. "But what about now? I can't wait a week."

Olivia placed her hand on Hope's shoulder. "I know. I reached out to my church and made arrangements for you to stay with a woman named Beth. She's in her sixties, lives alone, and has plenty of room for you. I talked to her personally, and she's more than happy for you to stay with her. Free of charge, of course."

"Really?" Hope asked. "Are you serious? Why would she do that?"

"Because I told her you needed the help. I didn't provide details beyond telling her you were expecting."

Jess frowned but didn't say a word. Olivia was glad Jess was able to keep her thoughts about the church quiet for now.

"I'll take you over to her place whenever you're ready. Then we'll get started right away on the legal documents."

Hope threw her arms around Olivia in an unexpected hug. "I don't know how to thank you."

"Just knowing you'll be safe is enough for me. Let me know when you're ready."

"I'll run to the restroom, and then I'm good." Hope went down the hall to the restroom, and Jess turned to Olivia.

"I thought you said this wasn't going to be a religious mission on your part. If this is how you're going to operate, then I don't think I can be a part of it."

"Whoa, back up. Hope needed a place to stay. The center

wasn't an option. I did what I had to do. Beth isn't going to push her beliefs on Hope."

Jess huffed. "Yeah, whatever you say."

"And for that matter, you don't even know what Hope's views are on the topic."

Jess shrugged. "I guess, but it seems like an awfully convenient thing for you to do."

Olivia was a bit taken aback by Jess's strong response. "We will finish this conversation later, but I have no doubt I did the best thing here given the situation. A safe place for Hope is all I'm looking for here. If you can't get on board, then I suggest you quit now."

Hope walked back into the room. "I'm ready."

"Great." Olivia turned toward Jess. "Please start working on the order of protection. That is, if you're staying?"

"I'm on it." Jess walked to her office and shut the door.

"I didn't cause any problem between you two, did I?" Hope asked.

"No. Don't worry about that. You're going to love Beth. She's a very sweet woman."

As Olivia escorted Hope out, she couldn't help but wonder if God had a bigger purpose for her legal clinic.

———

MORENA HAD INVITED Stacey over for dessert and coffee. In Stacey's mind that meant Morena had something to talk to her about. She just wasn't sure what.

"Thanks for coming over tonight, Stace. I know you're juggling a lot right now."

"I'll always make time for you if you say you need to talk. You sounded kinda serious on the phone." Stacey prepared herself for whatever Morena had on her mind.

Morena lifted the ivory coffee cup to her pink lips. "I do think it's serious, but it doesn't have to escalate further. I wanted to have a heart to heart about something."

"I'm game."

"I know you've been spending some time with the Wiccans."

"Oh." So that's what this was all about. "It's not what you think. You don't have to worry about them polluting my thoughts."

"The thing is I do worry, Stace, and so does Layton. We want you to be able to explore and grow, but to do it with all the facts. I can't be sure what kind of thinking Eliza and her group of witches adhere to, but I know it's not exactly in line with our beliefs at Optimism."

Stacey took a bite of the chocolate pie before responding. "I'm glad you came to me because I want to share some things with you." Stacey recounted what had happened at Eliza's and the follow-up visit. "Eliza was completely freaked out. I think she's better now, but I don't think she realizes what she's doing."

Morena nodded. "I've talked to Layton and, ideally, we'd like to see if we could convince any of the Wiccans to start practicing our ways. They all have an interest in the spirit world and magic or they wouldn't be doing what they're doing."

"Yeah, it's a bit more complicated than that. They don't want true power and control and won't use their spells for any evil purpose. They're living in la-la land, if you ask me. I actually thought Eliza might be a fraud, but she does have some magical abilities. I'm the one who was able to show her what true power looks like."

Morena dabbed her lips with her napkin. "I'm glad Eliza saw that because I think we can use it to our advantage."

"I think it scared her half to death," Stacey said.

"She needs to realize that once she starts doing magic, it's all associated with the evil one. It's just a matter of whether she's going to let it spiral out of control or whether she will harness it for certain purposes."

"You think I could convince her to join us?" Stacey wasn't sure that was possible—or even a good idea.

"I'd love for you to try," Morena said.

She needed to level set Morena's expectations. "Like I said, right now she's spooked. She might even be too afraid to practice any magic."

Morena took another sip of tea. "Their numbers are growing. I've been doing some research, and they have about fifty active members right now. A year ago, it was less than ten."

"They're not a threat to us." Stacey didn't see how they could be.

"Not a direct threat, but if they pull our people away, that's a problem. Their kinder, gentler message appeals to some. We need to bring their members in, not the other way around."

Stacey understood the problem. "I can talk to Eliza, but I don't know if she will budge."

"Just invite her to our next party at Layton's. She'll see we're not a bunch of blood-guzzling animal sacrificers."

Stacey had participated in Optimism's special ceremonies before, but it was with a select few VIPs behind closed doors. The general membership didn't engage in the most hard-core of activities. "I get it."

"Good. More pie?" Morena asked.

Stacey laughed. "You'd have to roll me out of here. I'm good. It was delicious."

"Thanks. I love baking. One of my stress relievers."

"Why are you stressed?" Stacey asked.

Morena looked up at her. "I can't shake the feeling we're about to be hit by something big."

"Whatever it is, we're strong enough to handle it." Stacey was ready for a fight.

CHAPTER EIGHT

Nina Marie walked into church, her stomach a knot of nerves. She had to get over this fear of church. That was one place, Pastor Dan had told her, where she shouldn't be afraid.

When Dan had called her about volunteering, she decided to say yes. She still hadn't figured out her next career move. Since she left her company, she wasn't sure what she wanted to do with the rest of her life. Thankfully, she'd saved more than enough money over the years, so she could take her time and find something to do that helped people. She was learning she'd been doing life in a completely backwards way. At least her eyes were now open.

She let out a breath when she saw Pastor Dan in the hallway.

"Nina Marie, so glad you could come to help." He gave her a quick hug.

"Where do you want me?"

"We're in the rec room. Follow me."

Nina Marie walked with him past the main sanctuary and into the rec room. She wasn't sure what this volunteer opportunity would include, but Pastor Dan had promised it wouldn't be too taxing. She was still getting her strength back.

There were a few volunteers and many different huge piles of clothing. "Wow," she said. "Are these donations?"

"Yes. This is our clothing drive. We need to go through everything, sort it, and then pack it up to get it to the right people who need it."

This she could handle, right? How hard would it be to sort clothes?

Dan stepped forward. "Everyone, this is Nina Marie. She's here to help."

She made eye contact with the few other women and one man and held her breath waiting for the worst, but it didn't come. They smiled and welcomed her.

"Let me know where to start and how I can help." She smiled too, trying to be upbeat even though inside she was still nervous.

"Over here. You can help with our teen clothing," one woman said. "I'm Annie."

"Thank you."

Annie proceeded to show her their system, and they made small talk for the next thirty minutes. That's when Annie turned toward her. "Can I ask you something?"

Annie had been so nice that she felt like it was okay to say yes. "Sure."

"You used to be a member of Optimism, right?"

Nina Marie shook her head. "No. But I was a member of Astral Tech, their competitor, and I was CEO of the company."

Annie's hazel eyes widened. "Do you mind if I ask how you ended up here?"

Nina Marie couldn't blame her for being curious. "Believe me, I never thought I'd be here. I used to despise the church, the people, everything it stood for, but the Lord stepped into my life in a big way. I left that old life, and here I am. That's obviously the short version of the story."

Annie smiled. "You hear about these amazing transformations or testimonies, but I haven't ever met anyone who has a story like you. Have you considered sharing your whole story with the congregation?"

Nina Marie almost choked. "You mean like talking up in front of everyone?"

Annie nodded. "Yes!" Her eyes sparkled. "I'd love to hear your full story, and I think it could make a big impact on our members. This town has been infiltrated by forces of darkness. The occult runs rampant. We need to know we can withstand them and fight another day. You are the epitome of that story."

"It's not me. It's God."

"Even more important that you tell your story then. I think it could really touch and uplift our members. From the moment a person moves into this town, they know it's different here. And for those of us who have stayed and call this home, we have a battle to fight. I don't know why it's happening in this town, but I can feel the spirit of the living God in you, Nina Marie. He has changed you—I think your testimony is what this church needs right now."

Nina Marie folded clothes but didn't say a word. She was rendered speechless for a few moments. "I know this is going to sound strange. I used to talk in front of crowds all the time for work, and I had no problem with it, but this idea terrifies me."

Annie placed her hand on top of Nina Marie's. "You won't be alone, and the impact of your testimony could send a revival throughout this church."

"You really think that?"

"I do." Annie looked over her shoulder. "Pastor Dan, can you come here?"

Nina Marie thought she might become ill. She sat quietly as Annie told Pastor Dan all about the idea.

Pastor Dan listened and then turned to Nina Marie. "How do you feel about this?"

"Petrified!"

Dan reached out and patted her shoulder. "You don't have to do anything you're not comfortable with."

"But she would be great," Annie urged.

"I know she would, but this is her decision," Dan said. "Maybe one day you'll be ready. You can let me know if that day comes."

A wave of relief washed over her. "Thank you." She wasn't certain she could handle it right now. But if she was honest, there was a piece of her that longed to be able to spread the word and tell her amazing story of redemption. Maybe one day she'd be ready. *Lord, give me the strength to help others in this town.*

———

WHEN ELIZA'S DOORBELL RANG, she hopped up from her yoga mat and headed toward the front door. She wasn't expecting anyone so when she saw Stacey standing on the other side, a chill shot down her back.

Stacey had accompanied her back to the house the other day after they had met for coffee and tried to make sure there weren't any unwelcome spiritual beings. Eliza had made Stacey a deal— that she would teach her the Wiccan ways of witchcraft as long as Stacey made sure those demonic spirits didn't come into her house anymore. But Eliza had been having second thoughts. She wanted a way to break things off and not even go down that road with Stacey. Eliza was still having awful nightmares, even if she hadn't actually seen anything else in her house. The evil presence still lingered in her mind—or maybe she was going a bit crazy. That was always a possibility. She took a deep breath before opening the door.

"Hey, Stacey. I wasn't expecting you."

"Sorry to just drop by, but can I come in?"

Eliza hesitated for a moment. She really didn't want to invite Stacey in, but she couldn't shut the door in her face.

"Eliza, you don't have anything to fear from me. I promise you that."

Eliza wasn't completely convinced, but she let Stacey into her home anyway.

"What's going on?" Eliza asked.

"Can we sit and chat for a moment?"

"Sure. Come into the kitchen. I can make tea if you'd like." Eliza figured she would be welcoming and see what came of this visit.

"That would be nice."

They chitchatted while they were waiting for the tea, but once it was poured, Eliza looked at her. "So, what is it?"

"Well, I wanted to check on you, but it's more than that. How have things been since I was here?"

"Calm. Nothing to report." She didn't want to go into her nightmares. That was too much information, and she was still trying to figure out what Stacey's angle in this whole thing was. At first, she thought she was just a curious young woman, but there was something more to all of this.

"Good. The last thing I'd want is for you to be uncomfortable in your own home."

"Thank you. I appreciate you saying that." Now if only she could actually rewind the clock and have it go back to the way it was before.

Stacey picked up her cup. "There's something else though."

Here it comes. "All right."

"You saw what you saw, and you're not denying that. You also realized for the first time there are such things as demons. It's not something made up."

That wasn't in question. "Oh, yeah, I definitely saw them. There was no doubt in my mind what they were. I'd never seen or felt anything like it before."

"Maybe the reason they appeared to you was because of my presence, but I believe they were already here. You're a practicing witch. So whether you like it or not, you're fair game. Just because you'd never seen them before didn't mean they weren't here. They were making a point by revealing themselves to you."

Eliza shook her head. "I told you when we first met I only practice white magic. I have never—and I repeat *never*—invited anything demonic into my life."

"That's the thing, Eliza. It doesn't matter what you think you're doing. By going down that path, you did it."

"You realize how you sound right now, don't you? I get the same lecture from my Christian friends who tell me not to play with my Ouija board or practice magic. I'd expect that type of argument from them, but not you."

Stacey sat in silence for a minute.

"If you want to say something, now's the time to say it." Eliza's frustration level was building.

"You're living in your own fantasy world. We're in a cosmic battle here, and you're trying to have your cake and eat it too. If you want to practice magic, then you have to realize you're on our side whether you want to be or not."

No. Eliza refused to take that as an answer. "I don't believe that. I really don't."

"It doesn't matter what you believe. It's a fact. And you can try to blame this on me, but it was only a matter of time before you had some type of legit interaction with a spiritual being. My presence just sped up the process."

"What are you asking?" Eliza was at a loss.

"Come and meet some of my friends at Optimism. Layton is having a party this weekend."

Eliza's head was swimming. "I'm not sure that's a good idea."

"You can bring Randi and anyone else you'd like."

Eliza felt like Stacey wasn't going to take no for an answer, but she did have another question. "What do you want from me?"

"I like you, Eliza, and for your own protection, I think if you're going to continue like this, you need to understand the bigger picture. We can offer that."

"Let me think about it, okay?"

"Sure."

"You know, something just came back to me."

"What?" Stacey asked.

"I've been to various psychics before. There was one I went to over five years ago. She told me that I'd meet a young woman who would change my life. I didn't think much about it until this very moment."

Stacey smiled. "And here I am."

A shiver shot down her spine. What Eliza didn't tell Stacey was the rest of the reading. That the woman would bring her great pain and despair.

———

GRANT TALKED with his lawyer Scott O'Brien in the law firm conference room as they waited for the other side to arrive. This was the initial mediation, and Grant was hoping and praying this thing could get resolved.

"There's something I need to tell you," Scott said.

"What?" Grant braced for more bad news because that was the only type of news he was getting lately.

"Something strange has happened. The initial lawyer for Ms. Ramos is still on the case, but they've added a new attorney."

"Who is it?"

"Eli Morgan. He's a hot shot at one of the Chicago litigation boutiques. He does both plaintiff and defense work. He's the real deal though."

"Why in the world would he take a case like this?" Grant asked.

"I was hoping that you'd have a theory because I've got nothing."

Grant racked his brain and the name didn't mean anything to him, but he did have an inkling of an idea about this late addition, and it wasn't good news.

"A guy like Eli isn't cheap. He wouldn't take a case like this on contingency especially if split with another attorney. And in my mind that means that someone has to be actually paying his hefty billable rate. Ms. Ramos certainly can't pay it. There has to be another explanation."

As Scott talked, a knot grew in Grant's stomach. If what he was now thinking was right, then this thing just went from bad to worse. Who would have the money, power, and motivation to do something like this? He knew the answer. "I've got another ex-client that doesn't like me. He's rich and powerful. Maybe he thought this would be a good way to get at me, and he helped bring him on."

Scott frowned. "That's not good, man."

"I know." Just when Grant had thought he was at the bottom of the barrel, now this.

It wasn't long before the mediator arrived along with the other side. Including the new attorney Eli Morgan.

"Eli." Scott shook his hand. "Surprised to see you on this case. A bit outside the norm for you, huh?"

Grant knew that Scott was fishing and eagerly waited to hear Eli's answer.

"A bit, yes, but it's not every day that I have the opportunity to work on a legal malpractice case. This one presented such an interesting fact pattern that I couldn't turn it down—and once I met Ms. Ramos, the deal was sealed."

Ms. Ramos was at the mediation, but she hadn't said a word to anyone. Grant knew better than to try to talk to her. She'd already taken a seat and seemed completely uninterested at pleasantries or other introductions.

Grant did do the right thing though and shook Eli's hand. The man had a strong grip. Grant studied Eli's eyes and wondered if Layton was truly behind this. Grant couldn't help himself. "Eli, I think we have a mutual acquaintance—Layton Alito."

Eli smiled but it was a sinister one. "Yes, we do. Layton and I go way back. I believe you represented him at some point, did you not?"

"I did. The case ultimately settled."

"Settlement usually is preferable, isn't it?" Eli asked.

"Yes, it is." The mind games were already starting.

Eli's eyes narrowed. "Unless, of course, the parties are too far apart."

That didn't sound good. Everything about this stunk, and he

felt like Layton had his dirty fingerprints all over it. Another wave of sickness threatened to make him gag.

"I think everyone is here," the mediator said. "Why don't we begin?"

Each side gave preliminary statements that the mediator listened to attentively. Grant took copious notes to make sure he knew all the arguments Eli was making. It wasn't lost on him that the original lawyer barely spoke a word, but one thing was to his advantage—there was no jury here. The mediator didn't care about lawyering skills. The mediator's job was to get the parties to strike a deal.

This mediation was very telling though. If Grant did have to take this thing to trial, he was toast. Scott was a perfectly capable, relatively young lawyer, but Eli was on a different level. After hearing him speak, Grant even thought himself guilty of malpractice.

The moment of truth was about to arrive. The numbers. The complaint had asked for two million, and his policy only covered a max of one.

Eli gave a sly smile before he spoke. "Our settlement demand is one point seven five million."

Grant almost choked on his coffee. That was almost the full demand of the complaint.

Scott seized onto that. "Eli, that's not a good-faith demand in the settlement context, is it?"

Eli crossed his skinny arms in front of him. "Just because we're in mediation doesn't mean we're going to cave. As you know, I'm new to this case, and I would've asked for much more than two million if I had drafted the complaint. And let me remind you that a jury has discretion in what it can do."

And that's exactly what frightened Grant. A jury could nail him to the wall, but the problem was that he didn't have seven hundred and fifty thousand dollars lying around to pay the difference between the settlement demand and the offer. What was he going to do?

"I think you're blowing smoke," Scott said.

Grant bit his tongue as Scott started to spar with Eli. He feared Scott was going into the deep end and didn't realize a great white was right there. Grant almost grabbed onto Scott to ask for a break, but Eli started talking again.

"I hear you, Scottie."

Scottie? Where had that come from?

Eli continued. "We are in the stronger negotiation position here. It's not smoke. It's actually fire. And if you think long and hard, you'll agree to our offer and move on with life."

Grant started to rack his brain and wonder whether he could somehow scrounge up the money. It would require cooperation from the bank—a lot of cooperation. Some loans and equity lines of credit. Putting up his house and rental condo, but maybe it could be done. He couldn't exactly ask Olivia after he'd basically bailed on her the other day.

He hated himself for that, but on the other hand, he still thought he may have done the best thing for her in the long run. He shouldn't bring her into his troubles. They were a couple, yes, but they weren't married. Although he felt like they were headed that direction. He'd been the one to hit the brakes and throw her out of the car.

"Are you saying that's your best offer? Because if so, we should stop wasting our time and get out of here right now," Scott said.

Grant shifted in his seat. He didn't know if it was appropriate to intervene—after all, the insurance company was on the hook for the first million. This was ultimately Scott's call.

Eli unbuttoned his gray suit jacket and looked at Scott and Grant. Then he turned his attention to the mediator. "It appears we are at an impasse here, gentlemen."

Scott fought back. "Only because you're being unreasonable about the initial ask. We're here to negotiate in good faith, but it doesn't appear that we can say the same thing about you."

Eli smacked his lips together. "Pity, really. I'd like to get this case off my docket."

Grant thought that was actually the last thing Eli wanted. He didn't take on this case to settle it. No, he took it on to make a spectacle of things—and his settlement offer proved that.

They bickered back and forth for the better part of two hours before calling it quits.

After the other side left, Grant sat alone with Scott.

"I'm sorry, man. I did my best to push him," Scott said.

"I know. Unfortunately, for both of us, I think this is bigger than one case."

"What do you mean?"

"I can try to explain, but it would be helpful to know where you stand on issues of faith."

"I'm a holiday kind of churchgoer, but I believe in God. I think it would be foolish not to."

Grant took a breath. "Let's get some food. I've got a lot to tell you."

CHAPTER NINE

Eliza stood outside Layton Alito's mega-mansion and questioned her sanity. Why was she here?

The ultimate answer was that she was afraid to turn down Stacey's invitation. Ever since the demonic infiltration, Eliza had been constantly on edge, and rightfully so.

When she'd started embracing Wiccan beliefs, she thought she was doing no harm. That's what she was told Wicca was all about —doing no harm. That she was spreading peace and love into the world. Never once had she attempted to cast an evil spell or speak evil over anyone—just the opposite.

But now she was learning that apparently there was actually a spirit world out there that latched onto whatever she was doing. That was not her intention. She had been telling Stacey the truth. Before they had connected, Eliza thought angels and demons were some make believe idea of Christians. She didn't think they existed.

She believed in a spirit world and that those spirits could be good and evil, but they weren't tied to the notions of the Christian faith. As soon as she had started that spell the other night, a sense of unease had crept through her. Maybe Stacey was a bad apple who had brought evil spirits into her life, although her gut told her she had stumbled onto something much greater. More troublesome and much more dangerous.

But here she was, standing on the doorstep of a man she didn't know and didn't really want to know. She rang the doorbell, and a bead of sweat ran down her back. Stacey had told Eliza that Layton's parties tended to be on the fancy side, so she wore a black cocktail dress. The last thing she wanted to do was be at Layton's, but she didn't feel like she had a choice. She worried that if she turned down the invite, Stacey would've retaliated somehow.

A moment later the door opened, and a very handsome man with blond hair and ocean blue eyes answered the door. He was older than her, but still not *that* old.

"Hi, there," he said.

"Hi, I'm Eliza Fitzpatrick. Stacey invited me," she said quietly.

He grinned, revealing a killer smile. "Ah, yes. I've heard a lot about you. I'm Layton Alito. Welcome to my home." He took her hand in his and placed a gentle kiss on it. His touch was warm and inviting. His hand lingered on hers as their eyes locked.

She'd heard that the enigmatic Layton was quite a charmer, but nothing had prepared her to feel quite this way.

"Please come on in and let me show you around. I'm so glad you made it."

"Me too," she responded before she even realized what she was saying. This man was magnetic, but she thought it might be more of a manly nature than a magical one. She stepped into the foyer and couldn't believe her eyes. "Wow."

"So you like it?" he asked proudly.

"I love it. I've never seen anything quite like it." The décor was a mix of modern and classic.

He stretched out his hand. "I literally just had it redone. I wanted a fresh start. You can probably understand that feeling, right?"

She could. "It's gorgeous. Don't even come to my place. I'd be embarrassed." She giggled and wondered where in the world that had come from.

"I've got an amazing interior decorator. I can't take all the credit." He placed his hand on her lower back and guided her into the expansive living room. "Let me find Stacey. I'm sure you two will want to chat."

"Thank you."

"And I'm not stuffy about my house. Feel free to roam around and make yourself at home. Most of the people are in the living and dining areas, but don't let that stop you."

"You're such a gracious host." And she meant it. She'd had this picture of him as some crazy-eyed creep, but he was about as far from that as she could imagine. He was enchanting.

When her eyes met Stacey's, she smiled. Stacey walked over to the two of them.

"Layton, I see you've met my guest."

He beamed. "Yes, and what a lovely guest she is. I'm going to attend to some other things, but I know the two of you will fare plenty good without me." Layton turned to her. "It was truly a pleasure to meet you."

She felt her cheeks redden as she accepted his kiss on her cheek. "Thank you," she said.

He left the two of them alone, and she looked back toward Stacey.

"Wow," Stacey said.

"What?"

"There were some serious sparks between the two of you."

Eliza huffed. "I'm sure he acts that way with all the ladies. He's way out of my league, and I know it."

Stacey raised an eyebrow. "I think you're selling yourself short. You're really pretty and there's something unique about you. I can't quite put my finger on it, but I think Layton would be interested."

"Like I said, way out of my league." She threw her arms out wide. "I mean, look at this place! It's a freaking mansion. I've seen nice homes before, but this is on a different level."

"As amazing as this place is, Layton doesn't actually measure people by their material standing. He looks inside to what someone's potential is. And judging by the looks of it, he's taken a liking to you."

Eliza's heartbeat thumped loudly. She hadn't had a guy hit on her in long time, and it seemed implausible that Layton could actually be interested. "You really think that?"

"I do, but don't stress about it. Tonight is a party, so let's party." Stacey grabbed onto her hand and took a step back. "And you look stunning."

"Really? This was one of two black cocktail dresses I own. I've had it for ten years."

Stacey nodded. "Yes. You look gorgeous."

Over the next hour, Eliza met many people from all walks of life—she had been surprised at the range of personalities and professions. She was learning quickly that maybe she'd been too quick to judge.

"What do you think?" Stacey asked.

"It wasn't anything like I had expected."

Stacey laughed. "That's what a lot of people say. They think we're vampires drinking blood or something, but I can tell you that hasn't ever been my experience."

Eliza couldn't help herself. "What has been your experience?"

Stacey blew out a breath. "I won't lie. It was rocky at the beginning. There was a bit of a battle over where I would end up, but I didn't let any of that faze me. After I got over the initial shock, I made the decision myself. It was a decision of freedom, of independence. I don't need man-made rules supposedly from God to tell me how to live my life. *I'm* in charge."

"But does that line up? Haven't you still given your life up to be able to get your power?"

"Technically, yes, but that act doesn't have the same implication as someone who has dedicated their life to God. The whole point of our belief system here is to have the type of freedom and autonomy that you wouldn't have if you abided by the beliefs of those who were believers."

Eliza pushed further. "But what about someone like me? I'm definitely not a churchgoer. I consider myself a practicing witch."

Stacey bit her bottom lip. "I don't want to offend you, Eliza, but I told you that I'd be straight with you."

"Please do. I like having the truth spoken to me." She didn't want things sugar coated.

"I believe you. I think that you believe you're a witch, but you're just at the tip of the iceberg."

"And why do you say that?"

Stacey's eyes locked onto hers. "Because you're embracing ideologies that are limited. You've cracked the window instead of opening it all the way."

"I'd say it was pretty open the other night."

Stacey nodded. "Yes, because I was there. You don't have to give up your way of doing things. Just be open to enhancements. I can help you with that."

Eliza pondered what Stacey was saying. The problem was she didn't know how to put it into practice. "I'll admit I'm a bit confused." And scared, but she didn't want to say that.

Stacey wrapped her arm around Eliza's shoulder. "I say enough of this for now. Let's have some drinks, eat some of the amazing food, and worry about these details later. There are still a lot of other people I'd love to introduce you to."

"All right. Show me the way."

————

STACEY THREW BACK another glass of fancy champagne. Layton didn't skimp on the quality of the alcohol, and for that, she was forever grateful.

Eliza was turning out to be quite the handful. She'd been assigned as her babysitter for the night, so Stacey had to buck up and handle it.

It had only taken a few minutes with Layton before Eliza had melted. She'd expected her to hang a bit firmer to her whole Wiccan-lifestyle mantra, but after seeing those puppy dog eyes, Stacey figured she would be able to execute on this assignment ASAP.

All she needed was for Layton to give Eliza a bit of one-on-one time, and she was confident Eliza could be part of team Optimism.

She chuckled about it because Eliza had given off such a strong vibe that she was set in her ways and wouldn't be swayed. All it took was a visit from the spiritual realm and a smile and kiss from Layton and she'd folded.

Stacey would never be that easily swayed. Ever. She wanted power. Control. And she never wanted to cede that to someone else—especially a man. That had been one of the reasons she'd been intrigued by Nina Marie. The sad end of that story was enough to depress Stacey though. Now Nina Marie was nothing and no one. She'd heard that Nina Marie had dedicated her life to God, but she found that so hard to believe. The woman who had offered to teach her witchcraft had been amazingly strong and fiercely independent. Stacey had truly believed Nina Marie was as strong as, if not stronger than, Layton.

Word on the street now was Nina Marie was living in exile. That could never happen to Stacey. If it meant ultimately fighting Layton, then so be it. She'd be more powerful than Nina Marie ever was and ready for battle. Stacey was intent on growing her magical repertoire. She needed to be ready. She would stick close to Eliza to see if she could gain any knowledge from her. Stacey could use every tool in her magical arsenal to get where she wanted to be.

Eliza walked back up to her after mingling. "Stacey, I must say, I had no idea it would be like this."

"See, I told you we weren't a bad group."

Eliza placed her hand on Stacey's arm. "But what exactly do you believe? What do you do here? I feel like I'm missing something."

That was a very tricky question and one that Stacey knew she needed to be diplomatic in answering. "We're a diverse group with a variety of beliefs, but at the core, we fully embrace New Age ideologies."

Eliza nodded. "I get that, but what does that actually look like? Because I consider myself also embracing New Age ideologies."

"It means we're not beholden to any other human. It goes beyond that for Optimism though. Our loyalty is to Lucifer." Stacey figured there wouldn't be any better opportunity to lay it on the line.

"And by that you mean what Christians consider the devil?"

"Not just Christians. We obviously believe in Lucifer too. He has many names. I'm not sure how well-versed you are on the biblical nature of this whole thing. I grew up in Windy Ridge Community Church and know the whole story, but if you didn't grow up in a church, then maybe you'll need some additional information to make sure you have all the pieces to the puzzle."

"You're definitely coming from a different place than me. I've been to church for weddings or special occasions, but that's it."

"Really?"

"Yeah. My parents were pretty agnostic, in general. Not much talk about any religion in my house."

The enormity of that statement hit Stacey. Eliza had zero idea what she was dealing with here, and that could end up being highly dangerous. "Then I think we should talk more, but now isn't the time."

"Even if I never deal with Optimism again?"

"Absolutely. You think you can live this Wiccan lifestyle in a bubble, but nothing could be further from the truth. There is much more out there you're blind to, but it is impacting your entire life."

Eliza's face paled as she digested Stacey's words. "That sounds ominous."

"I'm not trying to worry you. I want you to understand the full picture here. I think you got a taste of things the other night, but it's so much bigger." Stacey patted her shoulder. "C'mon. Let's enjoy the rest of the party, and we can handle the heavy stuff tomorrow." Once Stacey got through with Eliza, she felt certain she'd be able to bring her over to their side. Now the issue was whether Eliza would be able to convince others in her coven to also turn.

CHAPTER TEN

Olivia sat in her office at the clinic a bit dismayed that her eleven o'clock had been a no-show. Unfortunately, in this type of work, that was bound to happen. It broke her heart to think about the circumstances these women were living in. She could only do her part in helping but wished she could help even more.

The good news was that her pregnant client Hope had settled in with Beth from the church and was doing great. They'd also been granted the protective order by the court, so Olivia felt that was their first real victory and they could build upon it.

When the bell Olivia had placed on the door jingled, she thought for a moment that maybe her no-show was really late. Jess wasn't working today so it was just Olivia.

"Be right there," she called out. The last thing she wanted was for the woman to get cold feet. She left her office and rushed into the waiting room.

Her stomach dropped. This was not one of clients. "Layton, what are you doing here?"

"I could ask you the same thing." He took a step closer to her.

"I'm being serious. What do you want?" Her patience was waning.

His big, sparkling blue eyes focused in on her. For a moment they stood, staring each other down. On the outside, this man had it all going for him. He was incredibly handsome, impeccably dressed, highly intelligent, and a smooth talker. But underneath that exterior was a monster. A man who had truly sold his soul to the devil and had never looked back.

"I'm here because when you told me about this clinic of yours, you never told me that it was going to be in *my* backyard. I can't help but think you have something up your sleeve here."

She shook her head. "I actually can't take credit for that. I had nothing to do with getting the lease and office space. I didn't realize it was located here given how the addresses were numbered and named. I was just as surprised when I drove here the first time."

Layton quirked an eyebrow. "Really? I find that hard to believe."

"It doesn't matter whether you believe it or not. It's the truth. Not everyone operates with hidden agendas." She paused. "And what's it to you, anyway?"

He moved yet another step closer. "Because I don't want you using this clinic as a ruse for something else."

"And why would you think I would do that?" She stood her ground, refusing to give him any ground.

"Because I've heard that you already sent one of your clients to live with someone from the church." The accusatory tone came through loud and clear.

She sucked in a breath. How had he found that out? That wasn't good. She needed to make sure Hope was protected. "Layton, don't you dare mess with that woman. She is completely innocent and has nothing to do with you."

He smiled revealing his pearly whites. "Do you really think I'd waste my time? I have bigger issues, but I don't want you sniffing around my building and trying to get people to visit here."

She couldn't help herself. "Are you saying that your members are victims of domestic violence and would need my services?" She was letting her anger get the best of her.

He crossed his arms. "That's beneath you, Olivia."

"You tried to kill Nina Marie. I know exactly what kind of man you are, Layton. I'm not fooled for one second." She clenched her fists tightly by her sides as the memory of what happened to Nina Marie came flooding back to her.

"You believe in the justice system, right? I was found not guilty by a jury of my peers."

"Because you rigged the system." Her voice rose with each word.

"My, my, Olivia. Something has gotten into you." Layton smirked. "This side of you is unexpected. Where's the loving and understanding do-gooder that I'm used to?"

Layton was right about one thing. She was going too far off the deep end and needed to rein it back in. Getting upset at Layton and lashing out wasn't going to help anyone. Where was all the frustration and anger coming from? Then it hit her.

She looked around and didn't see anything visible to her eyes, but she knew as she stood there that Layton had brought his demonic friends with him.

Layton laughed. "I can't believe it took you so long to figure out that I wasn't alone. You're really off your game. Maybe it has something to do with your boyfriend's lawsuit."

Her head snapped back to attention. "Leave Grant alone."

"Or what?"

She fought the urge to lunge at him. That wasn't her. *Lord, I need your help right now. Protect me from evil.*

A shriek sounded in her ear, but she still saw nothing. After a moment, though, she realized she was now alone with Layton. "Not as big and bad without your backup, huh?" she asked.

"Olivia, I could crush you like a fly if I wanted to."

She straightened up. "We both know you're lying. If you could've, then you would've already done it."

Layton cocked his head to the side "Spiritually, you may be right. But physically, I could kill you. No question about it."

"What's your point? I answer to a higher power, the only one true God, and He decides if I live or die. Not you."

Layton took a big step back. "Now, who's the one calling in reinforcements?"

Olivia looked around and didn't see anything, but she could feel the presence of God's protection solidly surrounding her. "Layton, you should go."

"You've been warned." He walked to the door and turned. "If you start messing with my members, there will be consequences."

As he shut the door, she let out a breath. "Thank you, Lord." She was never fighting alone. She could take Layton's shots, but what he said about Grant really bothered her. What was Layton's role in that?

———

WHEN GRANT HEARD a knock on his door, he got up from the kitchen table and went to answer it. He saw it was Olivia on the other side.

"What's going on?" he asked.

"We need to talk."

"Come on in." He stepped aside so she could enter. "What's wrong?" He immediately worried something bad had happened.

"I think Layton is involved in your lawsuit."

Ah. Yeah. "Well, funny you say that because the plaintiff brought on another lawyer—a big-time guy from a Chicago litigation boutique—an attorney who has no business being on this case. And it turns out he knows Layton."

"You're sure?" Olivia asked.

"He told me as much, but I don't know that we can blame this entire thing on Layton. I think the lawsuit was brought without his intervention. I'm guessing he found out about it and decided to try to turn the screws and make my life more miserable than it already is."

Olivia took his hand. "Grant, your life is not miserable."

He dropped her hand. It was too painful to feel her touch right now. "Olivia, you have no idea what is happening in my head." He was conflicted because in a way he wanted her to know the despair he was facing, but on the other hand, he wanted to protect her from that. "You don't understand."

"I'm trying, Grant, but you have to meet me half way."

"Don't you see I don't want to?"

She recoiled from him.

"I didn't mean it like that. Everything I'm doing, I'm doing to protect you from this. From me. From all of it."

Olivia closed the distance between them. "I do *not* need protection from you, Grant. I never could."

"That's where you're wrong. Just look at how much pain I'm causing even now. I appreciate you giving me the heads up about Layton, but I haven't changed my mind about where we stand."

"So that's it? We break up and pretend like we never happened?"

He needed to do this for her sake. "I'll always remember what we had, but I become more convinced by the day that I'm not the man for you."

Olivia lifted her chin. "I refuse to believe that. Maybe you need help I can't provide you to face down these issues, but I want you to get that help. Don't shut me out and think that's going to solve everything."

"I know it won't solve everything, but at least it gets you out of my web."

"You're talking crazy. You have no web. You're not a bad man, Grant. You're a good guy. A guy who needs the people who love and care about him in his life."

"Sounds more like Pastor Dan talk again," he couldn't help but say.

"You're trying to get me to go away by pushing my buttons, but after everything I've faced down in my life, I am not going to give up on you. I love you too much, and I'm not going to give up on us. If you believe you need time, then I'll give you space, but know this, Grant Baxter. I'm not just going to leave and forget about you. Our story is far from over."

He loved her so much it hurt, but that was why he had to stay strong. "At least we can agree on me needing some time to work on my issues." He breathed in deeply. "And you should know they basically asked for the full two million at mediation. The insurance company wants to take the deal and have me pay the remainder."

"Would you even be able to do that?"

He looked away. "It would require a lot of asset consolidation and some major bank financing. But now that this ringer has been brought in, the fear is that if we go to trial the amount could be even more, and that could completely destroy me."

"Do you actually think a settlement offer is on the table?" Olivia asked.

"Yeah. They made it clear at the mediation."

"Maybe because they thought you'd turn it down. Layton's endgame is to break you—both mentally and financially. He would want a trial."

Grant hadn't fully figured that out. It showed he was not on the top of his game right now. "You might be right."

Olivia looked up at him. "If you'd take that deal, I think you need to act quickly before they can weasel out of it. And I know you'll say no, but if you need my help in securing funds, all you have to do is ask. My sizable salary from the BCR would whet the appetite of any bank."

"You know I wouldn't have you do that," Grant said softly.

"And you know I would do it for you in a heartbeat."

Once again, they stood staring into each other's eyes, but he couldn't will himself to look away.

"I love you, Grant. Please know I would do anything and every-thing for you."

And that's exactly why his heart was breaking.

———

ELIZA PACED around her kitchen waiting for Stacey to arrive. After the party at Layton's house, Eliza realized she needed to get the full download from Stacey to understand what she was dealing with.

Eliza had never believed there could be such powerful spiritual forces. Yes, she was a practicing Wiccan, but she saw that more as harnessing energy and using it for good. But what she had experienced literally felt like it was from another world—and it definitely didn't seem to be what she understood as good magic. The question was, what was she going to do about it?

According to Stacey, Eliza had already opened a door she couldn't close. She couldn't help but think that Stacey had some agenda. A big agenda. Layton hadn't been what she was expecting at all. He'd been charming. There was a magnetism about him. Something that made her want to know him better. It had been a long time since she'd felt attraction like that. Could it possibly be that a man like him could actually be interested in her?

First, she had to handle Stacey, so when the doorbell chimed, Eliza stood up from her chair and walked to the front door. She opened it fully expecting to see Stacey on the other side, but she sucked in a breath when she saw it was Layton instead. She was kicking herself for not putting on more makeup and a cuter outfit instead of the ultra-casual sundress she had bought from the thrift shop.

"Layton, what're you doing here?"

He gave her a warm smile. "I'm sorry to show up unannounced. Can I come in?"

She stepped aside. "Of course, but I should warn you that my house is small and not fancy at all. It won't be like what you're accustomed to." She felt her cheeks flush as she spoke, and embarrassment flooded through her. What was this high-society guy going to think of her little home?

Layton patted her shoulder. "Don't give that a second thought. It's actually quite charming."

She found that hard to believe, but she knew he was being polite. "Would you like some tea? I also just made some cookies."

He followed her into the kitchen. "Cookies sound delicious."

Baking was something she was good at. Thankfully, she had goodies to offer him. "Is Stacey okay?"

Layton nodded. "She's perfectly fine. She mentioned that she was coming to talk to you about Optimism, and I thought, why not have the conversation with you myself. Go straight to the source."

She fumbled around the kitchen. "Please, have a seat. I know you're busy. You didn't have to do this. I'm sorry if I caused any inconvenience."

Layton surprised her by grabbing onto her hand. His touch sent a jolt of electricity through her.

"You are *not* an inconvenience. I knew from the moment we met that you were special."

"Really?" Her heartbeat sped up.

He squeezed her hand. "Absolutely."

"Can I tell you something?" she asked quietly.

"Sure."

She placed a few cookies on the blue pastel plate and placed it in front of him. "You are nothing like what I expected."

"How so?"

She decided to be transparent with him. "Frankly, I'd heard some not-so-flattering things about you, but I haven't seen any of that."

"Like what have you heard?" He picked up a chocolate chip cookie.

"That you are cold and calculating and don't care about your members. You're just power hungry and in it for yourself." As the words came out, she couldn't believe she was saying it to his face, but for some reason, she felt oddly comfortable with him.

Layton laughed. "It's funny how that works, right? You become successful and then everyone tries to come at you and spread foul rumors. Nothing could be further from the truth. Optimism and its members mean everything to me."

His sincerity showed through his words and, more importantly, how he had treated her. "I'm glad I've gotten an opportunity to judge for myself. Given some of the things that people say about us, I can empathize."

"That you're a bunch of crazy women who think they're witches, right?"

Now it was her turn to laugh. "Yeah, that about sums it up. Throw in a few black cats and we're the perfect caricature—especially around Halloween. But we're not like that. Just like I can see you don't match the rumors either." She placed a few more cookies in front of him and poured the tea.

"I'm an open book. What would you like to know? You can ask me anything." He took another bite of the chocolate chip cookie. "Mmm. These are amazing."

"Thank you." She tried to sort out her thoughts. "I'm not sure where to begin. Stacey said I didn't have the background knowledge or understanding of the Optimism world-view because I wasn't raised in the church and didn't know how it all worked."

"There are pluses and minuses to that. At least you weren't indoctrinated in some of their insanity, but Stacey is right that you might be lacking in some of the ideas that shape who we are and why we do what we do."

She wanted to go down this path and see what happened. "All right. I'm ready to hear what you have to say."

And she did. For the next hour, she got a tutorial in the biblical battle of good and evil. She was certain Layton was putting his own spin on it, but she also knew enough to know that he was giving her a lot of good information.

Now she had some questions. "But I struggle with understanding why you have turned to the dark side. It doesn't seem to match up with the man sitting here in my kitchen right now."

"Because evil gets a bad rap since it's viewed through the Christian lens. Once you view it through a different lens, you see that evil is just what we've been called to justify our oppression and subjugation to those who believe differently."

"You're losing me a little bit here."

Layton had finished the initial offering of cookies, and she provided him with a few more, which he eagerly took before continuing the discussion. "God didn't like Lucifer because Lucifer threatened him. He didn't want to be challenged. He wants blind acceptance. We aren't about that. We are about independence and making our own choices. Using the powers of darkness to maximize our time on this earth. Yes, we dedicate our lives to the Prince of Darkness, but he gives us everything in return, and he doesn't ask for blind acceptance. He appreciates those of us who are shrewd individuals who can think for ourselves. At the end of the day, our lifestyle and beliefs are about self, autonomy, and living in the now. Not planning for some absurd afterlife. This is it."

"But you can still use these powers for ill, right? Not just for good."

"The whole point is that what is ill may be different for you and me. And, I'm not going to hide it from you. We are in a battle. So, yes, if we have to use our powers to inflict harm or gain a tactical advantage on those who would try to destroy us and our way of life, then yes, we fully embrace that."

She sipped her tea as she reflected on his words. "This is all fascinating. I'm not sure where I fit into this."

Layton leaned forward. "And that's one of the reasons why I'm here. Like I told you before, I sense something special in you. Stacey told me what happened the other week. The fact you had that experience let me know you were one to watch. Then when I met you myself, I could feel your spirit energy." Layton paused. "Now it's time for me to be brutally honest with you. One of the reasons why no one has told you that is because the women you surround yourself with are rank amateurs. I'm not one to mince words. I'm telling you the truth. They want to believe they're real witches, casting feel-good spells, and putting positive energy into the world, but they're fooling themselves. They're not the real deal. They don't have the ability to be the real deal, either. And that's all well and good, but we can't take them seriously in the realm we work in."

"You really think we're all delusional?" her voice squeaked.

Layton shook his head. "Not all. But many, yes. Not you, though. That's why I'd love to give you the opportunity for more, but you have to want it. Have to embrace it. If you're happy going about it with your friends and your little coven, then you can keep doing that and never have to be subjected to me again."

She bit her bottom lip as her mind swam with conflicting thoughts. "Hypothetically, if I wanted to be a part of Optimism, what would that look like?"

"We're not dabblers, Eliza. We're an all-or-nothing, take-it-or-leave-it group."

That sounded exciting and daunting at the same time.

"You don't have to decide today. I want you to fully consider what it would be like to join us."

"Thanks for spending the time and being so kind to me."

He placed his hand on top of hers. "You could add a lot to Optimism."

She had to keep bubbling romantic feelings in check. He probably didn't see her in the same way she saw him. "You're too nice."

"Only for people I like." He grinned. "I mentioned our battle against those in town who believe differently. We're in a struggle, that's for sure. We could use you and any other like-minded women in your group that you think would be interested, but only if they could accept our ways. The last thing we want is friction between our groups, especially if you decide not to join us. That would never be my intention."

"I think some of our members don't have the highest opinion of Optimism or Astral Tech—although, I guess that group is now defunct, I hear."

"Yes, it is. We have obtained the members who have potential from there, and the rest of the group has dissolved."

"You've given me a lot to think about. Thank you for coming over."

"I should be the one thanking you for such hospitality. I think I ate almost a dozen of these cookies. You have a real gift for baking."

Her cheeks burned at his compliment. "I love baking. I'd do it as a job if I could."

"Next time we have an event, you're going to have to bring some for the group. People will go crazy over them." He stood up. "I think I've taken enough of your day."

"No, I appreciate it." She rose to meet him. "I feel like all we did was talk about me. How are things with you?"

"I've had an unexpected development happen with a legal clinic that opened near our office."

"Oh, is that the domestic violence clinic?" She remembered meeting the woman at the festival.

His eyes narrowed. "Yes, how do you know about it?"

"I met the lawyer running it at the summer festival. She was going around telling people about it. She seemed very nice." She thought for a minute. "Why would you have an issue with the clinic?"

"I obviously support a domestic violence clinic, but my fear is that Olivia has an ulterior motive and that she wants to use the clinic as a front for her own religious agenda."

Ah. Now that made sense. "Oh, yes. She and I actually had a conversation at the festival about it."

He took a step toward her. "Really?"

"Yes. Why do I feel like I'm missing something here?"

"Olivia Murray is basically our number one enemy."

She found that hard to believe. "Her? She didn't seem very threatening to me."

He placed his hands on her shoulders. "You cannot underestimate her. She has something that I've never seen or experienced before."

"Wow. I would've never known."

Layton frowned. "That's one of the reasons she's so dangerous."

"And what do you think she's doing now?"

"Hopefully nothing but her legal work, but we've been through a few rounds together, and I know her better than to think that she's just acting as a lawyer. She's never *just* a lawyer. I don't want her polluting the minds of women who are already vulnerable."

She bit her bottom lip. "Come to think of it, she did warn me about Optimism."

Now that made him smile. "What did she say?"

"Basically to stay away from you guys. I told her I was a practicing Wiccan. She didn't push, but she left the door open for conversation."

Layton's jaw locked.

"What's your big beef with Olivia?"

He looked her in the eyes. "That she wants to destroy Optimism, and even more than that. Me."

CHAPTER ELEVEN

Olivia and Jess sat at the clinic having finished up a full day of consultations. Olivia was starting to feel like they were making a difference. And while she and Jess didn't see eye to eye on some things, they were a good team advocating for these women.

But when she heard the bell on the clinic door, Olivia's heart dropped. She could only hope that it wasn't Layton paying her another visit. She really didn't need that especially with Jess there.

When she went to meet the visitor though, her heart actually warmed.

"Nina Marie, what a pleasant surprise." She hugged Nina Marie but was careful not to grasp too tightly.

Nina Marie gave her a slight smile. "I've wanted to come down sooner, but honestly, some days I have a hard time even getting out of the bed. Thankfully, I've been feeling better lately."

Layton had taken away so much from Nina Marie, but at least she still had her life. "Nina Marie, this is Jess. She's a law student helping me out here."

Jess took her hand and gave her a smile before turning to Olivia. "I'm going to head out unless you need something."

"No. I'm all set. Great work today."

Jess beamed. "It was a good day." Jess grabbed up her bag and laptop. "Nice meeting you, Nina Marie."

Once they were alone, Olivia couldn't help but give Nina Marie another quick hug. "I'm so happy to see you."

"I know I don't look it, but I'm actually getting physically stronger. Mentally, well, that's still a work in progress. Abe has to be the most patient and kind man in the world."

"I'm glad the two of you are together. He's not going to let you down." As she said those words she couldn't help but think of Grant.

"Have you talked to Grant?"

"Yeah. But nothing has changed."

Nina Marie looked at her. "Just give him time. I believe he'll come back around."

"I hope so," she said softly.

"How are things going here?" Nina Marie asked.

"Really well. We've already been able to get almost a dozen protective orders."

Nina Marie looked out the window. "It's sad that there are so many cases. You know how important this cause is to me. Maybe one day when I'm in a better place mentally, I could be of some use."

"Absolutely." An idea popped into her head. "You know it could be very therapeutic for you to help others. You'd be an invaluable asset. Unfortunately, that's because you've lived this yourself."

Nina Marie nodded. "Something I'll never be able to forget."

"You're stronger than you realize."

"Speaking of that, I have started volunteering at the church. I've only done it once so far, but I plan on going back."

Olivia loved to hear that news. "That's wonderful, Nina Marie."

"Thanks. I enjoyed it, and I think it will be good to force myself to get out more. I can't live shut up for the rest of my life." Nina Marie turned to face her. "A little close to Optimism here, aren't you?"

Olivia sighed. "Yeah. That wasn't by design. Layton has already been here threatening me to mind my business."

Nina Marie quirked an eyebrow. "And are you?"

"Honestly, right now I have my hands full with the legal issues and getting these women the practical help they need, but if God opens a door for me to walk through, I'll do it."

Nina Marie smiled. "I have no doubts about that." She took a seat on the small sofa. "There's actually another reason I came by too in addition to wanting to check out the place."

Olivia joined her on the couch. "What is it?"

"I heard an interesting rumor that I thought might be of interest to you."

"Tell me."

"I don't know how familiar you are with the Wiccan presence in town?"

"Not very. I met a woman at the summer festival who said she was a Wiccan, but that didn't surprise me given who that festival targets."

"Well, I think Layton might be making a play for some of their members."

"Really? Why?"

Nina Marie tucked an auburn strand of hair behind her ear. "I'm not sure, but the de facto leader of the group is being courted. A woman named Eliza."

"Wait, I think that's who I met."

"And Stacey is knee-deep in this," Nina Marie said.

She didn't like where this was headed. "What a mess. I wish I could have some time with Stacey away from this craziness and the influences of Optimism."

"She has to make her own choices. You know that. Maybe one day she'll come around. If I can change, then I think there's hope for anyone."

"Do you think the rest of the Wiccans are supportive of this Optimism effort or against it?"

"There's disagreement," Nina Marie said knowingly. "A core group of their members believes they are doing good and refuse to engage in anything that could be construed as dark magic or sorcery that could hurt anyone. We know Layton is the epitome of all of that."

"Why would Eliza and the others consider going to Optimism?"

"Maybe they got a dose of powers the dark side can hold? Or maybe they're drawn in by Layton's smooth-talking and fancy parties. That kind of thing can be very alluring to people."

"You realize that from my standpoint, Wiccans are also problematic."

"Yes, but Layton is even worse," Nina Marie replied.

Olivia wanted to be clear. "I'll give that to you, but we can't sanitize the situation. The Wiccans may or may not realize what they're doing, but they're aligned with evil whether they understand it or not."

"You can't give up though. Shouldn't you try to talk to Eliza at least?" Nina Marie asked.

"You think she'd listen to me? I wouldn't just be saying that she shouldn't go to Optimism. I'd also be encouraging her to give up witchcraft completely."

Nina Marie patted Olivia's hand. "Do I need to remind you how convincing you can be? I was a lot further gone than Eliza, and I was able to change my life."

"You want me to do this? Why?" Olivia asked.

"Because I believe in you."

Olivia shook her head. "It's not me. It's the Lord." Olivia thought for a moment. "I'll talk to Eliza on one condition."

"What?"

"You come with me."

Nina Marie's eyes widened. "Me? Who am I?"

It seemed like the best solution. "You're the perfect person to talk to her. You made the point a minute ago without even realizing it."

Nina Marie paled. "I'm not good at sharing my faith, Olivia. I'm still getting my own bearings."

"We'll do it together. We both bring something to the table here."

Nina Marie averted her eyes. "If you really think I could be of any help."

"I definitely do. What do you say?" Olivia asked.

"Let's do it."

———

ON SATURDAY, Olivia had a meeting with a new potential client who had sent her a cryptic email. She had said in the note that it was important they met soon, so Olivia had made the time. She hadn't asked Jess to come in on the weekend, but Olivia didn't have any issues with it. Spending almost ten years as a BCR lawyer, she often worked weekends and long hours.

Right at ten o'clock on the dot, the door opened, and she went to meet Katy Leonard.

"You must be Katy?" Olivia provided her hand to the pretty, young blonde.

"Yes. Thanks for meeting me." Katy turned and closed the office door. "Are we safe here?"

"Yes." That was the first thing that let Olivia know this was serious.

"Can you lock the door? Especially since it's the weekend. You're not expecting anyone else, are you?" Katy's voice shook as she spoke.

"Just you." A sense of unease washed over Olivia, and she locked the door before turning her attention back to Katy. "Can I get you anything? Coffee, water, tea?"

"Water would be great."

Olivia went to their mini fridge then gave Katy the bottle. "Come on into my office."

Katy followed her and took a seat. She clenched the water bottle tightly. A tell-tell sign of nerves.

"Katy, take a deep breath and get comfortable. No one is going to harm you here."

"I know logically that's right, but it's a lot harder than you may think to feel safe."

Olivia looked into Katy's light brown eyes that were full of fear. "Please start at the beginning. I need to know everything in order to best help you."

Katy drank some water before setting the bottle down on Olivia's desk. "I met this guy about six months ago. At first, things were amazing. He was super handsome, had a great job, wonderful personality. Basically, he was like the total package. He told me ran a company that did really well, but we never got into a lot of details about his work. Mainly, he was focused on me, and always was very attentive."

"All right." Olivia took down some basic notes. She knew enough to realize that this dream guy was going to turn out to be a nightmare.

"He was a bit older than me, but I've always been mature for my age, and I was so tired of dating deadbeats who didn't have jobs or were still living at home."

"And how old are you?"

"I'm twenty-eight."

"So you're with the guy and things are going well."

Katy nodded. "Yeah. He bought me nice gifts, and he always knew the right thing to say. I was swept off my feet." Katy looked down. "But then we didn't see each other for a few months. When he called me a couple of weeks ago, that's when things started to change."

"How so?" Olivia feared it would be a similar story to all the others she heard.

"He started getting really possessive and jealous. He wanted to know my whereabouts all the time, who I was texting, everything. It was like my dream guy became my worst nightmare."

"And then what happened?"

Katy clasped her shaking hands in her lap. "He started getting violent."

Olivia leaned forward. "You're not alone, Katy. I'm right here, and we can get you help."

"It's not just the violence."

"Is he emotionally abusive too?" she asked.

"Not in the way you're thinking."

"Tell me."

"He was into some weird stuff," Katy said softly.

"Do you mean sexually?" Olivia feared where this might be going.

Katy shook her head. "No. Not like that. You're going to want to commit me after I tell you this."

Olivia wanted Katy to feel like she could tell her the whole story. That was the only way she could really help her. "I am not going to judge you. I promise you that. I'm here to help. Here as your legal counsel. Whatever you tell me remains confidential unless you give me permission to share."

Katy sat silently, and Olivia didn't push her. She needed to give Katy time to get comfortable, and she had all day, if need be. This was exactly the type of work Olivia wanted to do. Really help those that needed it the most.

Katy looked back up at her. "I think he was into some weird black magic."

Olivia's gut clenched.

"See, you think I'm psycho."

Olivia shook her head. "No. That's not it at all. What is this man's name?"

"Layton. Layton Alito."

Of course. Olivia thought back to Katy's description of the guy. It all made sense now. "Did he try to get you involved in his New Age group?"

Katy paled. "How in the world could you've known that?"

"Because unfortunately I know all about Layton and

Optimism."

"You actually believe me?" Katy's voice cracked.

"Absolutely. What did he try to get you to do?"

"Some weird séance or something. I don't even know. When I got to his house, there were other people, and there was some type of ceremony he wanted me to take part in. Thankfully, I was able to sneak out, but then he broke into my house the next night, and things got out of control."

Olivia seethed inside. "Layton is an evil man, Katy."

Katy's eyes filled with tears. "I didn't figure that out until it was too late, and now I don't know how to get him to leave me alone."

"That's what I'm here for."

Katy leaned over the desk. "Do you believe he actually has magical powers?"

"Unfortunately, Layton does have power that is derived from a spiritually dark place."

Katy's eyes widened. "I didn't think much about this stuff. I haven't been to church since high school."

"You see now with your own eyes that there is spiritual darkness in this world, Katy. We are often surrounded by darkness, but God is stronger than Layton or anything else." Olivia didn't know how much to discuss this topic with Katy. She didn't want to scare her off, but she also wanted her to know what she had gotten into. "This is bigger than just you or me."

"What can I do?" Katy asked.

"There are a few things that we can do. Obviously, I'll file for an order of protection against Layton, but I want to be completely transparent with you."

"You don't think he'll leave me alone, do you?"

"Layton isn't deterred much by the law, and he has a lot of friends in high places."

"Then what in the world can I do? Just be a sitting duck?"

Olivia shook her head. "You could consider trying to reconnect with God. Go to a church service. I'm not saying you should jump into something, but you've seen enough with Layton to know you will want God on your side. He can provide protection I can't."

Her eyes filled with tears. "Do you really believe that?"

"I do."

"Why?"

"Because I've seen God work in my own life. He's protected and provided for me in my times of need. When I literally thought I might not see the next day, He was there."

Katy gripped her hand. "I'm scared. Can you please help me?"

Olivia's heart broke into pieces. "I'll get this paperwork filed with the court right away. In the meantime, where did you leave things with Layton?"

She blew out a breath. "After he hit me the other night, I haven't seen him. He did send me some texts acting like nothing had happened, but I ignored him."

"Absolutely no contact with him, okay? No calls, texts, emails. Nothing."

"You don't have to worry about that. I don't want to be with him."

Olivia felt like she had to say something else. "I'm fully aware of how convincing Layton can be. He's a charmer, and he may come back to you with an awfully sincere sounding apology. Probably with some extravagant and very thoughtful gifts. He's a master of manipulation."

"I don't care. I've had enough. This whole cult ceremony was the final straw. I can't be a part of his demented world."

"Layton doesn't take no for an answer. We have to be prepared that he will lose it over us seeking an order of protection. Is there anyone you can stay with until we get through this patch, so you won't have to be alone?"

"Not really."

Olivia tapped her pen on her legal pad as she tried to think through options.

"If he knew I was here, he would hurt me again. That's why I wanted to come in on a Saturday when he wouldn't be working. I couldn't believe how close the clinic is to his office."

Olivia couldn't argue with that. "How did you find out about this clinic?"

"I saw the flyers at the grocery store."

Jess had taken flyers out to the local businesses the other week. "I should also say that because Layton and I have such a tumultuous history, that having my involvement may make things worse for you. Maybe I should get you a referral."

Katy shook her head. "No. I can tell by listening to you that you're not afraid of him. You'll stand up for me and do what's right. That's what I need."

"Are you certain? I could find you another lawyer who isn't connected to any of this." Maybe Olivia should've suggested that the moment she heard Layton's name.

"No. No one else will believe me. They will think I'm delusional. I can tell that you get it."

Olivia knew what she had to do. "Then you should come and stay at my place. You don't need to be alone."

Katy shook her head. "No way. You're already doing all of this without pay. I couldn't do that. I will be fine."

"Layton isn't one to underestimate. I can't guarantee your safety if you go back to your house alone."

Katy relented. "I do have one person I could reach out to. We used to be really good friends in college. She'll let me crash with her."

"Why didn't you mention this person earlier?" Olivia was wondering if this friend existed.

"Because we didn't part on the best of terms, but if I tell her that I need her, she'll come through. That's the type of person she is."

"I suggest you go pack a bag and visit your friend, and if you decide you want to go to a church service, just let me know."

Katy smiled for the first time since she entered the office. "Thanks, Olivia. You're a good woman."

"I haven't done anything yet."

Tears filled Katy's eyes. "Yes, you have. More than you could know."

———

LAYTON WATCHED with interest from the parking lot as Katy walked out of Olivia's clinic. Now wasn't that something? There was a reason he'd put that tracking software on Katy's phone. They'd started casually seeing each other months ago, but he had cooled things off while he was preparing for the trial. Thankfully for him, Katy had been oblivious to his legal troubles.

He liked Katy, but he wasn't into serious relationships. Yeah, he'd gotten a little rough with her the other day after they had reconnected and had actually felt a little bad about it. That was until now. Because she'd committed the worst type of offense—she'd sought help from the enemy. Olivia was up to no good. Now he'd have to take care of this situation before it escalated.

One thing he'd learned was not to underestimate Olivia's legal skills. If she came after him over what he'd done to Katy, then that could cause him a lot of negative publicity he didn't need, especially after the Nina Marie fiasco.

Layton made sure he gave Katy enough of a head start to her house. Knowing Olivia, she had probably counseled Katy to get somewhere safe. That's another reason Layton didn't have time to spare.

When he'd met Katy, he'd instantly wanted her. She was not only gorgeous, but she was able to carry on an enjoyable conversation. It wasn't a combination he saw every day. He'd made the mistake of inviting her to an Optimism ceremony. Why he couldn't learn his lesson and keep the two things completely separate, he didn't know. It was one of his weaknesses and something he had to be more careful about, and now he had another mess to clean up.

But his feelings for Katy weren't like those for Nina Marie. Katy made the mistake of seeking help from the wrong person, but that's all it was—a mistake. One she'd have to pay for, but not in the same way he made Nina Marie pay.

A few minutes later, he arrived on Katy's street. He parked a few houses down and started to make his way to her house. He was almost there when a small gray sedan pulled up in her driveway. He sidestepped behind one of the neighbor's cars.

He watched as Katy came out of her house and embraced the tall, wavy-haired brunette who got out of the car.

The woman turned. *What was this? Some sick joke?*

Why was Eliza at Katy's house? His day had just gone from bad to worse. He turned around and walked back to his car. He'd have to figure out another way to handle this situation—and fast.

———

"KATY, ARE YOU OKAY?" Eliza looked into the eyes of her old college roommate whom she hadn't spoken to in months.

Katy's eyes darted back and forth looking at the street. "Please come inside. It's not safe out here."

"You're scaring me."

Katy grabbed onto her hands and pulled her into the house.

"Katy, tell me what's going on," Eliza demanded.

"Come with me as I pack a few things, and I'll explain."

Eliza's mind scrambled with awful thoughts as she followed Katy into the bedroom.

Katy pulled a suitcase out from under the bed and started grabbing clothes from her drawers.

"Talk to me," Eliza said.

"I've been in an abusive relationship, and I found out from the legal clinic some even scarier things about the man."

"Did you go to the new domestic violence clinic?" Eliza asked.

"Yes. Do you know anything about it?"

"Yeah, I met the lawyer in charge at the summer festival."

Katy folded a couple of shirts and placed them into the suitcase. "We're going to file for some type of restraining order, but this man is powerful, and he is scary."

"In what way?"

"I know you believe in magic stuff, so maybe you'll get it. He belongs to some occult group."

Eliza's heartbeat sped up. "Wait a minute. Are you talking about Optimism?"

Katy stopped and turned. "You know them too? Am I the last person in this town to hear about this group?"

Eliza started feeling sick. It was like she knew the answer before she asked.

Katy stared at her. "Please don't tell me you're involved with them? I thought you said your witchcraft didn't hurt people."

"It doesn't," Eliza shot back. "I've been approached by them, but I haven't joined their group."

"Good. Don't. Stay far, far away. Especially from their leader, Layton Alito."

And there it was. Her worst suspicions were confirmed. "He's the one who hurt you?"

"Yes."

"Physically?"

"Yes. On multiple occasions." Katy turned toward her. "Do you not believe me?"

"Of course I do. It's just I never would've thought that."

"That's what makes abusers like him so powerful."

Eliza felt she might get ill as she remembered feeding Layton cookies and them having long talks together—all alone. She could've ended up like Katy.

"What are you thinking?" Katy asked.

"That I could've just as easily been you."

Katy started to cry. "My life is a mess, Eliza. Thanks for helping me out here."

"I know we've had our ups and downs, but I wouldn't leave you alone to deal with this." The question was how she was going to manage this situation. First, she had to make sure Katy was okay. Then she could deal with the fallout.

Katy quickly finished packing, and Eliza did what she could to help. When they were in Eliza's car, Katy started sniffling again.

"I'm sorry. Everything is hitting me."

"You have no reason to apologize. I should've listened to my initial gut instinct about Optimism, but, like you, I was drawn in by Layton."

Katy turned to her. "You weren't dating him too, were you?"

Eliza gripped the steering wheel. "No. It wasn't like that." At least it hadn't gotten to that point, thankfully. "But I did experience things with one of their members that scared me to death."

"I knew I wasn't losing my mind. They're really a bunch of devil worshippers."

A chill shot down Eliza's arm. "A few weeks ago, I would've disagreed. I didn't even think there was a devil, but I've reconsidered that point. I'm supposed to go to some events to get to know them better."

"Is that what you want?"

"I'm not saying all the people in the group know what Layton's capable of—I didn't. But now that I do know, I can't support them in any way, shape, or form. Like you said, my goal has always been to use magic to help people."

Katy blew out a breath. "I'm beginning to think there isn't such a thing as good magic."

"I've heard that before," Eliza muttered.

"I haven't been to church in years, but I know the difference between right and wrong. I believe there is a God, and apparently, that's a good thing given the situation I'm in now."

"I'll admit I'm feeling a bit out of sorts about everything."

"You and me both," Katy said.

Eliza feared the path she had been on was one that would lead to destruction. She wondered if she had already taken the wrong turn and was doomed.

CHAPTER TWELVE

Olivia had convinced Nina Marie to share her story with Eliza to try to make sure she didn't get pulled into Optimism's dark hole. Olivia sat in the driver's seat as they rode to Eliza's house to pay her a visit. It hadn't been that difficult to track down the address.

"I can't believe I let you talk me into this. I don't know if I'm ready," Nina Marie said.

"There's no time like the present. You know better than anyone how fragile this life is. If we can make an impact on one woman's life, let's put forth our best effort, okay?"

Nina Marie nodded. "You're right, as usual."

They pulled into Eliza's driveway. "After we're done here, I'm taking you to get food." The least Olivia could do was make sure Nina Marie had a good meal.

"Don't you have better things to do? How are things going with Grant?"

Ugh. "I'm trying my best not to be that girl who is too needy."

Nina Marie turned to her. "As hard as it is, you have to be patient. It might take time."

Nina Marie was right. "I get that, but it's hard. It's not something where there is an easy fix."

"You aren't alone through this. I've had my fair share of guy problems in my life. You know you can confide in me."

Nina Marie's kind offer touched her. "Thank you." Olivia took a breath. "But for now, let's put my problems aside and go talk to Eliza."

The two women got out of the car and walked up Eliza's steps. Olivia knocked on her door.

"Showing up unannounced is a bold move," Nina Marie said.

"I didn't want to give her the opportunity to say no." She had been afraid Eliza would've politely declined their visit. That was much harder to do in person.

The door opened but it wasn't Eliza. "Katy, what're you doing here?" Olivia asked.

"What are *you* doing here?" Katy eyed Olivia and then Nina Marie.

"Who's at the door?" Eliza's voice rang out before she appeared. "Come on in."

Eliza quickly ushered them inside.

"What's going on here?" Katy asked. "Is this about me?"

Olivia shook her head. "Actually, Katy, I had no idea you'd be here. We're here to visit Eliza."

"Katy, maybe it's best if you finish up the cookies. I'll be out on the back porch. I need to speak to Olivia for a minute."

Katy frowned. "All right." Katy walked toward the kitchen.

Olivia and Nina Marie followed Eliza outside to the porch.

"I don't believe we've met," Eliza said.

"I'm Nina Marie. I used to be CEO of Astral Tech."

"Ah. Yes, I know who you are. I didn't recognize you, but I think we did actually meet some years ago."

Nina Marie nodded. "Yes, I believe that too."

"Katy told me that you were her lawyer," Eliza said to Olivia.

"When she said she had an old friend who wouldn't let her down, I didn't know it was you," Olivia said.

"Would you have told her not to come?"

"I would've warned her that you knew Layton"—Olivia took in a breath, not wanting to sugarcoat it—"the man who has been abusing your friend."

Eliza held up her hand. "I get it. I had no idea what that man was capable of. I was fooled, but I'm on Katy's side here. If that's why you came over, then this can be a short conversation because I have her back one hundred percent."

"Like I said before, I didn't even know that you knew Katy. I'm working on Katy's legal issues, and I appreciate you taking her in, but you need to understand what type of man you're dealing with. That's one of the reasons I brought Nina Marie with me."

Nina Marie took a seat in one of the patio chairs, and the other women followed suit. "Sorry, I get weak if I stand too long these days." Then Nina Marie looked directly at Eliza. "That wasn't the case before Layton stabbed and left me for dead."

Wow. Nina Marie wasn't pulling any punches.

"I read that he was found innocent," Eliza said.

"Not guilty," Olivia responded. "There's a big difference under the law. Plus, he had help from an insider who gave him an alibi, but there's no point rehashing his case. Nina Marie is sitting right here. She's known the man for years—been both an ally and an enemy of his. She speaks the truth."

"I'm not saying it didn't happen. Especially now after I've heard Katy's horror story. Where does this all leave Katy? Do you think she's safe here?" Eliza asked.

"That depends." Olivia knew this next topic of conversation was going to be dicey. "We want to talk to you about something else."

"If you're wondering if I'm going to join Optimism after all of this, I think I can safely say that won't happen."

Olivia let out a sigh of relief, but that wasn't enough. "That's good to hear. It really is."

"So, what's the problem?" Eliza asked.

Olivia looked at Nina Marie, urging her to speak. Thankfully, Nina Marie took the hint.

"I thought I could provide you with a unique perspective on things," Nina Marie said.

"What things?" Eliza asked.

She wasn't going to make this easy. Maybe Olivia should intervene to set up the conversation. "Nina Marie used to be a practicing witch among other things as leader of Astral Tech."

Eliza sighed. "But that isn't what type of magic I practice. How many times do I have to tell people that?"

"That's it," Nina Marie said. "You think there's this thing out there called white magic and that you're helping people, but you're as much a part of the evil one's flock as those in Optimism. And the fact that you don't even realize it means you're in danger—of either eventually ending up like them or continuing to think what you're doing is innocent when in actuality you have already invited forces of darkness into your life." Nina Marie took a big breath and shut her eyes. "In fact, they're still here right now."

"What?" Eliza's eyes widened. "Stacey told me that they would leave me alone now."

Nina Marie's hazel eyes popped back open. "Stacey was wrong."

Eliza groaned. "I can't believe this. I can't have them around me. This is my home!"

"They are free to hang around you as long as you continue witchcraft and whatever else you're practicing," Olivia said. "You've opened that door for them to walk into your life."

"But I'd been living peacefully until Stacey came into this house. If what you're saying is right, they could've been around for years."

Nina Marie cleared her throat. "It's possible that Stacey's presence was like a magnet, but it was probably just a matter of time before they visited you, that is, unless they have been here the whole time and you didn't realize it. Demons can be dormant and docile when they want. You were doing what they wanted. Practicing magic, divination. They had no reason to interfere."

Eliza drummed her fingers on her patio table. "This all sounds crazy."

Olivia needed to push her. "Under regular circumstances, we wouldn't be here, but because I know how dangerous Optimism is and what they bring to the table, I can't be silent."

Eliza leaned forward. "Then tell me what you really want to say."

Olivia took a breath. "There are only two sides here, Eliza. There is no magical middle ground. No white witches."

Nina Marie nodded. "Take it from someone who has been deep into this world. You have no idea the danger and darkness you're bringing into your life."

Eliza frowned. "Even if that's never been my intention? I've always only wanted to spread love and help people—not do any harm. I've not once used any magic for a bad purpose. And if someone in our group did that and I found out about it, I would tell them they were no longer welcome in our coven."

"You're being naive," Nina Marie said, playing bad cop.

"And I think you're being a bit harsh," Eliza responded.

Olivia held her tongue. She didn't know whether Nina Marie's tough love approach was going to work, but she would defer to her given what she had lived through.

Nina Marie looked directly at Eliza. "I'm not trying to upset you. I don't want to gloss over it. I almost died because of the life I led, Eliza. I want to prevent the same hardship from coming to you. It's not too late. There is another way," Nina Marie said softly.

Olivia felt the outdoor temperature rise. Her hands grew clammy as she started to sweat. She didn't think this was from the summer day. This was something sinister. A heavy weight descended on her shoulders. "We've got company on the porch. Eliza, do you want them here?"

Eliza shook her head. "No, of course not."

"They don't believe you want them out of your life," Nina Marie said. "Take that crystal off from around your neck and any other New Age items you might be wearing."

Eliza didn't move for a moment. Then slowly, she removed the necklace and a ring. "That's all I have." Eliza stood up. "Get out of here. You're not welcome."

"They're not going to listen to you," Olivia said. The sweat started to drip down the back of Olivia's neck. She could see no visible signs of evil, but the presence of darkness was unmistakable. Even on that bright and sunny day, they were surrounded by darkness.

Eliza spent the next five minutes telling them to leave to no avail because her approach was wrong. Eliza didn't have the power to tell the demons what to do, but at least this demonstrated to Eliza that things were more serious than she could've imagined.

Olivia looked at Nina Marie and then at Eliza. She knew what she needed to do. She had to act before someone got hurt and the situation got completely out of hand. *Lord, help me.* She closed her eyes and started to pray aloud asking for help from the Lord. Only in His name would these demons flee.

After a moment, a breeze blew through the screened in porch. Olivia opened her eyes, and she saw that all the color had drained out of Eliza's face. Nina Marie also looked pale. "Are you both okay?"

Nina Marie nodded but Eliza still didn't speak.

"Talk to me, Eliza."

"I—I... saw them again," Eliza stuttered. "Evil creatures with big, bright, burning eyes."

Nina Marie took ahold of Eliza's hand. "They can take many forms, Eliza. Some days they look beautiful to the human eye, and other times their true heinous form comes out. And I didn't see anything, did you, Olivia?"

Olivia shook her head. "No. They just made themselves visible to you, Eliza."

"What have I have done?" Eliza asked. "I tried to talk myself into thinking that the experience with Stacey was a fluke. That I was hallucinating or something, but after today, I saw them as clearly as if they were standing here." Eliza's voice started to shake.

"Eliza, remember what Nina Marie said. It is *not* too late, but if you want to cleanse your life of this evil, you've got to do it all out. There is something I am going to ask of you."

"What?" Eliza asked.

"I'd like for you to sit down with Pastor Dan."

"The one you defended?"

"Yes. I think it would be good for you to hear from him about this stuff and not just me and Nina Marie. There's a lot I think you need to consider and contemplate."

"Why would he meet with me given my beliefs?"

"He'll meet with anyone," Nina Marie said. "He won't judge you."

"I'll listen. I admit I'm a bit confused. I know for certain I don't want any part of this evil."

"But you're not ready to change your current lifestyle, right?" Olivia could clearly see Eliza's struggle.

"You set up the meeting with the pastor, and I'll be there."

It was only a first step, but Olivia would take it.

———

LAYTON WAS TYPING AWAY on his office computer when his intercom buzzed loudly, indicating his secretary wanted to talk to him.

"Yes, Ingrid, what is it?"

"There's someone here who says he has to see you personally. He has a package delivery."

"Fine. Send him back." He wasn't expecting anything, but he'd welcome the break from the financials he was reviewing. Optimism was actually doing quite well from that perspective, but he always wanted to do better. That drive was one of the things that had made him such a successful businessman.

A few moments later, a young man walked into his office. "Are you Layton Alito?"

"Yes." Layton looked up at him.

The man handed over a large envelope that Layton accepted. "You've been served."

Layton cursed under his breath, and the man walked out of his office. He should've known better, but he'd learned long ago with the litigation he'd been involved with over the years that there was no point in trying to evade service. They'd always be able to get to you. The question was, what exactly he was in legal trouble for this time.

He tore open the envelope and pulled out the pages. Letting out another string of curses, he took the papers and walked down the hallway. When he got to Morena's office, he didn't bother knocking before walking in.

Morena looked up from the pile of documents and put down her pen. "Layton, what is it?"

"Take a look at this." He slammed the papers down on her desk.

She took a moment and scanned the documents, a deep frown pulling down on her lips. "This is a summons for you to appear before a judge. Some dispute with a woman named Katy Leonard. Who is she?"

Layton ran a hand through his hair. "A woman I've casually dated. Katy's not the point. Look who Katy's lawyer is."

Morena flipped the page and blew out a breath. "Of course, it's Olivia. Layton, this appears to be through the work Olivia is doing at the clinic. What does this Katy woman have on you?" she asked pointedly.

He didn't miss the hint of disdain in Morena's voice. There was no reason to be dishonest with one of his staunchest allies. "Katy and I had a fight that got a bit out of hand. She's fine though. She wasn't seriously injured."

Morena shook her head. "Layton, I thought you were supposed to be laying low after your trial. Why in the world would you put yourself in this compromised position?"

Now Morena had moved to straight up lecturing him. He had to be careful and hold his tongue because the last thing he needed was for Morena to decide she didn't want to work with him. "I *wasn't* thinking, okay? I reconnected with her after the trial, and things got a bit out of hand."

Morena tapped her pen on the desk. "Wait a minute, is this the woman you brought to one of our services the other week?"

"Yeah, that's her."

Morena groaned. "Layton, sometimes I think you need a babysitter. How can a man as brilliant as you continue to do such stupid things?"

"I'd watch your tone, Morena. Remember who you're talking to."

"And you remember what your place is! You haven't just put yourself at risk here, Layton. You've risked Optimism's operations and reputation. What if this Katy woman starts talking to the judge about what she saw happen at your home?"

"I'll deny it, and it will be her word against mine."

"Your word isn't as solid as it used to be. You just stood trial for attempted murder."

"Now you're starting to get hysterical."

She shook her head. "No. I'm apparently the only one around here thinking straight. We've got to fix this." She rose from her chair and started pacing. "Money. We need to offer her a payout."

"Do you really think Olivia's going to let that happen?"

"Olivia doesn't have to know about it. Let me approach Katy myself. See if I can clean up your colossal mess."

Layton stood. He'd had enough lecturing from Morena, but at the end of the day, her bottom line was right. "Good. Let me know how it goes and how much she's going to cost me."

———

GRANT SAT with Scott in Grant's office. Scott had wanted to meet face to face. Grant knew that wasn't a good sign.

"Give it to me straight," Grant said.

"When I tried to accept their settlement demand, I was told it was no longer on the table."

Grant held back what he really wanted to say and instead pushed forward. "How's that possible? They made the offer, and we accepted. Done deal."

"It's not a done deal until it's inked, and Eli claims Ms. Ramos is no longer interested at all in settlement. She wants her day in court, and according to Eli, it's a fight about principles."

Grant groaned. "I moved mountains to get the money to pay this settlement. Now you're telling me there is no way we can get this thing done out of court?"

Scott looked down at his legal pad. "I'm sorry, Grant. This is highly unusual. I think Eli has fanned the flames of passion in his client. This has become even more personal for her. She wants to see you pay."

"Could I have done a better job? Of course. But the way they're treating this thing is crazy." And that's why this was about so much more than Ms. Ramos. For all he knew, Layton was paying Ms. Ramos to push the lawsuit.

"Listen, I know when you told me the entire backstory I was a little skeptical. Well, a lot skeptical. But given how this is all unfolding, I'm thinking that you're probably right about Layton's involvement. I'm not sure if it's spiritual or not, but we know there's a connection between Layton and Eli. And the fact that the plaintiff won't even entertain sure money is unheard of in these types of cases."

"Where does that leave me, though? Totally screwed?" Grant could no longer hold back his frustration. "I'm in a no-win situation here."

Scott didn't immediately respond and that didn't instill confidence.

"I think we need to be a bit more aggressive than I would normally prefer," Scott said.

"How so?"

"Going after Ms. Ramos. Really searching for the skeletons in her closet and trying to use those as leverage."

"And if there are no skeletons?"

"Everyone has skeletons," Scott said flatly.

"Man, I'm not looking to destroy her life."

"We're at war here, and the last thing I want is for *your* life to be destroyed. Sometimes you must take drastic action. She's not all innocent here either if we're right about her involvement with Layton. Don't go soft on me now. We have to fight or you're as good as done. What do you say?"

"Fire away."

CHAPTER THIRTEEN

Olivia stood in the lobby of the courthouse waiting for Katy to arrive. She was a little worried that Katy might not make it, but she knew how difficult this was. At the end of the day, if Katy didn't want to go through with it, Olivia would be disappointed but she would understand. She tapped her foot to a song she was singing to herself.

"Hey," a voice said from behind.

She turned and there was Grant. Her heartbeat sped up just seeing him.

"Hey," she said.

A moment of awkward silence hung between them. "You have something going on today?" Grant asked.

"Yeah. A hearing for an order of protection." She didn't say against who.

"The clinic work must be going well for you." He shifted his weight from side to side.

The tension between them was palpable but it wasn't unfriendly. Just not their normal, easy connection. "Yeah. It's fulfilling, but it's also a lot of pressure to do the best I can for the victims."

He took a step closer to her. "Are you holding up?"

The fact that he seemed so concerned about her made her heart melt. "Yes," she said quietly. "How about you?"

Grant ran his hand through his hair. "They pulled the settlement demand off the table."

She snapped her fingers. "I knew it. Layton is up to his old tricks."

Grant nodded. "That was my thought too. We've got the deposition of the woman who sued me coming up."

That was big. She knew how important that moment would be. "I'll be praying about the case. For your lawyer and you." She wanted so badly to reach out and touch him, but she held back. He had asked for space, and she was trying to respect his wishes.

"Thanks." He looked over her shoulder. "I think your client might be here."

Olivia turned and saw Katy walking their way. "Yeah, that's her."

"I'll let you go then. Hope it all goes well in there."

"Thanks." She paused. "It was good to see you."

"You too," he said.

As Grant walked away, she tried to compose herself. Katy approached, and her cheeks were flushed.

"Katy, are you all right?"

Katy nodded. "Yeah, but I need to tell you something. I was getting coffee yesterday and was approached by a woman named Morena."

Olivia's stomach sank. Layton was now sending one of his people to do his dirty work. "I know Morena. What did she tell you?"

"She offered me money if I dropped this case and left Layton alone."

"How much money?"

"Twenty-five thousand dollars," Katy whispered. "Morena told me to keep it between us, that you would just complicate matters, but I couldn't do it after all you've done for me."

"Are you considering taking it?" Olivia knew how that amount of money could change Katy's life.

"Morena told me I could have a completely new life. Move out of town and start fresh." Katy paused. "But I don't know if I can." Katy looked directly at Olivia.

"This is a delicate situation. At the end of the day, it's your decision if you'd like to settle this matter. As your attorney, I can't make that decision for you."

"I couldn't sleep at all last night. If I don't say anything and just go on with my life, then what's the chance that Layton will hurt another woman?"

Olivia couldn't lie. "There's a high likelihood he will keep hurting women. Unfortunately, the only way to stop him is to lock him up, and the current case we have is about keeping him away from you—it isn't the state bringing criminal charges. Does that make sense?"

"How do we get the state to do that?"

"We would need a prosecutor to step up, open an investigation, and then bring charges. Given the fact that he went through the attempted murder trial, though, finding a prosecutor to take it on could be tough." Olivia didn't think that would happen anytime soon. "But let's take things one step at a time for now. You need to do what is best for you. There's a good chance Layton will end up leaving you alone regardless, given how this issue has flared up, but having an order in place demanding it would make me feel a lot better. If you want to move away and start a new life—taking the money—then I will be here for whatever you decide."

Katy's eyes filled with tears. "Taking his money doesn't seem right. Yes, I could use it, but I want to be able to look at myself in the mirror and not second-guess my decision. I want to move forward with the hearing, assuming you're still on board."

Olivia let out a sigh of relief. "You know I am."

"Then let's do this."

LAYTON WALKED into the courtroom ready to take on a new challenge. This was becoming an all too familiar occurrence for him. At least today he wasn't facing an attempted murder charge, but it was a big hassle, nonetheless.

He'd opted not to have a lawyer here with him today and instead brought Morena. From the conversation he did have with one of his many attorneys, this type of hearing was much more informal than what he was used to. And he was hoping the fact that he came without a lawyer might help his case. A guilty man would never show up unrepresented.

Layton turned to Morena. "You weren't successful in your attempt to make this go away." She had always been more optimistic about that prospect than him, especially since he knew Olivia was involved in the case.

"I gave it my best shot, but you messed this woman up, Layton," Morena said in a hushed tone.

Layton shrugged as he took his seat in the courtroom and waited for the judge to arrive. "I've faced much worse."

Morena gave a knowing nod of agreement, but he could tell she was royally ticked off at him. He was mad at himself for not being more disciplined, especially in the current climate. But today he planned to try and make Katy look like a crazy, desperate woman. He'd see if the judge would bite.

When Layton heard the sound of heels clicking loudly down the courtroom floor, he knew Olivia had arrived. If he was being honest with himself, this was all about him and Olivia—not Katy. She was a casualty in his larger battle.

Olivia didn't speak to him as she ushered Katy to the other table, and they had a seat. Katy glanced over at him and then quickly averted her eyes. The woman was scared to death.

After a few moments, the judge walked into the courtroom. Layton let out a breath when he saw it was a male judge. He figured a woman would've been worse for him given the circumstances. The gray-haired judge looked to be in his fifties and had pudgy red cheeks that probably reflected his elevated blood pressure.

"Good morning, I'm Judge Lowe. This is a hearing for an order of protection filed by Ms. Katy Leonard against Mr. Layton Alito. Is Ms. Leonard present?"

"Yes," Katy said quietly in response.

"And Your Honor, I'm Olivia Murray, Ms. Leonard's attorney."

Judge Lowe nodded. "Thank you." He turned and looked at Layton. "I presume you are Mr. Alito?"

Layton stood to address the judge. "Yes, Your Honor."

"And do you have legal representation here today?"

"No. I didn't think that was necessary."

"Very well." The judge shifted some papers in front of him. "I'm not sure whether everyone involved here is aware of how these hearings are conducted, so I'll set out some ground rules. Basically, I'm going to want to hear from Ms. Leonard and Mr. Alito directly. Ms. Murray, you're free to speak, but you won't be examining witnesses. I'll find out the information I need and then render a decision."

This guy seemed practical enough, but Layton would have a much better idea once he heard the types of questions the judge asked.

"Ms. Leonard, I'd like to start with you."

Layton leaned back in his chair and tried not to give off any hostile vibes.

Katy walked up to the witness box and was sworn in.

"Ms. Leonard, even though we're going to be very informal here, do you understand that you are under oath?"

"Yes, sir," Katy said.

"Very good. I've read your court filings, but I'd like to hear everything in your own words." He paused. "I know that talking about these issues can be very difficult. At any time if you need a break, just let me know. I've got all day and am in no rush."

Layton didn't like the sound of that, but he kept his facial expression neutral.

"I met Layton about six months ago. Initially I was swept off my feet."

"Tell me more about that."

Katy looked at the judge. "Layton seemed like the perfect gentleman. Always very professional and charming. He would open doors for me, bring me flowers and other gifts. The gifts did get nicer as we started dating. I knew he was wealthy, so I didn't think there was anything wrong with that."

"And you're saying at this period, you didn't feel threatened by him?" the judge asked.

Katy shook her head. "No, Your Honor. Like I said, he was a guy right out of my dreams. Unlike other guys I dated that wanted to immediately jump into bed, Layton wasn't like that. He actually wanted to talk to me. Get to know me. He would ask me a lot of questions about my day and my feelings. He didn't make it about him at all. It was really a breath of fresh air."

"When did things start to change?"

"It was strange because he said he needed a break a few months into things. I figured he was getting tired of me. I always felt he was out of my league, but then a few weeks ago, he called and wanted to see me again. I wasn't dating anyone, so I was happy to reconnect."

"And what happened when you started dating again?" the judge asked.

Katy blew out a breath. "He seemed like a different man almost from the start. He started getting very possessive and jealous. Demanding to know where I was going and what I was doing. Who I was calling and texting. He hadn't acted that way before. At first, I thought that maybe he actually wanted to get really serious and that's why he was acting that way, but then things took a turn for the worse."

The judge looked at Katy. "Did you want a serious relationship?"

Katy bit her bottom lip. "Yes. I did. That was until he started acting like a different man. The original Layton I knew was amazing. The new Layton was scary. It was like he wasn't even the same person."

"Did you convey your concerns to him?"

"I tried to, but when I started to question him, that's when he became aggressive. That side of him was completely new to me, and it scared me to death. I'd never been in a relationship before with someone who acted like that."

Layton let her words sink in, and frankly, he didn't think he'd been like that. But this, of course, was her side of the story.

"Did it escalate from there?" Judge Lowe asked.

Katy nodded. "Yes. One night Layton got mad at me and slapped me hard across the face. On another occasion he threw me to the ground." Katy's voice started to shake. "I was afraid he was going to hurt me badly."

Layton gripped the sides of his chair. She was starting to tick him off.

The judge picked up the paper in front of him. "I read in the filing your attorney submitted about some incident at Mr. Alito's house. Can you tell me more about that?"

Katy shifted in her seat. "I'm not sure what all Layton is into, but it's not something that I'm comfortable with. It was like a black magic séance he was trying to get me to participate in. Thankfully, I was able to sneak out, but I paid the price later when Layton hit me again. That was the last straw. I feared for my safety." She paused and looked at Layton. "I still do."

Layton had to stop a smile from spreading across his lips. Katy had no idea how much her words thrilled him. He only got stronger by sensing her fear. He looked at Olivia, and she was focused intently on Katy. Layton was anxious to have the judge hear his side of the story.

The judge asked a series of additional questions, but Layton became preoccupied with what he was going to testify to. Finally, the judge thanked Katy and turned his attention to Layton.

Layton was sworn in, but he obviously had no qualms about

lying. Katy's version of events had basically been accurate, but of course, he would never cop to that.

"Mr. Alito, just as I told Ms. Leonard, you are under oath. Do you understand that?"

"Yes, Your Honor." Layton looked directly into the judge's eyes.

"Now it's your turn to tell us what you believed happened here. But right off the bat, I have to ask. Do you dispute Ms. Leonard's account?"

"Absolutely, Your Honor. Ms. Leonard is a wonderful woman, but it became clear to me after spending some time with her that she has some mental health issues."

"Like what?"

"I'm not a doctor, but she had extreme mood swings, bouts of depression, and severe paranoia. She always thought someone was watching her or was out to get her. I tried my best to calm her fears and say that I would protect her, but it only got worse the closer we got."

"You bought Ms. Leonard numerous gifts, did you not?"

Layton nodded. "Yes. I'm fortunate to have a thriving business, and it gave me great happiness to be able to give Ms. Leonard nice things. She was always very appreciative." Layton looked down, preparing to start the real acting. "I'm honestly very concerned for her mental well-being. When I got served with these papers, I read in extreme surprise the allegations she was making. I've never laid a hand on her."

Layton stopped and tried to read the judge's response, but he wasn't easily read.

"Ms. Leonard," the judge said. "Have you ever been treated for any mental health issues?"

Katy didn't immediately respond, and Layton was relieved she'd confided her weaknesses in him.

"I—I have been treated for depression in the past," Katy stuttered. "But that was a couple of years ago."

"You're not currently seeing anyone for that?" the judge asked.

"No," Katy responded.

Layton decided to push the issue. "I encouraged her to seek treatment, Your Honor. When we reconnected, I was hoping that she would've taken my advice. I told her I would be by her side." The lies rolled off his tongue so easily. He was almost enjoying the story he was weaving on the fly. She had told him about her past struggles, but that had been the end of the conversation.

"Let's get back to you, Mr. Alito," Judge Lowe said. "What do you say about Ms. Leonard's allegation that you tried to force her to participate in some type of séance."

Layton let out a little laugh. "Your Honor, I have absolutely no idea where that came from. I do run a New Age company where we market and sell a variety of products, but I think Ms. Leonard misunderstood what we do and jumped to the crazy conclusion that spiritual well-being had to do with séances. Nothing could be further from the truth. My company is highly respected. When I read those words, I did wonder if Ms. Leonard was having some sort of break with reality. Yes, I did host a dinner party that evening with many esteemed members of the community, including a sitting judge. Ms. Leonard did leave unexpectedly, and I followed up with her the next day to check on her. I never hurt her. Not once. I only wanted what was best for her—and still do. That's another reason I didn't come here with a lawyer today. I don't want this to be adversarial. I want her to get the help she needs, and if that means she doesn't want me in her life, then I can abide by that."

Olivia frowned deeply. He was scoring big points right now, and this wasn't going according to Olivia's plan.

Layton wanted to add one more thing to try to push the judge over to his side. "I also have a colleague here today, Ms. Isley, who was at the alleged event in question. She can provide additional information on that evening if you need it."

The judge nodded. "I don't think that's necessary."

"One last thing. While I'm not a lawyer, there appears to be no physical evidence supporting her story, which, even coming from a non-lawyer like me, seems to be an issue worth factoring into your decision." He hoped he hadn't pushed too far. He also felt like if Katy had pictures of what he'd done to her, those would've been front and center.

"Thank you. Mr. Alito, please return to your seat."

"Your Honor, may I speak?" Olivia asked.

"Yes," he answered.

Layton knew that Olivia was going to make an attempt to change the narrative.

"Whether Ms. Leonard sought counseling years ago shouldn't have any bearing on the issue at hand today. The issue before you today is whether Mr. Alito physically assaulted my client."

"And you don't see any interconnection? What about her credibility?" Judge Lowe asked.

Olivia looked at the judge. "Your Honor, with all due respect, that's starting to sound like blaming the victim. Mr. Alito has no credible argument to rebut my client's allegations beyond a stark denial. He's provided no plausible reason why Ms. Leonard would make this up and put herself through this troubling ordeal."

"Mr. Alito, I'll give you a chance to respond," the judge said.

Layton straightened up in his seat. "I didn't want to have to go there, but given the seriousness of these claims, I feel like I have to." He paused. "I didn't reach out to Ms. Leonard. She called me." And didn't it feel good to have that fun fact in his back pocket.

"Is that true?" the judge asked Katy. "I believe you previously told me Mr. Alito was the one to reinitiate contact with you."

Katy sat silently, her face flushed.

"Your Honor, my client has been through a traumatic ordeal. Physical abuse. Her memory may not be on point on those types of details."

"Mr. Alito is directly contesting whether those events ever happened," the judge said.

"I realize that, Your Honor." Olivia's voice got louder. "But in these situations, it's often one person's word against another. The fact that we don't have pictures or other physical evidence shouldn't be determinative."

"Then what should be determinative?"

"As I said before, my client has absolutely no reason to make this up. Having to be here and testify and relive these events is tremendously difficult. We all know that a hearing like this isn't about a monetary outcome. It's solely to issue an order of protection to keep Mr. Alito away from Ms. Leonard. The only reason she would be motivated to try to get such an order was if she had truly lived through this horrific experience and wanted to get away from this man." Olivia took a breath. "And given how long you have been a judge in this area, I know you have seen instances where a witness presents well, but underneath is a completely different person."

Judge Lowe looked up at Olivia. "Ms. Murray, may I have a word?"

"Of course, Your Honor." Olivia stood and approached the bench.

Layton had a feeling the tide had turned back in his direction. The judge and Olivia spoke in low tones for longer than he would've liked. Anytime Olivia got to open her mouth, it wasn't a good thing. She was probably trying to spin her own web of lies against him.

He tapped his foot nervously as they continued to talk for way too long. But when Olivia finally turned around, her cheeks were red. She was not happy.

"I'm denying the request for an order of protection," the judge said. "Mr. Alito, no further action is required from you today. Thank you for your time. Ms. Leonard, I think you'll need to have some discussions with your attorney and then decide how to proceed. Thank you both."

And with that, the judge rose and left the room. Layton had no idea what had happened, but he knew one thing—he'd just faced down an adversary and won big time.

CHAPTER FOURTEEN

That night Olivia sought comfort and advice from Pastor Dan. She needed somewhere to turn, and she didn't want to bother Grant. Now, sitting in Dan's living room, he was trying to talk her down from the rough day she'd had and provide her encouragement about the Grant situation.

Dan came back into the room and handed her a cup of coffee. "I'm sorry about everything, but you know Grant is doing the best he can. This isn't easy for him."

"I believed that if I told him I needed him, he would be there for me. I really do think that."

"I do too," Dan said.

"But I also know that sometimes things don't work out." She sniffled, trying to hold back her crying. "I'm sorry to dump all of this on you, but you're one of the only people that fully understand everything here."

"You're not dumping anything. My door is always open for you —and for Grant."

"And I appreciate all you've done for both of us, but I wanted to talk to you about what happened with Layton."

"I'm ready." Dan took a sip of his coffee.

Olivia explained what had transpired at the hearing. "Then the judge asked to speak with me privately—true to form, Layton had him convinced. It didn't help that Katy had lied about the initial recontact. I don't know why she felt the need to lie. Maybe she thought it was somehow her fault since she reached out to him. But regardless, that lie negatively impacted us. The judge strongly urged me to have Katy see a mental health professional. I tried to explain to him that Katy was perfectly stable, but to him, her allegations about the séance seemed crazy. Especially when Layton was able to play the Louise card once again. How many times will he get to do that before someone figures out the truth? We have to expose Optimism for what it is."

Dan leaned toward her. "Be patient, Olivia. Their time will come."

She ran her hand through her hair. "I know. I'm upset. I feel like I failed Katy, and she couldn't just take the money that Layton had offered her. Now she has nothing, and she's been victimized a second time. I need to do better. I *have* to do better."

"You are doing your best, and we all know these are not normal circumstances." Dan raised his cup. "And speaking of not normal, I had a talk with Eliza."

"And?"

"I listened to her story. We're still in the getting-to-know-each-other phase. I can't launch in without understanding her, but she seemed open to continuing our dialogue, so I took that as a big plus." Dan squeezed Olivia's hand. "You are facing some huge obstacles right now, but you still have God on your side. Never forget that."

"You're right. It's not like me to wallow this much. Where do you think Eliza's head is really at right now?"

"I think she's convinced herself that her Wiccan practices are harmless, and she enjoys them. She's not ready to give them up. She knows Optimism is bad news, but she still isn't making the connection."

"If she keeps going down this path, she could end up in the crossfire."

"All we can do is try to guide her. We can't make her change."

Olivia knew that fact all too well. "She's been shaken up, that's for sure, but it hasn't gotten real enough for her yet. I'm glad that she and Katy are friends and she was able to avoid getting personally involved with Layton. That would've been a complete and utter disaster."

"See, there's one thing to be thankful for." He smiled.

"Thanks for the company, Dan."

"Olivia, you can't let this thing with Grant defeat you. I believe the two of you are supposed to be together. I think this is just one more trial the two of you have to face. You'll both come through it stronger. He loves you."

"And I know that. I love him so much too. It's hard when you can't immediately fix something. Fixing things is what I do. It's my job and my way of handling things. I think he's having issues that go beyond me. He's struggling with where he is with God."

"You're worried he's doubting God?"

She nodded in agreement. "He's being tested. This lawsuit is personal because it calls into question his actions as an attorney. That goes to his very identity. It's more than the money, although that financial exposure is also big."

"Don't give up on him."

"I'm not. I'm just trying to give him the space he asked for."

"And that's good, but you should also make sure he really knows you're on his side, no matter what."

"You're right. I have to show him I'm willing to wait on him, but also that I'm not going to run away because times got tough."

"Seems like you may need to make a stop on the way home tonight." He stood up. "Give me your coffee cup and hit the road."

She got up from the sofa, knowing exactly what she needed to do.

———

WHEN HIS DOORBELL RANG, Grant groaned. He wasn't sure who would be at his door, but he didn't want to see anyone tonight—or really at any time right now. People were annoying him. Maybe he should ignore the doorbell and they would go away. Each day he seemed to get more bad news, and his attempted prayers were falling on deaf ears.

He couldn't blame God, could he? Grant was basically giving up on himself, so why should God care about him?

The bell rang again. Someone was persistent, and there was only one person who he figured it could be. It was with a mix of emotions that he walked toward the door and opened it.

"Olivia."

"Can I come in?" she asked.

He stepped aside, allowing her to pass. "Are you all right?"

Olivia brushed by him, walked into the living room, and took a seat on the couch.

He could tell she was flustered, and that made him concerned because it took a lot to frazzle her. He sat down next to her. "What happened? Was it your hearing today?"

Olivia nodded. "What I couldn't tell you at the time was that the protective order I was trying to get today was against Layton."

"What?" No wonder she was upset. "Did you get it?" he asked, already knowing the answer.

"No." Her voice cracked. "I failed."

Seeing her in such pain broke his heart. He went against his better judgment and wrapped his arms around her. She needed him right now, and he refused to be selfish. He wanted to do the right thing by her. "What happened?"

She looked up at him, her eyes glistening with tears. "Layton lied and the judge believed him. That's the short version."

That evil man had brought pain to so many. Grant couldn't understand why God would allow him to have such a free rein in Windy Ridge. "I'm so sorry, but you can't blame yourself. You know how convincing Layton is. He's a master manipulator."

"But this time it wasn't about a business or money. It was about a woman's safety, and I let her down."

Grant wanted to try to bring some perspective, but he didn't know how she'd take it. "If you're going to do this type of work, then this thing is bound to happen. It's completely natural for you to be hurt, but you can't let it consume you." As he said the words, he realized the irony in him giving her this kind of talk.

She realized it too, but she didn't say that. She sat quietly for a moment.

Finally, he stood up and walked over to the fireplace, putting a little distance between them. Even though he was comforting her, his bottom line hadn't changed.

"You know I love you, Grant."

"I do," he said softly. "But I still think I'm undeserving of your love. That's the truth. It's how I feel."

"You have this crazy idea in your head that you're not good enough for me, and that's a lie."

Olivia rose from the couch and joined him. She wrapped her arms tightly around him. Even though he should run away, feeling her in his arms was too much to pass up. Because he was madly in love with her. He was also a very damaged man about to go to trial for legal malpractice. His livelihood could be taken away from him. "I wish it were a lie."

She looked up at him with her big brown eyes focused in. "I still believe in what we have together. Sometimes you have to fight for the things that matter the most, and I'm fighting for you."

He didn't know what to say. Once again, her kind words both touched him and made him feel like crap because he couldn't reciprocate. "Olivia, I'm numb."

"And that's okay."

"How can you say that? It's not okay!"

"If that's what you're feeling, then who am I to deny that?"

"That doesn't mean you have to embrace it. You need to be telling me that I'm messed up and not worth your time."

Olivia shook her head. "I would never think that."

He blew out a breath.

She rested her head on his chest, and he allowed himself to accept the love she was giving him—even though he didn't deserve it.

———

A CHILL SHOT through Eliza as she wrapped the blanket tightly around her. She sat on her couch with her friend Katy by her side.

"I can't stay here forever. Now that the judge has denied the restraining order, I will probably try to get out of town," Katy said.

"There's no reason for you to do that. You'd need to find a new job, a new place to live. Do you have the money for that?" Eliza asked.

Katy sniffled. "Not really, but I also don't want to be hanging around Windy Ridge when Layton decides it's time to have his revenge."

"Given everything, don't you think he'll stay away from you? He got lucky at the hearing, but if something happened to you, it would all come back to him."

Katy picked up a freshly baked chocolate chip cookie. "Yeah, I guess that's a good point. I can't thank you enough for letting me stay here. I know you'll want me out of your hair soon enough. Once I get everything figured out in my head, I'll get out of here."

Eliza shook her head. "You are not a burden on me. In fact, I'm actually glad you're here so I won't be in this house alone."

"Why?" Katy asked.

Eliza hadn't filled Katy in on everything that had happened because she already had so much on her mind, but maybe it was time to tell her about her experience. "You got a taste of what Layton was involved in when you got roped into the event at his house."

Katy shuddered. "Yeah, and that was freaky. I couldn't get out of his place fast enough."

"Well, something disturbing happened here at the house." Eliza recounted the story to Katy in vivid detail, including her seeing the demonic forces.

"Right here in this room?" Katy's eyes widened.

"Yeah. I know it sounds far-fetched, but I saw them with my own eyes. I've never been so afraid of something in my life, and now Olivia and her friends are trying to tell me that my Wiccan beliefs are allowing those types of forces to continue to come into my life."

"And do you believe them?"

"Honestly, Katy, I'm not sure what I believe anymore—about almost anything. I had my own world going, and I was enjoying my lifestyle. My Wiccan beliefs ground me and are completely compatible with the type of person that I am."

"How?"

"I'm not a fighter. I want peace. The spells and meditations I practice are for those types of things. For healing, peace, love. Not for hate, anger, and violence. But ever since those evil spirits came into my home, I've been off kilter. I'm lacking clarity. I went back to crystals to try to get re-centered, but no matter what I try, nothing works." Eliza knew she was venting, but it felt good to be able to explain this to someone who she felt wouldn't be judging her.

Katy continued to nibble on her cookie. "What are you going to do?"

"I'm not sure. What do you believe in?"

"Do you mean like God?" Katy asked.

"Yeah."

Katy didn't answer immediately. "I do believe in God, but before this happened, I wasn't thinking about it."

"You don't think I'm completely nuts for saying I saw these demonic spirits in my house?"

Katy shook her head. "No, but I surely hope I don't see them while I'm here. I have no interest in that."

"Me either. I'm hoping they've left for good, but I can't shake the feeling they're lying in wait."

"Then why don't you stop with the whole witchcraft thing? Is it worth it if it brings about these troubles?" Katy asked.

"I'm not convinced that there is a direct association like Olivia and the pastor say."

Katy crossed her legs under her. "I'm the wrong person to be asking for faith advice, but it seems to me it's reasonable to think practicing witchcraft could have unintended consequences."

"Then why was I able to do it for years without it happening?" That question was bothering Eliza.

"Maybe things were happening to you that you weren't even aware of?"

Eliza had considered the possibility. "I guess so. I plan to stay far away from Layton."

"You seem to be really confused. You can't live in limbo or in fear. Life is too short."

Katy was right. She couldn't keep living like this. She needed to take action.

———

GRANT ADJUSTED his tie as he took a seat in the law firm conference room. Today was Ms. Ramos's deposition, and that meant Grant was just a spectator. He had to place his faith in Scott to get the job done.

Scott hadn't shared with him all his findings into Leslie Ramos's life, but he had hinted that he had some stuff that would make the deposition interesting.

Grant still had mixed feelings about aggressive tactics, but he also knew this wasn't a level playing field. Everyone was out to get him, and he needed to do all he could to protect himself. He had to trust that Scott wouldn't cross any lines he shouldn't.

When Eli Morgan walked in, Grant didn't even bother to get up and shake his hand. They had dispensed with the usual pleasantries, and everyone was ready to get going.

Ms. Ramos sat at the head of the table wearing a microphone, and the court reporter was by her side, ready to take down every word that was said in the deposition. Most people thought depositions sounded exciting, but the truth is that they were usually boring. The question and answer format was much more sterile than a court environment, but today he did not need sterile. He was hoping for fireworks. Something to get some leverage to press for settlement.

Ms. Ramos's dark hair was pulled back in a bun, and she wore a navy sweater and pants. She had her hands clasped tightly in front of her, which showed her nerves. He couldn't blame her. Being deposed was nerve wracking. It was show time.

"Ms. Ramos, we've met before, but I wanted to reintroduce myself. I'm Scott O'Brien, and I represent Grant Baxter in this case. I'm going to be asking you some questions today, and you will need to answer verbally so the court reporter can take down what you're saying. Do you understand?"

"Yes," she answered.

"And you can always ask at any time if you need to take a break."

"Thank you," she responded quietly.

Scott cleared his throat. "All right. Then let's get to it."

Grant listened intently over the next two hours, and Scott went methodically through the details of Ms. Ramos's life and her accident. They had just returned from a break when Scott started a new line of questioning.

"Ms. Ramos, I know we went over the details of your accident already, but I want to circle back to that and get a few more questions in, okay?" Scott asked.

"Sure," she responded.

It wasn't like she had a choice. She had to answer anything Scott asked or have her lawyer tell her not to answer and get a judge involved. Eli had been playing it cool. He hadn't objected one time thus far.

Scott scribbled something on his legal pad and then looked up.

"Ms. Ramos, after your fall when you were taken to the hospital, do you know if they performed any drug screens on you?"

Ms. Ramos's eyes widened and before she could say anything, Eli spoke up. "Objection. Calls for speculation. There's also no foundation."

Scott turned to Ms. Ramos. "I know this is the first objection of the day, but even when your attorney makes an objection, that's just for the record. You're still required to answer my question unless your attorney directs you not to answer, and then we'll take it from there."

She nodded. "I'm not sure I understand what you mean by a drug screen."

Scott sat up in his chair. "Let me ask it again." Scott basically repeated the question word for word back to her. He wanted an answer.

Ms. Ramos shrugged. "I don't know. If they did, they didn't tell me about it."

"Is it true, Ms. Ramos, that you were taking prescription pain pills on the day you fell?"

So this was the dirty laundry Scott had found.

"No," she said without the same confidence she'd been showing in the last section of questions.

"Should I remind you, Ms. Ramos, that you are under oath? That you need to tell the truth here. It's as if you're testifying live in a courtroom under oath."

"I don't remember taking any pills," Ms. Ramos said without much conviction.

"Now that's a different answer all together than no, isn't it? So did you or did you not take prescription pain medication on the day of the accident before you went to the store."

Ms. Ramos's skin paled. "I don't remember."

"So, it is possible that you were on pain medication when you fell that day."

"Objection. Argumentative and speculative," Eli said.

Eli's body language had noticeably changed. It was clear to Grant that Eli had no knowledge about this beforehand.

"I told you, already, that I don't remember that," Ms. Ramos said.

"Just a couple more questions, Ms. Ramos," Scott said. "Isn't it true that you had been taking pain medication on and off for years before the accident—sometimes obtaining those pills without the proper prescriptions?"

"Don't answer that," Eli said.

"What's your objection counselor?" Scott asked, knowing he had Eli in a corner.

"Objection. Compound. Argumentative and prejudicial."

"You know this isn't trial, right? That's where those objections come in. Ms. Ramos, please answer."

Grant had to stifle a laugh. This was the first good thing that had happened in this case.

Ms. Ramos looked over at Eli, and he gave her the nod to answer. "I don't recall not having a proper prescription."

"That's all I have," Scott said. "Thank you for your time."

The normally cool Eli's cheeks turned red. Eli didn't speak to Scott and instead helped Ms. Ramos get untangled from the microphone and escorted her from the room.

Grant couldn't help it. He went over to Scott and gave him a huge bear hug. "Where did that come from?"

"Sometimes you have to take a chance," Scott said.

"What do you mean? Seemed like a slam dunk."

Scott laughed. "Because, man, I was going on a hunch based on all the documents I reviewed. I figured we didn't have anything to lose."

That made Grant laugh too. Laugh so hard he almost started crying. Maybe God was looking out for him after all.

CHAPTER FIFTEEN

Olivia had sat through a day-long continuing legal education class on domestic violence issues, and now she stood at Nina Marie's front door and knocked loudly.

A minute later, Nina Marie opened it, wearing her fuzzy purple robe and a towel on her head. "What's going on? I just got out of the shower."

"Can I come in?" Olivia asked.

"Sure." Nina Marie ushered her inside. Olivia followed her down the hallway to the bedroom.

"What's wrong?" Nina Marie asked.

"Nothing is wrong." Olivia had to try to contain her excitement.

"Now I'm confused." Nina Marie pulled the towel from her hair and grabbed a brush off her dresser.

"I took a continuing legal ed class today and it all came together in my mind, but I need to make sure you're on board."

Nina Marie pulled the brush through her auburn hair. "On board with what?"

"Guess what one of the topics was today?"

"Whatever it is, it clearly has you excited."

"Civil litigation."

Nina Marie laughed. "I still feel like we're talking two different languages right now. Remember I'm not a lawyer. Connect the dots for me."

"We sue Layton for assault and battery—in a civil case."

Nina Marie's hazel eyes widened. "Oh."

"Yeah. That's why I need your buy in."

"But what would that help anything? He's already been acquitted in the criminal case."

Olivia started pacing back and forth, trying to stay calm. "That was in a criminal court. There's a different standard there— remember, it's guilty beyond a reasonable doubt. The civil standard is lower. And full disclosure, the remedy available is monetary damages, and that's the only remedy here, but hear me out because it's bigger than money."

Nina Marie nodded. "I'm listening."

"This is our chance to expose Layton, and Optimism, for that matter. As we sat in court for the criminal trial, I was sick about not being able to question them. The prosecutor wouldn't dare go down the roads that we could. Even if we weren't able to get a favorable verdict, just putting them on the stand and asking the questions could be huge."

Nina Marie sighed. "But, Olivia, they'll lie like they always do. You know Layton and Louise have no issue with that. You'll ask them things, they'll deny, and we'll be right back to square one."

"I can do this, Nina Marie. I know I can. They're too cocky, too confident. I can catch them in their web of lies. They might be able to fool a run-of-the-mill prosecutor, but not me."

"You feel like this is what we need to do?"

"Yes, but if you are strongly against it, then I won't do it. You're the plaintiff here, Nina Marie. This would be your case. You suing Layton. There will be repercussions." Olivia realized as she spoke that maybe she hadn't thought this fully through. "It could put you right back in Layton's crosshairs."

"I'm not blind to the changes that have happened to me since the attack, but I am stronger than I look. I've faced down death, and I truly believe God saved me for a purpose. I also believe God uses you, Olivia, for things much bigger than yourself or me."

This woman who was once her enemy was now one of her closest friends. God had changed both of their lives using the craziest of circumstances. "I appreciate that so much. Let's make sure we're both doing this for the right reasons. I don't want this to be about revenge for either of us. I want it to be about justice and about trying to expose the evil behind Optimism."

Nina Marie smiled. "Olivia, no one would ever call you vengeful —me, on the other hand..."

"You'd have every right to feel that way. Layton did try to kill you."

"I can't live in the past. I have to use what happened and move on." Nina Marie paused. "I can tell you think I think Abe will be against this. He's hyper protective of me these days."

"And rightfully so." Olivia was thankful for Abe's protective and loving presence in Nina Marie's life.

"What will Grant think of this?"

Olivia thought about that. "Even if he's still figuring things out between us, he's always supported me in my cases. He will help if we need it. I know that."

Nina Marie grabbed onto her hands. "Let me talk to Abe, and if he's okay with it, then I'm all in."

———

THAT NIGHT, Nina Marie sat at her kitchen table as Abe finished up the dishes. They had fallen into such a nice routine. They often had dinner together, then went for an evening walk. Abe was always the perfect gentleman, never pushing things like the men she'd been with before. He was completely patient with her after the attack, but the biggest difference between Abe and the other men she had dated was that Abe was a true man of God.

Her ordeal had caused him to grow close to the Lord again, and he had embraced that journey fully. But now she had to tell him about the lawsuit, and she figured he might not like the idea.

"Abe, can we talk for a minute?" She gripped onto her cup of iced tea.

He turned around from the sink and looked at her. "Should I sit?"

"Yeah. I think that would be better."

Abe sat beside her at the table and took her hand in his. "Is everything all right? Are you feeling okay?" His dark eyes showed his concern for her.

She had to get up the nerve to tell him. "It's not me. I'm actually feeling better and stronger. And a large part of that is you. Abe, you're my rock and a ray of sunshine in my life that was so dark before."

"Then what is it?" he asked.

She took a minute to recount the conversation she had earlier in the day with Olivia. "I'd like to do this, Abe."

Abe frowned but didn't immediately respond. After a moment, he squeezed her hand. "This man tried to kill you. I found you here that night, bleeding out and certain you were going to die in my arms." His voice started to crack.

She had to hold back tears. "I know, and I realize this is asking a lot, but I feel like this is the right thing to do."

"To get revenge?"

Nina Marie shook her head. "No. But to use this opportunity to finally try to expose Layton for the monster he is once and for all. He's going to continue spreading evil and hate in this town. We have to put a stop to it, and this is an opportunity to do that."

Abe let out a breath. "Nina Marie, it's no secret that I've fallen hard for you. I believe the Lord brought us together under the most unlikely of circumstances, but we're here now. And if you really think that this is what you need to do, then I will be behind you one hundred percent. But..."

She knew there would be a catch.

Abe pulled her up out of her seat and wrapped his strong arms around her waist, pulling her close. "I plan on being beside you the entire way. I will not let that monster get near you again. He will never touch you."

This time a stray tear fell down her cheek. "Abe, I thank God every day that He spared my life and brought you into it." It still boggled her mind that God was so good and so forgiving, especially after all the awful things she had done in her life.

"I'm thankful too. I was wandering through life until I met you. We are going to do things greater than ourselves here in Windy Ridge, and if that means taking some risks, then I will be there to protect you each step of the way."

Nina Marie realized she had fallen completely in love with Abe. Having his support in this fight against Layton meant everything to her. She needed him to know how she felt. "Abe, I love you." She held her breath, waiting to see how he would respond.

"I love you too." He leaned down and pressed his lips to hers. And she finally felt truly loved.

———

THREE DAYS LATER, Layton sat at his desk reviewing the quarterly financials. He was waiting for Morena and Stacey to arrive to check in on how things were going.

He didn't have to wait long because about five minutes later the women entered his office. "Well, don't the two of you look sun-kissed? Did you spend the weekend at the pool?" Layton laughed.

"Just Saturday afternoon," Morena said. "What did you want to talk to us about?"

"I've been working on the business plan for next year and running the numbers. The company is strong and only growing. Never could I have imagined that we would be this successful. There is a continuous demand for our products. But I didn't ask you here to talk about that. Have either of you spoken to Eliza? I'm sure this unfortunate episode with Katy has clouded her vision." He had been so close to winning her over—it had almost been too easy. Then the whole Katy debacle had completely derailed his plan.

"She's hard to figure out." Morena twisted a curly lock around her finger. "I think she's fine with us if we leave her alone."

"And as long as she doesn't get any more demonic visitors at her house," Stacey said. "That's really her biggest concern."

Layton realized Eliza had no clue how deep she had gotten into things. "We can't control where the demons go. Granted, we could encourage their presence, for sure, but we can't forbid them to do things. Especially when she opened the door to their presence in the first place."

"We tried to explain that to her, but she remains convinced we are the problem, and that before us, she was living a perfectly peaceful life," Stacey said.

"Do you two think this is going to be an issue?" Layton asked.

Morena looked at Stacey and then answered. "I think she's fairly harmless, but if Olivia riles her up, then she could be an issue. The good thing is that she doesn't seem to be swayed that much by Olivia's beliefs. Her beef is that she wants to be left alone. I don't necessarily see her becoming a bible thumper out there crusading. Eliza wants to live in her little Wiccan bubble."

"Then I say for now, we let her be," Layton said. "I'd prefer not to cause any trouble if I don't have to. If she starts actively working against us, then we can revisit."

Layton's intercom buzzed with his secretary interrupting their discussion.

"Yes," he said.

"You have a messenger here to deliver something."

"Send him back." Then he looked at the ladies. "Last time a messenger was here, I got served."

"Do you think you're being sued again?" Stacey asked.

"At this point, nothing would surprise me. You know how tenacious Olivia is. She got embarrassed at Katy's hearing. I shouldn't toot my horn, but it was a complete victory. Morena can attest to that."

After a minute, the messenger walked in and, sure enough, it was another lawsuit. He opened the package and let out a long string of curses.

"What is it this time?" Morena asked.

"It's Olivia, but not what I expected." He thrust the papers into Morena's hands.

She took a moment and skimmed the page. "You know what this means."

Layton felt his cheeks burn in anger. "It means war."

———

STACEY SAT ALONE in her apartment, and her mind was over-loaded. This latest lawsuit was just another annoyance they didn't need. Layton was getting into way too much legal trouble, and even if he kept managing to escape, there would come a time when things would start to have an impact. Not just on Layton, but on the morale of Optimism.

She didn't think it was her time to make a move yet, but life didn't have perfect timing, and you had to act when it was necessary. Given her age, she didn't think she could pull off taking on the CEO position of the company, but she did believe she could convince the members that she could be the spiritual leader.

Morena would be the natural person to take over as CEO, but she didn't think Morena had the temperament needed to be a spiritual leader. But Stacey did. She felt deep in her bones that everything that had happened to her over the past year had led to this point.

She was becoming much more powerful. What she hadn't told Layton, or Morena for that matter, was that she had grown tremendously from her secret online meetings with powerful group leaders in other parts of the country. Every single night she'd been practicing her craft and seeking the evil one. She'd been putting what they taught her into practice, and she was ready to take her magical efforts to the next level.

She'd been batting an idea around in her head, and she grabbed her keys and headed out the door.

When she arrived at Eliza's, she knocked on the door.

"You don't look thrilled to see me, but can I come in?" Stacey asked when Eliza answered the door.

"Yes."

"Is Katy here?"

"No, she's at work," Eliza answered.

"Good. I was hoping to talk to you alone."

"What's going on?" Eliza led her into the living room and took a seat on the couch.

"Layton's in trouble. You probably don't know this, but Nina Marie filed a lawsuit against him and, Olivia is her attorney."

Eliza opened her mouth in surprise. "For what?"

"Basically, a civil case as a result of the attack."

"Can you do that? Wasn't there already the criminal case?"

"You can. I'm no expert, but I did some reading, and he could definitely be held liable for damages even if a jury found him not guilty."

"What does all of this have to do with me?" Eliza asked skeptically.

Stacey wanted to choose her words carefully. "What I'm about to say, you cannot repeat, and if you do, I'll deny I ever said it."

"All right."

"I think that Optimism is going to take a hit here, and it's Layton's fault."

Eliza didn't immediately answer but rose and went to the kitchen. Stacey didn't follow and instead waited patiently for Eliza to return.

"I think we need tea and cookies for this," Eliza said.

Stacey would never turn down Eliza's cookies, so she ate one quickly.

"Why are you coming to me?" Eliza asked.

"Eliza, I've liked you since the moment we met. I still think you have a ton to offer, and I believe in a more friendly and open environment, you could find your true voice. Layton is amazing at many things, but he has some really high negatives. I worry that his indiscretions are going to sink the entire group. And as a woman, I don't want to stand behind an abusive man. We have a voice, and we should be able to stop him."

"And what do you plan to do about it?"

"It's all about timing, but say, hypothetically, that an opportunity arose. Would you join with me?"

"Join with you in what?"

Stacey was about to put it all out there. "In taking over Optimism's spiritual arm. I realize being CEO of the business right now might be a stretch as that would most likely fall to Morena, but I think I could become its spiritual leader."

Eliza raised her eyebrows. "You don't need me."

Stacey didn't think that at all. "I disagree. I think we could band together and do good things, but to do that, you need to give up any fanciful delusions about Olivia and her way of life."

Eliza shook her head. "I don't have any delusions. I've told you many times that I don't believe in what Olivia does. I have my own path."

"And there will be space for people like you within Optimism. Those who want to practice the Wiccan ways. Layton is intolerant, but I'm not. I think we are stronger when we ban together, not as a fragmented body." Stacey wasn't sure how far she could push it, so she let those words sink in.

Eliza sat back in her chair. "What do you want from me?"

"Nothing right now. But if the time comes, I'd love to know that I could count on your support. We could remake Optimism into something better than it's ever been." She locked eyes with Eliza and realized Eliza was actually considering this proposition. It was time to seal the deal. "Layton has hurt too many people, we can do things in a new and different way. When given the opportunity, we can make a big change."

"I don't want those things in my house," Eliza whispered.

"I can help you with that. I can protect you. That will not

happen again on my watch." Stacey might be overselling, but this was all for the greater good, in her opinion. "Believe me. I know I'm young, but I do have special gifts."

"I can feel that about you. I want to trust you. I really do."

"But?"

"I am afraid."

"Enough of that fear. Here and now, let's do a cleansing ritual." Stacey was making this up as she went along, because if demons wanted to come into Eliza's house, this ritual wouldn't stop them. But if it helped convince Eliza, then Stacey was going to put on a show. Yes, this was all happening much faster than she could've imagined, but sometimes you had to strike when the iron was hot.

———

LAYTON SAT with Eli Morgan in his fancy downtown Chicago law office. When Layton had gotten the lawsuit, his first call was to Eli. He wasn't sure if Eli was going to take the case or refer it, but he was anxious to have this meeting.

"I've read over the complaint." Eli's lips pulled down into a tight frown.

"And what do you think?"

"The good news is that your criminal trial went well, and that evidence could be used in the civil case. The bad news is that, optically, this looks really bad. In civil cases, the rules are completely different. You don't have the criminal defendant protections built in. The discovery process is much more onerous." Eli cleared his throat. "What do you think their endgame is here?"

Layton cursed. "They want to make me feel pain. I don't think this is about the money. Nina Marie has done well for herself over the years."

Eli shifted the papers on his desk. "That's what I was afraid of. This could be a PR blitz against you, against your company. And if it's not about money, then settlement isn't a realistic alternative. I have to ask you this."

"You want to know if I did it."

Eli laughed. "I think I already know the answer to that."

"You have that little of an opinion of me?" Layton had to ask.

"I didn't get this far in life by playing by the book, and you didn't either. There was obviously a falling out between you and Nina Marie, and you took it too far. The question is now, what are you going to do about it?" Eli twirled his pen in his hand. "But you have to realize that as long as she's around, this is going to be a problem. She's going to drag you through the mud."

Layton couldn't believe Eli's insinuation. "Are you saying what I think you're saying?"

"And what is that?"

"That I need to get rid of her for good."

Eli didn't respond.

"Your lack of a response is all the response I need."

"The problem is that you can't withstand a murder trial. A jury won't be so forgiving a second time around so that isn't an option."

"Then what do you suggest?"

"If we can't squash her like an ant, then we crush them in the litigation. We need to gear up for this case and the discovery requests that just came in. They aren't wasting any time."

"Does that mean that you're going to take this on?" Layton asked.

"I like a challenge. We have to match them on how aggressive they are. I'm assuming you'll be good with that."

"Absolutely and we have one major tactical advantage." Layton was already starting to feel better.

"And that is?"

"Olivia Murray is a rule follower."

Eli laughed. "My friend, I haven't met a rule yet that isn't meant to broken."

CHAPTER SIXTEEN

Grant knocked on Olivia's door and held his breath. If she opened and then slammed it in his face, he'd accept that. He'd been in such a foul mood lately that he would deserve any treatment she would give him.

He still wasn't ready to change their relationship status, but he did have something he wanted to share with her. The first good news he'd had in what seemed like months.

Olivia opened the door, and her eyes widened in surprise. "Grant."

"Yeah, I know I'm probably not welcome."

She shook her head. "You're always welcome." She grabbed onto his hand and pulled him inside. "Is everything okay?"

Finally, he could give a positive answer. "Yes. I have some news I wanted to share."

"Let's sit."

He followed her into the living room and sat down beside her on the couch.

Olivia turned toward him. "Do you want some coffee or something?"

"No. I won't be staying too long."

A flash of disappointment hit her pretty brown eyes. "What's on your mind?"

He couldn't wait to tell her. "We reached a settlement. A very positive settlement."

"Really? How?"

"Turns out the plaintiff had some damaging baggage, and my attorney was able to capitalize on that."

"I know your settlement is confidential, but can you share anything?" Olivia asked.

"It's within the insurance coverage." Five hundred thousand to be exact. Which meant he wouldn't have to pay out of pocket. Thank God for malpractice insurance. Maybe God had finally heard his prayers.

She threw her arms around his neck. "That's amazing news."

He accepted her embrace and then pulled back, putting a little space between them. "Yeah. Not gonna lie. I needed something to go my way."

"And it did. I'm so happy for you."

"I also owe you an apology for being such a beast lately. I still can't say that my ultimate feelings on us have changed, but I never want to hurt you."

"You need more time," Olivia said softly.

He ran his hand through his hair. "Yeah."

"I can handle that."

Once again, this woman took the high road. "Anything new with you?"

She smiled. "Actually, something big."

"Go on."

"We've sued Layton."

"What? Who is we? For what?"

"I filed suit on behalf of Nina Marie in a civil suit against Layton. The flip side to the criminal case."

"Wow." He didn't even know what to say. "Do you think that's a good idea?"

"I didn't undertake it lightly. Civil litigation was a topic at a continuing ed class I went to, and it hit me once I heard them talk about it that this could be a viable option."

"And you think Nina Marie is ready for this? Last time I saw her, it looked like a slight wind would blow her over." The woman wasn't the fiery and confident woman he had once known.

"She's improving. I think this lawsuit will give her a purpose and drive her to get out of bed each day."

Grant took a moment to process everything Olivia had told him. "So, you're seeking damages for assault or something like that?"

"Yeah, but it's not all about the money. It's bigger than that, Grant." Her eyes lit up.

"You think this is an opportunity to get to Layton."

She nodded. "Absolutely. The criminal justice system didn't allow us to put the true Layton on display. We were constrained by the system and prosecutor, but those rules don't apply to a civil case."

"You'll depose him, I'm sure."

"Of course. And before you say that he'll lie, I'm more than ready for that, but we're going to outsmart him this time. Him and Louise and whoever else I need to expose to bring down Optimism."

"That's a mighty feat."

"Have you ever known me to back down in litigation?"

He laughed. "Never." Then he turned serious. "What can I do to help?"

"Nothing right now. I want you to focus on your issues and getting your head on straight."

"I've been messed up. I'll fully admit that, but I don't know if there is a solution. Would you really ever want me again?"

"Grant, I never stopped wanting you. You're the one who keeps pushing me away, not the other way around."

"I hear you. Why don't we take this victory and move on from it, right? One step at a time."

"I'm more than willing to do that. I'm going to push as hard as

I can on this case. I sent out discovery earlier today and deposition notices."

"You're not playing around."

"No, I'm not," she said flatly.

Looking into Olivia's determined eyes, Grant felt like Layton's time of evading justice might finally be up.

———

STACEY SAT in the Optimism meeting in Layton's den surrounded by Layton, Morena, and Louise.

"Who all here got deposition notices?" Layton asked.

Everyone spoke up but Stacey. "I guess Olivia doesn't think I'm important enough to bother with."

Morena looked at her. "Or she still holds onto the delusional belief that you'll go back to the church."

"Like that's ever gonna happen," Stacey said under her breath.

"We need to make sure everyone's on the same page here and has legal counsel," Layton said.

"As you can imagine, I'm going to push back hard on my deposition," Louise said. "I probably can't avoid testifying, but we'll cross that bridge when we get to it. For now, I'm going to have my lawyer file to squash the deposition. But Layton and Morena, you will have to get deposed."

Morena groaned. "Although the good thing is that I literally don't have any personal knowledge about what happened that night. Should be a short deposition."

"Not so fast," Louise shot back. "Everyone needs to take this very seriously. Olivia's strategy isn't a big payout for Nina Marie. It has to be something else, which means in these depositions, you need to be prepared for her to go on a major fishing expedition trying to air out all of our dirty laundry."

Stacey let Louise's words sink in. "This could be a very real threat to our group."

Layton swatted his hand. "We do not need to overreact. We've faced down litigation before and always come out on top. The criminal trial went off without a hitch. I don't see why this would be any different. It's not like anyone from Optimism is going to admit to anything we shouldn't. We're all solid as a rock. They won't have any proof to discredit us."

The room fell silent for a moment as everyone was probably thinking about the subject. Stacey started to realize that maybe her best move right now was to sit back and listen as opposed to being an active participant. It appeared to her, though, that Louise was miffed.

Ideas brewed like a strong espresso in Stacey's mind. She settled in and waited for the conversation to continue.

Layton leaned in. "I still feel by the look on your faces that this group needs a pep talk. In the grand scheme of things, this is truly a blip on the radar."

Louise cleared her throat. "I'm afraid I have to report on one additional piece of unrelated bad news."

"What's that?" Layton asked.

"Grant's lawsuit settled. Eli did everything he could, but the plaintiff had some issues in her past."

Layton shrugged. "I'd much rather have Eli focused on my case right now, so that all works out fine."

"Grant is still weak," Morena said. "I think we should focus some spiritual energy on him. Getting to Olivia directly is most difficult, but he doesn't have the strong foundation of faith that she has."

"I can help with that," Stacey piped up.

"Good," Layton said. "Do it. No holding back, Stacey."

Louise picked up her coffee cup. "Back to your case, Layton. Is Eli going to try to delay?"

Layton shook his head. "No. Actually, he thinks it's better to quickly push through this, at the same time, keeping up the pressure on them as well. You all seem worried about your depositions, but let's not forget that Eli will get a crack at Nina Marie. And I'll have a front row seat to that train wreck. The quicker this thing goes to trial, the better. We can't allow this to string out for months and months. That would have a more negative impact than ripping off the bandage. We defeat this thing and move on quickly."

Stacey fought the urge to ask more questions, but she remained quiet.

"Remember, though," Louise said, "I can't stress enough how important it is to take this seriously."

It was clear to Stacey that Louise was very concerned about this. Would Louise ever turn on Layton? Could the women of Optimism take out their male leader?

Morena placed her hand on top of Louise's. "Let's not add additional pressure to Layton. We've gotten this far and look how we're thriving. We will come out on top of this too."

Louise nodded and gave a weak smile. "I know, I know. It's my job to worry about these legal matters and the protection of our group."

"And for that we are eternally grateful, Louise." Layton leaned back in his chair. "Eli is on the top of his game, and I think he's going to make Olivia feel the pain. He's not constrained by the rules like she is."

"He can't let up on her. You give that woman one inch and it's all over," Morena said.

Stacey had seen just how impressive Olivia was, not only as an attorney, but also as a person. In a way, Stacey admired her, but Stacey would never go back to that type of belief system. She believed Olivia could have so much more in life. "If you all don't need anything else from me, I'm going to go home and hit the books. I'll also get started on those spells to see if we can keep Grant down."

Layton nodded. "Perfect, Stacey. Thanks again for everything."

She left the three of them and made her way outside. Once she reached her car, she had decided it was time to shake things up.

CHAPTER SEVENTEEN

The past few weeks had gone by in a blur, but Olivia was managing to keep up. The case against Layton was moving at lightning speed—and much to her surprise, his lawyer seemed to want to push the case along much quicker than normal. That meant she was about to defend Nina Marie's deposition.

She'd already taken Layton's deposition in which he sat there and lied for five hours. That was to be expected, but she would have that transcript when she faced him down in court and proved he was a liar.

Olivia had feared what this case might do to Nina Marie, but if anything, it was only speeding up her healing process. In this litigation, Nina Marie had a voice she didn't have in the criminal case. And Olivia openly strategized with her. It was not only good for building up their case but also their continued friendship.

Olivia was in the separate conference room with Nina Marie, and they were about to enter the main room where the deposition would be held. "Are you ready?" Olivia looked into Nina Marie's eyes.

Nina Marie smoothed down her black blazer. "Yes. It's like you told me. I have the truth on my side. I don't need to lie or hide anything."

"Right. The whole point is to get the true story out there. And to be completely honest, I'm not sure what tact Eli is going to take with you, so you need to be prepared for anything. Don't get too comfortable, even if he is a smooth talker."

Nina Marie lifted up her chin. "I can handle him, Olivia. I know you have every right to be nervous about this, but believe it or not, I feel good. You put in the time to prepare me, and I'll do the best I can."

They had spent hours on deposition preparation, mainly to make sure Nina Marie had back the confidence Layton had stripped away from her.

"I'm not worried. Just wanted to make sure you were comfortable."

Nina Marie laughed. "As comfortable as I'm going to get while sitting and being questioned for half the day."

Olivia escorted Nina Marie into the main deposition room. Eli was already in there scribbling down notes. When they arrived, he looked up and then stood.

"I'm Eli Morgan." He stretched out his hand to Nina Marie. "I represent Mr. Alito."

Nina Marie took his hand quickly before taking a seat.

Eli turned to her. "Nice to see you again, Olivia."

They'd met during Layton's deposition. "Looks like we have everyone and are ready to begin." And by everyone she meant the lawyers and the court reporter.

"Let's give Mr. Alito another minute. He should be joining us too," Eli said.

She took a moment to size Eli up. Average height, dark hair and glasses, and probably in his fifties. He wasn't an attractive man, but he carried himself with confidence she assumed came from his legal prowess. From her research, he had quite the reputation. She hadn't shared all those details with Nina Marie because she didn't want to psych her out, but that's one of the reasons she wasn't exactly sure how Eli was going to handle this deposition.

Olivia planned to be on high alert to make sure she was protecting Nina Marie. They didn't have to wait too long for Layton to enter the room. The energy shifted immediately upon his entrance. *Lord, please protect Nina Marie.*

"Hello, everyone. Sorry I'm a few minutes late." He gave Olivia a dazzling smile, but he didn't even attempt a handshake. Instead he took his seat and unbuttoned his gray suit jacket. His sparkling blue eyes locked onto hers. "Olivia, good to see you, as always."

"I think we're ready if you are, Eli," Olivia purposefully diverted the conversation away from Layton.

Eli proceeded to set the usual deposition ground rules and started his questioning with basic, boring background information. Olivia willed herself to focus because at any moment the line of questioning could change, and she needed to be sharp and on the lookout to make the right objections to preserve the record.

It took another good forty minutes before Olivia perked up to attention.

"Ms. Crane, isn't it true that you believe you are a witch?"

Olivia bit the inside of her cheek waiting for the response.

"No," Nina Marie said.

Olivia quietly smiled inside because she knew why Nina Marie had answered that way.

"So, you're denying that you were ever a witch?" Eli asked.

"Mr. Morgan, I believe that wasn't your original question."

Eli frowned for a moment and then smiled realizing his own mistake. "Let me try that again, Ms. Crane. Isn't it true that you used to believe you were a witch?"

Nina Marie nodded. "Yes, that is true."

"But you don't believe that anymore?" he asked.

"No. I can say with certainty that I am not a witch."

"And what made you change your mind?"

He was still conversational in tone. Olivia thought that based on how this was going he was trying to make her look crazy.

"I have left that life behind me. I became a Christian and was born again."

Nina Marie was following Olivia's instruction—just answer the question asked. Depositions were not the place to explain everything.

Eli tapped his pen on his notepad. She was fairly certain that even given his vast litigation experience he had never had a series of deposition questions on witches.

"How does one become a witch, Ms. Crane?"

"There isn't just one way."

"Humor me with one." Eli leaned forward in his seat.

"You could start practicing magic, engage in spells. That would be a start."

"But could a person believe that they were a witch but not actually be one?"

Nina Marie considered his question. "I think if you believe you are, you are. You may not be a very effective one though."

Olivia held back a laugh. This line of questioning wasn't going anywhere.

"Ms. Crane, is it your contention that you believe Mr. Alito is a witch?"

"No. I do not believe that."

"What do you think Mr. Alito is then?"

"A monster," she responded without hesitation.

"Finally, we're getting somewhere." Eli smirked. "You clearly hold my client in low esteem."

Olivia decided the tit for tat had gone on long enough. "Eli, are you going to continue editorializing or ask your questions?"

Eli nodded. "Fair point, Olivia. I will continue."

And continue he did. For the next three hours. But Nina Marie went toe-to-toe with him performing like a champion. Olivia could only hope Nina Marie didn't peak too soon. They still had a trial to get through.

"Ms. Crane, isn't it true that you're still in love with Mr. Alito?"

Nina Marie laughed. "No. I am not."

"But you were before?"

Nina Marie bit her bottom lip. "I think so, but I wasn't thinking as clearly back then as I am now."

Olivia wanted to kick her, but she couldn't and wouldn't. She should've never added that last piece of commentary.

"Let's drill down on that." Eli adjusted his cuff link. "At what time were you, as you used the term, not thinking as clearly."

"I meant the time period when I was dating Layton and working with the New Age groups versus after that."

"And at the time of the alleged attack, were you thinking clearly?"

"Yes."

"But you had just recently left Astral Tech at that point, correct?"

"Yes."

"But you contend that you were still thinking as clearly as you're thinking today."

"Objection to the form, argumentative, calls for speculation." Olivia knew Nina Marie had to answer, but she wanted to preserve the objection.

"I am thinking more clearly today, but I was thinking clearly that night. Especially when Layton stabbed me."

"I'm going to move to strike the last sentence of Ms. Crane's answer as non-responsive."

"Actually, it was very responsive," Nina Marie said.

Olivia had to decide whether to let Nina Marie keep going or try to rein her back in.

"Being stabbed multiple times has a way of bringing extreme clarity to the situation," Nina Marie said.

Olivia let her go because she wanted to see how Eli was going to handle it.

He stayed silent for a moment before continuing. "There's no dispute that you were attacked, Ms. Crane, and I have sympathy for you over that, but the issue here is whether my client is the man who did it."

"And I'm telling you that he is." Nina Marie shifted and looked Layton directly in the eyes.

The two of them engaged in an intense stare down that made Olivia uncomfortable. The air thickened with a heaviness that Layton brought with him. Olivia decided to intervene. "Maybe now would be a good time to take a break."

"Actually, that won't be necessary," Eli said. "I'm done here."

"All right, then." Olivia stood and went over to Nina Marie to remove the microphone and shield her from Layton. She didn't want there to be an altercation between them right now, and she could feel it brewing.

Olivia placed her hand on Nina Marie's shoulder and guided her out of the room. "Let's get you out of here."

But Layton being Layton had to have the last word, and he followed them out. "Nina Marie," he called.

"Don't engage him," Olivia said. "Let me handle it."

Olivia turned to face Layton and purposely stood in front of Nina Marie.

Layton stood proudly. "If I didn't know better I'd say that you're afraid of me, Nina Marie."

Olivia had to interject. "Layton, I'd ask that you stop harassing my client. This only continues a pattern of behavior on your part that we will be sure to discuss at trial."

"Olivia, you clearly want to take me down, but you're going about it the wrong way wasting everyone's time with yet another legal battle. Haven't you learned your lesson yet?"

There was so much Olivia wanted to say. Like the fact that she could tell Layton was on the run and afraid. That she was going to air all his dirty laundry in a court of law. That she planned to take down his New Age network in Windy Ridge, but she held her tongue and didn't say a word to him. Instead, she turned around and walked with Nina Marie down the hallway.

Once they got into the elevator, Nina Marie looked at her. "Why didn't you respond to him?"

"Because that's exactly what he wanted. In his own sick way,

Layton enjoys the sparring match. It's all a big game to him, and he thinks he has the edge. I want his overconfidence to continue."

"It took all my strength not to lose it on that lawyer back there. Thank you for preparing me so well."

"I'm really proud of you. You did great today." But Olivia also wanted to level set expectations. "We still have to get through the trial though, and as you know, that's a completely different ball game."

Nina Marie turned to her. "I'll be ready."

———

Eliza sat on her couch beside Stacey. She was having an internal debate about what she should do. Stacey was making a strong case against Layton, but Eliza also realized that if she went against Layton and their efforts failed, then she would have a huge target on her back. And she didn't want to end up like Nina Marie and Katy.

"Tell me exactly what you're thinking," Eliza said.

Stacey finished munching down on a cookie before she spoke. "I don't have an exact plan yet, but I know that I could help turn the tide against Layton."

"Aren't you afraid?" Eliza thought that was an obvious concern.

Stacey shook her head. "Maybe six months ago I would've been, but I've started to come into my own. Ideally, I'd have liked more time to make this happen, but opportunities like this don't come along every day."

"You're playing with fire. I worry this could go sideways and you could get hurt." Eliza felt an affinity for Stacey that she couldn't quite explain, and she was growing to dislike Layton more by the day. Men like him who abused women really ticked her off.

"You're forgetting that I have power too. Layton's not the only one who practices the dark arts, and he doesn't realize how strong I've become. I haven't told anyone at Optimism how much time and effort I've dedicated to expanding my repertoire. They thought I've been spending the summer taking a class and laying by the pool, but I've been meeting and working with a variety of people from across the country who taught me a lot."

Eliza had to give it to Stacey. She was ambitious and cunning. More so than Eliza would ever be, but to take down Layton would probably require just that. "What do you need me to do?"

"Be there when this all goes down and help me rally support. Many members of Optimism don't know how ruthless Layton can be. I need help spreading that word and also spreading the message that he's a big liability."

"I'm not even an Optimism member, though."

"Not yet. But you have credibility given your status in the Wiccan community. Our people will listen to you."

Eliza thought Stacey was vastly overestimating Eliza's pull, but she let her go on with it. If Layton could get removed, that would be better for everyone regardless of whether Eliza ultimately joined Optimism or not. "All right. I'll be standing by to help."

"If you want to bail, I'll understand."

"No. I'm in." Eliza hoped she wouldn't regret it.

CHAPTER EIGHTEEN

O livia had been pulling crazy hours to prepare for the trial. She had a sinking feeling that Layton thought he had an ace in the hole because he had been fully on board with an accelerated trial date. Eli said they were eager to clear Layton's name, but Olivia figured they had some other play.

"Are you ready?" Grant asked her as they stood outside of the courthouse.

"Ready as I'll ever be. Thanks for coming."

Grant gave her hand a reassuring squeeze. "You know I wouldn't miss this trial for anything. If you need me at any point, all you have to do is ask. But I know you have this completely under control."

He'd been much better since his case settled. They were still working through things, but she firmly believed they would be together. "Thank you." She let out a sigh of relief when she saw Nina Marie walking up the courthouse steps with Abe by her side. She never doubted Nina Marie's commitment, but it was still good seeing her there now and ready to go. Olivia greeted them and ushered everyone inside.

"Is this really happening?" Nina Marie asked.

Olivia's pulse began to ramp up and they hadn't even started yet, but she didn't want Nina Marie to feel her anxiety. "Remember it's going to be a long day. We have to pick a jury and get through the preliminaries before any witnesses will be called."

"But I will be called first?"

"Yes. You will be up first."

Nina Marie glanced over her shoulder. Grant and Abe were talking. "Abe is concerned, but he knows this is the right thing to do."

"Abe loves you and is trying to protect you."

Nina Marie smiled. "He really does, and I love him too. Sometimes I still can't believe how much I've changed literally from the inside out. I never thought I'd be able to break free of the chains of the past."

Olivia squeezed her hand. "But you have."

"With God's help." Nina Marie's eyes misted up.

Nina Marie's vulnerable reaction touched Olivia, and she had to hold back her own tears.

"Now, don't you start," Nina Marie said. "We've got a case to win."

Olivia nodded. "And there he is." Olivia turned and watched Layton strut into the courtroom with all the confidence in the world. It was time to change that.

———

GRANT SAT in the courtroom audience that afternoon and tapped his leg as he waited for opening statements to begin. For some reason, he was incredibly nervous. Maybe that was because he had dealt with Layton before in a courtroom and saw firsthand how dangerous he could be. But so had Olivia. She had taken him on before, but now there was so much more baggage between all of them.

The jury had been selected, and Judge Beck had been running a highly efficient process so far. First up would be Olivia's opening statement, which he had heard her practice.

The fifty-something-year old judge had a reputation for being right down the middle. Grant wasn't quite sure how he would take the introduction of some of the New Age elements, but they'd have to wait and see. The judge put on his glasses and turned his attention to Olivia.

"Ms. Murray, are you ready to proceed with your opening statement?"

Olivia stood. "Yes, Your Honor." Olivia walked up to the podium where she placed her notes. Grant would be surprised, however, if she actually used them. Olivia had this committed to memory—the story ingrained in her mind.

Olivia turned and faced the jury. "Ladies and gentleman of the jury. You met me this morning before the lunch break. Again, my name is Olivia Murray and I represent the plaintiff, Ms. Nina Marie Crane, in this litigation." Olivia paused a beat. "This case is about assault and battery, but it's actually more than that. The evidence will show that this case is about a man, the defendant Mr. Layton Alito, who has a pattern of abusing women. A pattern of using his power against others. A pattern of evil acts."

Eli shot to his feet. "Objection, Your Honor. Ms. Murray is going far outside the bounds of a proper opening statement with her argumentative editorializing."

Grant thought the same, but Olivia was doing this all for a purpose. Once the jury heard something, it couldn't be unheard.

Judge Beck's brown eyes focused in on Olivia. "Ms. Murray, consider this a warning. Please continue."

Score one point for the good guys.

Olivia continued. "Mr. Alito will point to many things to claim that he is not the man who viciously attacked and left Ms. Crane for dead on the night of February twentieth. But the evidence will show that Mr. Alito had the motive and intent to gravely harm or kill Ms. Crane and that he in fact did stab her multiple times."

Grant looked away from Olivia and studied the faces of the

jurors. They seemed engaged. The only good thing about this situation was that a case like this was more likely to keep the attention of the jury because of all the inflammatory issues that would be highlighted.

"Now, you're going to hear about how Mr. Alito was found not guilty in a criminal trial that took place only months ago, and no doubt there will be debate about what you should and shouldn't consider that happened in that trial. But you will hear evidence from witnesses in this case that you must consider. I will show by a preponderance of the evidence—which is the standard in a civil case like this—that Layton committed assault and battery. The evidence will show he went to Ms. Crane's house on the evening of February twentieth with the intent to harm her. That he did in fact stab her upwards of fifteen times and left her to bleed out on her floor. If her friend had not stopped by her house that night, Ms. Crane would not be sitting in this courtroom right now."

Olivia paused again. Her pacing was to ensure the jurors were processing all she was saying. "Finally, you might have already gathered from our jury selection questions that this case has some rather unusual elements to it. I ask that you listen to the evidence presented to you on those topics and evaluate it and the credibility of the witnesses. Once all the evidence is heard, I will ask that the jury find for my client, Ms. Crane, and award her damages to cover the actual medical expenses plus damages for pain and suffering. I appreciate your time and attention today and throughout the trial." Olivia returned to her seat.

"Mr. Morgan, are you ready? We can jump right into your opening," Judge Beck said.

Eli stood and buttoned his navy designer suit jacket. "Yes, Your Honor."

Grant already didn't like this guy because of his own lawsuit, and he couldn't help but want him to fail badly.

Eli didn't bring a single thing with him as he waltzed up to the podium and started talking to the jury. "Members of the jury, I'm Eli Morgan and I represent Mr. Layton Alito, who is the defendant in this case. As Ms. Murray already alluded to, this is a civil trial—not a criminal one. The remedy being sought by Ms. Crane is financial—meaning money, plain and simple. And I contend that once you hear all the evidence that Ms. Crane will be exposed for the fraud that she is."

Olivia shot up to her feet. "Objection. Argumentative, Your Honor. Move to strike that last sentence."

"I agree," Judge Beck said. He looked toward the jury. "I'm directing that last sentence to be struck from the record, and you are not to consider it."

It was obvious to Grant that both sides would be going all out. This was so much more than what evidence was in and out. It was about the full picture of ideas that the lawyers could get in front of the jury.

Eli didn't seem fazed as he continued his opening. "What you will hear about is a woman, Ms. Crane, who is a self-proclaimed witch. She and Mr. Alito had a romantic relationship years ago that ended badly, and she has held a serious grudge ever since. When she was attacked, she used the awful situation to try to get back at a man she despises instead of going after the real culprit. No one here is disputing that Ms. Crane was attacked in her house on the evening of February twentieth, but the evidence will show that the man who did it is not my client. Unfortunately, Ms. Crane has issues that have affected her judgement. Her obsession with the occult and witchcraft have colored her mind and impacted her rationality. My client, a completely innocent man, has gotten caught in the crossfire. I am confident that once you hear all the evidence you will find for Mr. Alito. Thank you."

Both sides had kept their openings short and to the point. The jury was still fully engaged, but now the real action would start. The witness testimony.

OLIVIA TOOK in a deep breath and looked at Nina Marie, who gave her a nod.

"Ms. Murray, we still have ample time today in the schedule so please call your first witness," the judge said.

"Thank you, Your Honor. Ms. Crane is my first witness."

"Very well. Ms. Crane, please approach and get sworn in."

Olivia watched as Nina Marie walked up to the witness chair. She truly hoped and prayed that Nina Marie was ready for this. They had practiced cross-examination for hours, but Eli was a different breed of lawyer. Olivia's strategy was to get out the questionable stuff in the direct and tell it their own way. She had no idea how the jury was going to react to all the supernatural elements.

Nina Marie was sworn in, and then it was time for questioning. "Ms. Crane, please begin by telling the jury a bit about your work and background. Do you have a college degree?"

"Yes. I have a BA in business."

"Any advanced degrees?"

"No. That's it."

"And did you at one time have a company that you started up?"

"Yes. The company is called Astral Tech."

"And what exactly is Astral Tech?"

Nina Marie looked at the jury. "Astral Tech is a New Age tech company."

"Let's stop right there. What do you mean by New Age?"

"New Age can have varying definitions, but in the context of my former company, we focused on a combination of things including meditative practices, astrology, and magic."

"Magic? Like hocus pocus type stuff?" Olivia asked.

"More serious than that. Members were versed in all types of spells, divination, and communicating with spirits."

"And you said members?"

"Yes. Astral Tech was a company, but it was also a spiritual group."

"And you say *was*?" Olivia asked.

"Yes. I'm no longer the CEO, and it is my understanding that the company has disbanded and the group itself has completely dissolved."

Olivia tried to determine how the jury was taking all of this. It was a lot to put out there. "So, in Mr. Morgan's opening statement, he said that you were a self-proclaimed witch. Is that true?"

Nina Marie didn't hesitate. "For years of my life, I was a witch. I practiced spells and was engaged in various dark arts."

"And who did you learn your craft from?"

"A variety of people."

"And was one of those people Mr. Alito?"

Nina Marie nodded. "Yes. Although I think I was already very developed in my skills by the time I met Layton, but I did learn certain things from him and him from me."

"And where does Mr. Alito fit into your Astral Tech group?"

"He runs the competitor to Astral Tech, a company called Optimism. Like Astral Tech, it's a company but there is a separate spiritual group as well. They are active participants in all aspects of magic and sorcery."

"Does it stop there?" They had gone over this many times, so Olivia was prepared for Nina Marie's next statement.

"No. Both groups also engage in satanic practices."

One of the jurors audibly gasped. Olivia let the silence fill the room for a moment. "And how do you know this?"

"Because I was a part of it."

"And are you still?"

Nina Marie shook her head. "No, and that's one of the reasons Layton and I had a falling out."

Olivia took a step forward. "Tell me about that."

"Layton and I did date years ago, but we broke up and then became competitors of sorts with our rival businesses. My business was more focused on technology with his being more old school. Optimism did have a greater market share for actual New Age products. We had a dispute between us over an app that Astral Tech marketed. That dispute was settled, and then he and I reevaluated our relationship. We formed an alliance of opportunity because we thought we were stronger together. But earlier this year, I had a change of heart. A change of soul, really. That led me to leave Astral Tech and become a Christian."

"Let's make sure the jury understands your testimony. You are saying that you used to be a practicing witch but you're now a Christian."

"Absolutely. I have given my life to the Lord and renounced everything that had to do with the occult practices."

"And Mr. Alito didn't like that?" Olivia asked.

"No. Layton hates anything to do with the church or God."

"Does Mr. Alito keep these occult activities to himself?"

Nina Marie cleared her throat. "Optimism as a company is legitimate and has a thriving business that sells New Age products across the country, but the spiritual group is much more secretive and includes prominent members of the Windy Ridge community."

"Really? Like who?"

"Judge Louise Martinique, for one."

With that, the courtroom was abuzz, and the reaction was exactly what Olivia was hoping for.

"You're saying a sitting judge is a member of this occult group?"

Eli stood to make his first objection. She was surprised it had taken him so long. "Objection. Lacks foundation. Calls for speculation."

"I can lay the foundation, Your Honor," Olivia said.

Judge Beck frowned. She was putting him in an awkward position given Louise's status on the bench. "I'll allow you to try."

That was an important ruling. "Thank you. Ms. Crane, what is your personal knowledge regarding Judge Martinique's involvement in Optimism?"

"I've been in many meetings with her, Mr. Alito, and others to discuss a variety of issues facing the community."

"So, under oath, it is your testimony that Judge Martinique is a member of an occult group that engages in satanic practices?"

Nina Marie looked directly at her. "That is absolutely my testimony."

Olivia let that hang for a minute as she planned to pivot. "So, on the night of February twentieth, you were at home and what happened?"

"I arrived home and Layton had picked the lock to my front door and was sitting in my living room having a glass of wine. At first, I was annoyed. I didn't want him there, but then he started to scare me. I realized this wasn't just a fight or conversation he wanted to have. He was in one of his angry tirades."

"What do you mean by that?"

"Layton has a way of convincing people that he's suave and professional, but I've seen him at times in a complete rage. So angry that I know he's capable of extreme violence." Nina Marie looked down.

"I know this is difficult for you, Ms. Crane, but the jury needs to hear what happened next that night."

"Layton was angry because I was leaving my old life behind. It enraged him that I would change my allegiance. Change my entire life and way of thinking." She took a breath. "He pushed me up against the wall. Then he pulled out the knife. He told me that I would die slowly." Nina Marie's voice cracked. This wasn't an act. Reliving this was awful for her, but Olivia had to keep pushing.

"And then what happened?"

"He slammed the knife into my stomach. The pain was horrendous, and then he kept stabbing me until I no longer felt anything."

"And what happened after that."

"Thank God that my friend Abe came back to the house to check on me. He found me unconscious and called 911. I was in a coma for quite a while, and it was touch and go. But I pulled through."

Olivia surveyed the jury. There was a mix of confusion, sympathy, and rank skepticism. This was quite the story, and she would have to find a way to make sure they believed it. Believed the truth.

"Thank you, Ms. Crane." She turned to Eli. "Your witness, counselor."

———

GRANT WATCHED as Eli strode up to the podium to face down Nina Marie. There were so many directions that Eli could take this. Grant held in a breath to see where Eli would start.

"Ms. Crane, I want to get right to the heart of the matter. You have testified both in your deposition and in your testimony today that you were at one point in time a full-fledged witch. Is that right?"

"Basically, yes."

"You realize that my client disputes and has done so on the record that he has any affiliation with any occult practices or anything of that nature. That he is purely the CEO of a company that provides holistic New Age products."

"Layton's lying," Nina Marie shot back.

"And why would he do that?" Eli asked.

"To protect himself and his empire. If the truth gets out about what and who Layton is, including his abusive streak against women, then that could hurt him and his business interests."

"You've openly called out a sitting judge here today. Why should this jury believe your word against everyone else's? Including a highly respected judge?" Eli's voice got louder with each word.

Nina Marie took a breath.

Grant could tell she was trying to determine the best way to tackle the question.

"I'm here to tell the truth. It's not easy for me to admit the things I've done in my life that I'm not proud of. But just because multiple people are towing the party line doesn't make it the truth."

Eli took a step toward the witness box. "What if I told you that I believe your boyfriend Abe Perez was actually the one who stabbed you that night in a moment of rage, but he had remorse and got you medical attention? Then you plotted this entire thing as a way to get back at my client. Pointing the finger at him because you're protecting your boyfriend?"

"I'd say that's completely ludicrous." Nina Marie's eyes shifted toward Abe, who was in the audience sitting next to Grant. "Men like Layton use their power and status to abuse women. Abe would never do that. He'd protect me with his life. Layton, on the other hand, tried to kill me."

Eli turned toward the jury. "Ms. Crane, do you have any other evidence to substantiate your claims about my client?"

"Objection," Olivia said. "Ms. Crane isn't in a position to know what other witnesses will testify to."

"But, if she does know, I want to hear it, Your Honor," Eli responded.

"Overruled. You can answer the question."

"I'm not sure whether anyone else will testify about these things. All I can do is name the people who I believe have that knowledge."

"All right. Please list those names for the jury."

"Morena Isley, Judge Louise Martinique, and Stacey Malone."

"Very well. And what happens if all three of those witnesses dispute your account of events?"

"I'd say they were all lying."

Eli shook his head. "We will see about that. That's all I have for this witness."

"Any redirect, Ms. Murray?"

"None, Your Honor," Olivia responded.

"Then we will adjourn for the day and pick up with the next witness first thing in the morning."

And with that, day one was in the books. Grant had no idea what tomorrow would hold.

CHAPTER NINETEEN

"What do you think?" Olivia asked Grant as they sat at her kitchen table having coffee.

"You're right. You'll have to win this case through the cross-examination of their witnesses."

She was glad he shared her opinion on legal strategy. "That means we'll rest, and they will start with their case tomorrow." She looked down at her notepad. "Their witness list includes the usual suspects—Morena, Louise, Stacey. And of course, Layton."

"You were great today with Nina Marie. She comes across as a very credible witness—even when Eli went after her."

"Did you get a read on the jury?" She had tried her best to watch, but she wanted to know what he thought.

Grant lifted his mug. "At times they seemed confused or in disbelief, but that's to be expected with all the talk about witchcraft."

"Enough about the case. How're you doing?"

He looked down and then back up at her. "Each day I'm feeling more like myself again. Honestly, Olivia, I'm not sure what happened to me, but Dan has been a big help. I've started going back to the men's bible study, and I've been speaking to Dan separately. I know his prayers mean a lot to me, as do yours. Because I know you've been praying for me."

She was thankful they were able to have this conversation. "Of course, I have. The tests we go through in this life make us stronger. You were depressed. It can happen to anyone, Grant, and you've been through a lot of stress with that lawsuit."

Grant took her hand in his. "You've been more patient with me than I ever could've deserved."

Lord, thank you for walking with Grant through this time of darkness. "I told you I would be here for you. Whatever ups and downs we face, we can make it through as long as we turn to God and put our trust in Him. And then we have each other to lean on."

"I wish I would've been able to open up more. I was almost ashamed at the weakness I felt. Does that make sense?"

"You don't have to justify your feelings. I appreciate how honest you're being with me." She squeezed his hand.

Grant looked down at his watch. "I should get out of here. You have a huge day tomorrow."

She nodded. "Yeah. I can't help but feel there's going to be some fireworks." The only question was how big.

———

OLIVIA TOOK a deep breath as Stacey Malone was sworn in. She was certain that Stacey would be the first in a wave of character witnesses for Layton. Having multiple women get on the stand and sing his praises was a calculated decision by Eli to try to win over the jury.

Stacey didn't look so much like a college student today, but a young professional. She wore a gray pantsuit, and her strawberry blonde hair was pulled back in a sleek ponytail.

Olivia listened and took notes attentively as Eli walked through a basic and straightforward direct examination. He only asked a couple of questions about her relationship with Layton and what he had done for her—helping with the internship and giving her the job offer. Then he sat down.

Olivia figured he was going to rely on the others for more substantive testimony, but he'd still opened the door enough for her to get in her line of questions.

"Ms. Murray, are you ready for cross-examination?" Judge Beck asked.

"Yes, Your Honor." Olivia took her time and gathered up her notes. Just like the others, Stacey would lie to protect Layton, but Olivia was going to do her best to try to catch Stacey in a trap.

Olivia walked up to her. "Ms. Malone, you're a college student, correct?"

Stacey nodded. "Yes, I'm currently a college student studying business, and I have an internship at Optimism."

"You're also part of the spiritual group known as Optimism, isn't that right?"

"Yes, I am."

"For now, let's put aside all of the talk about witches and New Age stuff and focus on something else. How did you meet Mr. Alito?"

Stacey glanced over at Layton. "I met him at the bookstore Indigo. We had an immediate connection, and he offered me an internship. I thought it was a great opportunity, and I started work soon after that."

"And it's also true that Mr. Alito has offered you full-time employment at Optimism post-graduation, correct?"

"Yes."

"Have you ever personally felt threatened by Mr. Alito?" Olivia knew this was a dangerous question, but she had to walk down this path if she was ever going to show discrepancies in the future.

"No," Stacey answered.

"Do you have any knowledge about Mr. Alito's attack on my client, Ms. Crane?"

Eli shot up. "Objection. There's no foundation for this, and it's argumentative."

"I'm merely asking if she does have knowledge. Let me lay that foundation, Your Honor," Olivia said.

"Overruled. Continue please, Ms. Murray."

"Ms. Malone, please answer the question." Olivia kept her voice even but stern.

"Yes," Stacey said.

Olivia wasn't sure where this was going. "Yes, you have knowledge?" She wanted the record to be clear.

"Yes," Stacey said.

"What kind of knowledge?" Olivia asked.

Stacey looked her in the eyes. "Layton told me that he attacked Nina Marie and that he wished he had finished the job."

Olivia stood in silence. Had she heard that right? "Ms. Malone, you're saying that Mr. Alito admitted to attacking Ms. Crane?"

"Objection, argumentative," Eli said.

"Your Honor, I'm just asking a clarifying question based on Ms. Malone's own words."

Judge Beck nodded. "I concur, Ms. Murray. Objection overruled."

Olivia looked over her shoulder and saw Layton's cheeks redden. Morena was slack jawed and the courtroom was full of mumblings. Could Stacey actually be turning on Layton?

"Ms. Malone, I'll repeat the question. It's your testimony that Mr. Alito admitted to attacking Ms. Crane?"

"Yes."

"Ms. Malone, do you believe Mr. Alito attacked my client?"

"Yes, I do."

"And why is that?" If Stacey was stabbing Layton in the back, then she had to get this all on record.

"Well, besides the fact that he told me as much, Layton has a violent streak. A really violent streak."

"How do you know that?" Olivia asked.

Stacey paused. "Like I said, he never hurt me, but I am aware that recently he assaulted a woman he was dating. He went to some sort of court hearing and convinced them that she was lying, but that's Layton's MO. He has enough power to ensure that he can get his version of the story out."

"So why are you going against him here today? You already told us that he offered you a job. I'm assuming that won't exist after this testimony."

Stacey nodded and looked directly at the jurors. "Because it's the right thing to do. Layton is an evil man, and he's hurt a lot of people. I was fooled by him at first too because he can be such a charmer, but I see the truth fully now." Then Stacey locked eyes with Layton.

"Are you worried for your safety after your testimony here today?" Olivia was used to making adjustments as she went, but this was a new test to her lawyering skills.

Stacey looked at the jury and then back at Olivia. "Yes, but I also realize that if something happens to me, then Layton would be suspect number one given that this is all out in the public now. I doubt he would take that risk."

It was almost like Stacey was reveling in this. It was at that moment Olivia realized Stacey had planned this. This was a calculated move not an on-the-spot decision. "Thank you, Ms. Malone. I'm done with this witness." Olivia returned to her seat, and Eli would take his best shot at trying to dig out of this mess.

Now she would see if this fancy trial lawyer was worth his billable rate. He'd just been thrown a huge curveball.

"Mr. Morgan, would you like re-direct?" Judge Beck asked.

Eli stood. "Yes, Your Honor. Ms. Malone, you were not at Ms. Crane's house the night she was attacked, were you?"

"No, I wasn't."

"So, you can't say for certain that Mr. Alito was her attacker?" Eli asked in a stern tone.

"I can say that based on what he told me and others."

"But you have no direct knowledge." It came out more as an accusation than a question.

Stacey took a breath. "Was I there? No. Do I believe he tried to kill Nina Marie? Absolutely. He was proud of it. Wore it like a badge of honor."

"Why should the jury believe you?" Eli asked loudly.

"Because I have absolutely no reason to lie," Stacey stated as a matter of fact.

"If Layton wasn't the CEO of Optimism, who would be next in line to run the company?"

"I don't know about a formal succession plan, but I'd guess it would be Morena."

"Any other possible candidates?" Eli asked.

"Maybe, but Morena would be the most obvious choice."

"What about yourself?"

Stacey looked at Eli. "I'm still a college student, so that's probably unlikely."

"Would you have any issue with Morena being CEO?"

Stacey looked out into the crowd. "No. Morena and I are close. She's been a mentor to me. My problem is solely with Layton and how he treats people, especially women."

"Your Honor, I'm done with this witness, but I'd like to ask for a brief recess."

"I imagine you would," Judge Beck said. "How brief is brief?'

"Thirty minutes?"

"Very well. We're adjourned and will return in half an hour. Ms. Malone, you may step down."

———

THE THIRTY-MINUTE RECESS turned into a request from Eli for a continuance until the next day. Olivia sat in her house with Grant and Nina Marie. When her cell rang and she saw who was calling, she wasn't surprised.

"Hello, Eli."

"Olivia, I'm putting an offer on the table, but it expires at midnight. Understood?"

"Yes, what is it?"

"One million dollars," Eli said.

"One million dollars," she repeated for Grant and Nina Marie's benefit.

"It's a great deal. If I don't hear from you by midnight, it's off the table. I'll await your call."

He ended the call without allowing her to respond. She turned to them. "Well, you heard the offer. It's only good until midnight."

"You have to take it," Grant said to Nina Marie.

"I think he's right," Olivia said. "I don't know that we'll inflict any more damage than we did today. We got our main points out about Layton's abuse, even if it was through Stacey's betrayal. I don't want to overplay things here."

Nina Marie nodded. "Yes, we'd talked earlier about justice versus revenge, and I don't want to be vengeful. I say we take the offer and hope that this whole thing weakens Layton's position in the community."

"We have time if you want to think about it more."

Nina Marie shook her head. "No. Abe should be here any minute to pick me up. This is the right thing to do."

"I'll make him sweat for a few and then call him back."

Nina Marie stood up. "Thank you, Olivia. For everything."

Olivia gave her a tight hug. "You're welcome."

Olivia waited half an hour before making the call. The settlement offer was accepted, and Eli said he'd have her a draft document in the morning to review—one of his associates was already working on it. Olivia could only pray that Layton wouldn't go after Stacey for her betrayal.

———

"I'M NOT HAVING a lot of luck so far," Stacey said as she looked at Eliza. Stacey sat numbly on her couch trying to figure out how this had gone sideways. "I can't believe people would want to stick by him after all of this." A sinking feeling grew in Stacey's stomach.

Had she severely miscalculated? Were these women so blindly loyal to such a dog of a man?

She'd fully expected loyalty out of Morena and Louise, but she was putting on the hard sell, working the phones, and the reactions she'd gotten so far hadn't been great. Layton and Morena had been even faster on the move trying to shore up support. They'd labeled her a traitor for helping Olivia—the chief rival of Optimism. She didn't care about Olivia. She cared about running Optimism's spiritual group.

"I'm not giving up on this fight yet," Stacey told Eliza.

"Well, I already told you that you're welcome in our coven. I know it's not what you're accustomed to, but I can guarantee that no one is going to hurt you in our group." Eliza gripped onto Stacey's hand.

Stacey thought she had gamed out all the scenarios, but now she was starting to doubt herself. There had to be a way to get the result she wanted. "I need you to start making calls."

"Me?" Eliza asked.

"Yes. The only way this is going to work is if I have reinforcements, meaning you. We have to explain to them why there's a better way."

A knock on Stacey's door caused her to jump.

"Let me see who it is," Eliza said.

Stacey feared it wasn't going to be anyone she wanted to see.

Eliza walked over to the door. "It's Morena. Should I let her in?"

"Yes," Stacey said. She hoped she was right in her gut instinct that Morena wouldn't actually do her harm.

Morena walked in and made a beeline for her. When Stacey stood up, Morena slapped her hard across the cheek.

"What were you thinking?" Morena asked. "After all Layton has done for you! You are an ungrateful, spoiled brat who thinks she can replace a man with more power in one finger than you have in your entire body."

"Are you done yet?" Stacey asked.

"No. You've made a complete mess of things." Morena's face reddened in anger.

"Then why are you here?"

"Because you have to fix it. You need to recant those statements and do it in front of the entire membership. Say that Olivia unduly influenced you to lie."

"You and I both know every single thing I said about Layton was true. I don't even know how you can still defend him. You were ticked off after that last domestic violence claim. I saw it in your eyes."

"Yes, I was, but he's still family. We are on the same team, and our mission is so much bigger than any of this. We are at war, Stacey. War. This town is a spiritual battleground, and you gave a big win to the other team. Do you even realize that? I'm beginning to think that you convinced yourself this was just a power move for you without realizing the huge implications this has for our work."

Stacey let Morena go on and on. There was no point in trying to silence her when she was this wound up, but Stacey had one more thing to get out. "I agree that it's about more than us, but why not take Layton out and then you'll be in charge of the company? I can work on the spiritual side, and you can run the business. We'll work together, but you'll ultimately be in charge of the company. Don't you see this is a huge opportunity for you? We don't need him. You're stronger than he is." Stacey didn't believe that, but she had to make this play right now. It was the best one she had.

"Do you really think that?" Morena raised an eyebrow.

"Yes. This is your time, Morena. Embrace it. I opened up a huge door for you. The least you could do is support me and get the other members off my back." The more she kept talking the more she understood that Morena hadn't thought this was a real possibility.

"Layton would kill us both," Morena hissed.

"No, he wouldn't. Look at the two of us. We have real power.

Imagine what you could do as the leader of the company. I know you've been loyal to Layton for years, but his recent actions have been reckless and negligent. You'd be doing the best thing for all members."

Morena bit her bottom lip.

"For what it's worth," Eliza said, "I agree with Stacey. You're a strong woman, Morena. I know that we haven't seen eye to eye, but from my group's perspective, we'd much rather have you in charge of the company than Layton, and Stacey would bring a breath of fresh air to the spiritual component of Optimism's work. Layton's violent tactics against women are totally unacceptable."

Morena lifted up her hand. "Even if I were theoretically to consider this, how in the world do you plan on actually implementing this idea?"

If she'd gotten this far, Stacey was confident she could get her all the way. Emboldened, she pushed forward. "We would start making phone calls. I know you've already been talking to people. You would say that you had a knee-jerk reaction, but now that you've had some time to think through all the facts, you believe it's best for Layton to go and you to replace him."

"And if people reject me?" Morena asked.

"They won't." Stacey was confident of that. "I think everyone is tired of Layton's games. They're afraid of the fallout. If we're all united, then there's nothing he can do. Get Louise on board and that will help too."

Morena shook her head. "I can't even believe I'm considering this."

"You know in your gut it's the best move for Optimism. Don't let Layton's grip on you cloud your vision here. You need to step up, Morena. It's your time." Stacey was laying it on thick. Morena would only reign a short while if Stacey had anything to say about it, but it was just the solution she needed right now. And Stacey planned to make it happen.

———

OLIVIA AND GRANT had finished dinner and went into his living room.

"You said you wanted to talk," Olivia said. She hoped that meant this was going to be a good conversation, but she was also fearful that he could backtrack on the progress they had made.

"I've been doing a lot of thinking."

Uh oh. She wasn't sure where this was headed. "And?" She held her breath waiting for the response.

"I love you, Olivia."

"And you know I love you too, Grant." She hesitated, wondering where the *but* was going to come in. "But?"

"There is no *but* this time. If you're willing to be patient with me as I continue to work through some things, then I want us to be back together officially."

Olivia sighed. "You know that's what I want."

"You've already been tolerant of my antics and mood swings. You've shown me what real love is, Olivia. I've never had anything like this before. Never had someone love me so completely and freely. Always putting yourself second. I can only strive to be a better man with you in my life."

Tears started flowing freely down her face. "I know it's not easy being here in Windy Ridge. Living this life fighting not only battles in the courtroom but battles for the hearts and minds of people in this town. But I truly believe God has called us both for that purpose."

Grant took her hand. "I can't promise life with me will be easy, but I can promise that I will love you the best way I know how."

She thought the conversation had taken quite a serious turn. "Grant, I don't want to push you on any grand declarations tonight. I want us to be together, and if we decide to take the next step, we'll know when it's right." She didn't want him to feel pressured.

Grant nodded. "I know now's not the right time for any of that. I have to show you that I am the man who will be there for you, and lately, that hasn't been what's happened. If you give me a chance, though, I'll show you I am willing to fight for you. For me. For us. For what we have together."

Her heart melted, and she leaned into him. "That's the best news I've heard in a long time."

Grant gently lifted her chin and their eyes locked. When his lips met hers, she knew this was the man she'd be spending the rest of her life with. And she was willing to wait as long as it took to make that happen.

———

LAYTON SAT AT HOME, still seething from what apparently was an attempt at a hostile takeover. Everyone he thought he could trust was turning against him—and the biggest traitor of them all was Morena.

In a sick way, he almost respected Stacey's power grab. She'd learned from the best watching him at work. So as mad as he was at her for blowing this whole thing up, at least he understood her motives and appreciated her desire for power. He'd almost been too good of a teacher, and he let his pupil get out of control.

Morena, on the other hand, was a completely disloyal woman whom Stacey had hoodwinked into thinking that she could run Optimism. *His* business.

Layton knew Stacey's ultimate plan was her taking charge, and Morena could be easily dealt with when the time was right. But now he had to figure out what to do about all of this.

He'd consorted with the darkness and was calling upon that power to help them. Yes, they all had those powers, but he had more. The years he had spent in service to the evil one had to pay off right now. That was the bet he was making.

He'd invited Morena over tonight and had promised her that he wanted to see if they could talk things through. But Layton wasn't going to let her take over Optimism. Not the company he had built and fought to make something of for a chunk of his life.

Morena arrived a bit later, and he welcomed her into his house.

"Thanks for coming over. I thought it best that the two of us have a chat given all that is going on."

She hesitated for a moment before following him inside. "I told you on the phone that I was willing to talk. So here I am."

"Coffee, wine, anything to drink?" Layton asked. "I'm having scotch myself."

"Count me in."

He poured them both a drink, and they sat down in his den—her on the couch and him in his favorite ivory armchair. He took a sip and then started talking. "You and I go way back, Morena. You've been there through thick and thin. Why now? Why would you turn on me after all we've been through? I thought of you like my sister."

Morena took a sip and placed the drink down in front of her. "I'm listening to what members are telling me, Layton. Everyone is concerned with your antics of late. I'm doing what I think is best for our business and our group—for spreading our beliefs in this community."

Layton didn't believe that for a minute. "Morena, this is a power grab. Pure and simple."

She shook her head. "No. It's not. If you took a vote today of our members, I would win overwhelmingly to run the company, and Stacey would have a majority on the spiritual side."

"And that's your first mistake, my dear. Optimism is *not* a democracy. It never has been. It can't function as one. The minute you start letting the people rule, you lose your grasp on power and the structure crumbles. The reason I rule with an iron fist is because it is absolutely necessary."

"I believe there's another way," Morena said. "This is checkmate for you, Layton. Just accept it. You overplayed your hand this time, and it's going to cost you."

"No, it's not. If you took over, you would fail, and I can't sit by and watch the two of you destroy everything I've built."

She threw up her hands. "What are you going to do about it? Stab me like you did Nina Marie?"

Layton had wanted to look Morena in the eyes to evaluate where her head was at. It was evident to him she would never be on his side again. She'd tasted a bit of power, and it had completely gone to her head. Now it was time to tell her what was really going on. "Morena, you're the one who has overplayed your hand. Now you have two options."

Morena laughed. "Okay, I'll play along."

"One, you leave town and never come back." He paused.

"Yeah, not happening. What's the second option?"

"You die from the poison you just ingested."

She looked down at the drink. "But you drank it too," her voice cracked.

"The poison was in your glass. I have an antidote that I'm more than willing to give you." He looked down at his watch. "But you have less than three minutes to make that call."

"Layton, I don't want to die!" Morena cried.

"Then agree to leave." He was giving her an out.

"You're a beast." She started to choke and her face turned pale.

"Yes, you should be feeling the effects right about now." He pulled the syringe out of his jacket pocket. "It's your call, Morena."

Her blue eyes locked onto his. "You would really kill me? After all we've been through together? All I've done for you?"

She was overstating her importance to him, but he let that go. "I'm giving you a way out. It's yours to take, but if you don't, then yes, I'm willing to do what I need to do."

"How would you explain my death?" she croaked.

"Do you want to sit around and try to figure that out? The clock is ticking." In a way, he hoped she would refuse and just die because he was losing his patience with her antics, but that would be much harder for him to clean up.

"Okay, okay," she whispered. "Give me the injection. I'll leave town. I don't care."

Layton walked over to her and squatted down. "I have to give it to you in the thigh." He plunged the syringe into her leg, taking pleasure in her pain.

After a minute, she looked much better, the color starting to return to her cheeks. She took a few deep breaths.

He looked her in the eyes. "Consider this a warning. If you go back on your word, I will kill you. I want you out of town tomorrow."

Morena nodded. She grabbed her purse and, still shaking, stood up from the couch.

Layton rose and walked back over to his chair. He lifted his drink to his lips and turned, ready to escort Morena out of his house and his life once and for all. Her actions showed why he had to rule with an iron fist. That was the only way to keep his hold on power. He took a big drink of whiskey.

When he faced her, he saw the revolver in her slim, trembling hand. He dropped his glass. It shattered loudly as it hit the floor. He lifted his hands in the air. "Morena, what are you doing?"

"You left me no choice."

Before he could make a move, she fired off a shot that hit him in the gut. A searing pain went through his body before his world turned black.

CHAPTER TWENTY

"I shot him." A wild-eyed Morena paced around Stacey's apartment. "He had just tried to kill me, but then I saw him on the ground and bleeding, and I panicked. I couldn't do it. I couldn't watch him die. I had to get him help."

"You called 911? Have you lost your mind?" Stacey looked at Morena and wondered how this woman could be so stupid. What a weakling she had turned out to be. Stacey would've never made that same mistake.

"I said it was self-defense to the operator. Then I bolted, but I think he'll make it. I called really quickly."

Stacey thought about how to respond. "A claim of self-defense might work from a purely legal perspective of getting you off the hook, but you went after him and didn't finish the job. He will come after you now."

Morena's hands shook and her face paled. "I want out. I'm leaving. Leaving this place. Going somewhere no one will ever find me. None of this is worth it."

Stacey couldn't believe her turn of fortune. Morena's idiocy could be just what Stacey needed. "If you flee, though, it will make you look guilty."

"I don't care. I'll get out of the country if I have to." Morena stopped pacing for a second. "Can you cover for me? If the police come to you, say that you haven't seen me."

"Absolutely. That's the least I could do." Stacey held back a smile.

Morena walked over and gave her a big hug. "I wish you all the best, Stace. I hate that things have ended this way. Maybe one day we'll see each other again, but don't plan on it anytime soon."

"I understand." And she did appreciate what Morena had done for her, but she had far outgrown what Morena could offer.

Morena grabbed her bag and rushed out the door. Immediately, Stacey grabbed her cell and called Eliza. "Layton's been shot."

"What?" Eliza asked. "Is he dead?"

"No. From what I hear he might make it. The less you know the better, but it wasn't me. I need you now though. We have the opportunity I've been waiting for. How quickly can you gather your coven?"

"Pretty quickly. We have an emergency signal."

"As does Optimism. It's time that we do this thing, Eliza. Are you with me?"

Eliza paused. "Yes. I'm in. I'll text you a meeting place."

Stacey hung up and knew what her next move had to be. She needed all the power she could harness to make this happen, and there was only one source to go to. The Prince of Darkness would provide everything she needed. There was no turning back.

———

BEN AND MICAH hovered over Stacey's apartment and watched as a flood of demons descended on the place. "This is worse than we expected," Ben said. "We haven't seen this level of demonic activity since last year."

Micah nodded. "We thought Layton was the strongest adversary yet, but Stacey is young and power hungry. She's shown that she will go to any length to reach her goal."

"Layton's still alive, though. His will to live is strong, and the doctors got to him in time. Do you really think he's going to let her be? Let her take over his kingdom?" Ben asked.

Micah shook his head. "No. But I don't want us to get into the middle of their power struggle if we can avoid it. Olivia and Grant have already been through so much. Whoever is the leader of Optimism, we'll have to deal with them, but it's not our job to determine that. All we can do is pray."

Othan flew over to where they were, his brilliant blue eyes shining in the night. "You two have no idea what you're in for. New blood, a new fight, a new day is about to dawn in Windy Ridge. And our first order of business is Olivia Murray." Othan laughed. "And you two fools are here. Wrong place, wrong time. If I were you, I'd be more concerned about being at Olivia's house tonight. Not Stacey's."

The warning rang true to Micah and Ben as they exchanged uneasy glances and immediately flew off to Olivia's house. They could only pray that they weren't too late.

————

A LOUD BOOM of thunder startled Olivia as she sat lounging on the couch with Grant watching a movie. Her light mood turned darker as a cool breeze blew through the living room. The lights started to flicker.

"Grant?"

He looked at her. "Yeah."

"Do you feel that?"

He nodded. "Yeah. Something isn't right."

Thunder shook the room again, this time even stronger. "Grant, this isn't just a bad thunderstorm."

Grant squeezed her hand. "I know." The lights flickered again and then went out. They were surrounded by darkness. "We need to pray."

Grant gripped tightly onto her hand and started to pray. She didn't understand why this was happening now, but they were under attack. An attack that had been completely unprovoked. A nice, relaxing evening and respite from everything had now become something sinister.

The room turned from cool to unbearably hot as beads of sweat formed on her brow. She moved even closer to Grant. "The Lord is my light and my salvation; whom shall I fear? The Lord is the strength of my life; of whom shall I be afraid?" Olivia started praying aloud using scripture because the Word of the Lord was their greatest weapon.

"Olivia, are you still all right?" Grant asked.

"Yes."

"Let's keep praying." Grant then took the lead in prayer.

As he started praying, tears rolled down her cheeks. This man who had his doubts was in this moment stepping up and stepping out in faith. *Thank you, Jesus, for answering my prayers. For your faithfulness in times of doubt.*

The rain pounded down, and the thunder boomed again loudly. She opened her eyes and gasped at the bright, fiery yellow eyes that were staring at her. They hovered in the darkness, but there was no mistaking the fact that they were locked onto her.

Grant opened his eyes too when he heard her reaction.

"Do you see that?" Olivia asked him.

"No. I don't see anything. Just the darkness. Complete darkness. It shouldn't be that dark in here."

But it wasn't only the darkness she saw. The yellow eyes were still there. She'd experienced these forces of evil before. Most of the times the demons were invisible, but they would show themselves in different forms when it helped their cause. They were trying to scare her. Trying to shake her. Trying to make her question everything she believed in and held dear.

Doubts started to bombard her. Awful thoughts about Grant, her life, her work. Her inadequacies. Her lack of faith. Her fears. Loneliness.

"Olivia?" Grant asked.

She couldn't respond, feeling paralyzed by fear and doubt. The yellow eyes moved closer and bore down on her.

The cackles of loud laughter sounded in her ears. The whispers of accusation hit against her. The pain brewed inside of her. It was all too much.

Yes, she'd faced spiritual attack before, but this one was so acute and focused. They were coming after her directly and doing it in the most hurtful way by targeting all her fears and insecurities. "Lord, please help me," she cried out.

Grant jumped up from the couch. She tried to call out after him, but no words came out of her mouth.

Why was he leaving her? Where would he go? Would he really abandon her now?

She heard lots of commotion but wasn't sure what was happening in her house.

"See," a deep voice said in her ear. "We told you that he'd leave you." She could feel the demon's warm breath on her cheek. "Now you're all alone. It's just us. Grant will always leave you. He won't stick by you. You'll be alone."

"No," she whispered.

But the accusations and threats still came at her. Her head pounded as if it were being squeezed from each side.

"You're alone, Olivia," the accusatory voice said.

Stop it. She couldn't speak. Couldn't make the voices stop.

"Olivia, look at me!" Grant grabbed onto her shoulders.

She opened up her eyes.

Grant sat beside her with her Bible in his hands. Using the flashlight on his cell phone, he flipped it open and started reading. "Put on the whole armour of God, that ye may be able to stand against the wiles of the devil. For we wrestle not against flesh and blood, but against principalities, against powers, against the rulers of the darkness of this world, against spiritual wickedness in high places. Wherefore take unto you the whole armour of God, that ye may be able to withstand in the evil day, and having done all, to stand."

As Grant spoke the words, Olivia watched the yellow eyes start to flicker as their strength was no match for the truth.

But the pain was still there. The fiery darts of the evil one were being hurled at her. *Jesus, help me.* "Submit yourselves therefore to God. Resist the devil, and he will flee from you." She repeated the verse a second time.

A great flash of light spread throughout the room. Not from the lightning but from the angelic beings bringing the power of the Lord with them.

"Now *that* I see!" Grant looked up in amazement.

The yellow eyes blinked and flickered and then faded away. The pain in her head stopped.

The room was illuminated with such a brilliant light she had to shield her eyes. The power of the Lord surrounded them, and she was no longer afraid.

"Thank you, Jesus," she said.

The two of them sat in awe and praised God for what He had done for them, but after a moment, the bright light was extinguished.

The electricity came back on, and the TV flickered back to life.

Grant wrapped his arms around her. "Olivia, are you all right? Are you hurt?"

She took a deep breath, trying to steady herself and stop shaking. "I'm okay." As the words came out, she still wasn't certain, but she didn't want to alarm him any further.

"That was a direct spiritual attack," Grant said flatly.

"Did you see anything?" she asked.

"Yes." Grant took a deep breath. "I saw two angels. Larger than life and so bright. I can't even put into words how majestic and mighty they were, but before that, the room was pitch black except for the light I had on my phone. I think I knocked over some stuff trying to get to your Bible. I couldn't see anything."

Wow. The enormity of everything was starting to hit her. "I

didn't see the angels, just a bright light. Before that I saw awful demonic eyes. They were taunting me. I couldn't stop them."

Grant frowned. "They were targeting you specifically, Olivia."

"But thank God you were here to help pray with me. For a minute, I couldn't do anything. The pain and the thoughts running through my head were indescribable."

"I believe you. I'm so sorry you had to experience that." He paused. "Why do you think I saw the angels?"

She thought for a moment. "After all you've been through, Grant, you demonstrated great faith and courage here tonight. Maybe that's why."

"I didn't know what to do, so the first thing that came to me was getting your Bible. I don't have as many verses committed to memory as you do. It's one thing I know I need to work on."

She squeezed his hand. "You did great. We put our faith in God and He sustained us. We can't fight this battle ourselves."

Grant wrapped his arm tightly around her, and they sat in silence for a few minutes.

When her cell started to ring, she saw it was Pastor Dan calling. "It's late. Something else must've happened." She picked up. "Hey. I've got you on speaker. Grant's with me."

"Olivia, Grant, have you heard?" Dan asked.

"No, what is it?" Olivia asked.

"Layton was shot tonight. He's in ICU. It's touch and go."

"Who shot him?" she asked.

"I don't know. One of the church members who works at the hospital heard about it and called me."

"I'm not sure what emotion I should be feeling right now, but I guess the right thing to do is pray for him, although I'll be honest, it's hard to do." She paused. "Also, tonight something happened at my house. A spiritual attack. It ended a few minutes before you called."

"Maybe Layton's attack set off the demonic forces and they came after you," Pastor Dan said.

"I'm not sure, but it's over now." Olivia looked over at Grant.

"If I hear anything, I'll let you know. If Layton doesn't make it, who knows what will happen to Optimism. I know Morena and Stacey made a power play."

"Stacey is proving to be a bit of an upstart," Grant said.

"Yeah," Dan said. "We all realize that now. After what she did to Layton at trial, she's willing to play hardball. I have to believe that the police will be questioning her given how that all unfolded."

"You don't think she would actually try to kill Layton, do you?" Olivia asked.

Dan sighed. "Honestly, I don't know anymore. She's no longer the young woman I knew."

Olivia's heart broke at that statement. "Thanks for calling."

They ended the call and Olivia looked over at Grant. "Do you think Stacey did it?"

Grant shrugged. "I don't know. Seems a bit against her strategy given she was already mounting a coup. I guess the police will figure it out."

"And we'll have to deal with the fallout from Optimism." She wouldn't back down. "The forces of darkness aren't going to let go of this town. We have to keep on fighting."

"And we will."

"Thank you again for everything you did tonight. You were there when I really needed you."

"Olivia, that's what I want more than anything in the world. To be the man you need me to be. I hope I can gain your trust back after what happened."

She looked into his blue eyes. "I love you, Grant. We're going to go through hard times if we stay together, and I believe we can face anything together."

"And I promise I'm not going to shut you out like that again. We are better together as a team." Grant placed his hand under her chin.

She leaned into him as he kissed her. They would live to fight another day. And tomorrow they'd be fighting this battle together.

DEAR READER

Do you want to read more books in the Windy Ridge series? If so, I'd love to hear from you. Please email me at racheldylanauthor@gmail.com or contact me at www.racheldylan.com. I'd love to hear from you!

WINDY RIDGE LEGAL THRILLER SERIES

Excerpt from Trial & Tribulations: A Windy Ridge Legal Thriller Book 1

When managing partner Chet Carter called, you answered—and you answered promptly. Just yesterday Olivia Murray had been summoned to Chet's corner office and told to pack her bags for a new case that would take her from Washington, DC to the Windy Ridge suburb of Chicago.

But this wasn't just any case. She would be defending a New Age tech company called Astral Tech in a lawsuit filed by its biggest competitor.

As she stepped out of her red Jeep rental, the summer breeze blew gently against her face. She stared up at the mid sized office building with a prominent sparkling blue moon on the outside, and she had to admit she was a bit intimidated. It wasn't the litigation aspect that bothered her, though. It was the subject matter.

She threw her laptop bag over her shoulder, adjusted her black suit jacket, and walked toward the door. Ready for anything. Or at least she hoped she was.

The strong smell of incense hit her as her first heeled foot stepped through the door. She thought it was a bit cliché for a New Age company to be burning incense in the reception area, but maybe it was to be expected. It reinforced her thoughts that this was all a money making operation—not a group of actual believers in this stuff.

The perky young blonde behind the minimalist glass desk looked up at her. "How can I help you?"

"Hi, I'm Olivia Murray from the law firm of Brown, Carter, and Reed."

The young woman's brown eyes widened. "Oh, yes, Ms. Murray. I'm Melanie." She stood and shook Olivia's hand. "Let me know if you need anything while you're here. The team is expecting you. I'll take you to the main conference room now."

"Thank you." Everything was already proceeding as normal. She couldn't let this whole New Age thing mess with her head. And besides that, she had her faith to get her through this.

Melanie led her down the hall to a conference room and knocked loudly before opening the large door. "Ms. Murray, please go on in."

Olivia didn't really know what she expected, but what she saw was a table full of suits arguing. She let out a breath. Regular litigation. Just like she had thought.

A man stood up from the table. "You must be our lawyer from BCR?" He wore an impeccably tailored navy suit with a red tie. He had short dark hair with a little gray at the temples and piercing green eyes.

"Yes, I'm Olivia Murray."

"Great. This is the Astral Tech leadership team. Don't let our yelling worry you. That's how we best communicate." He laughed. "I'm Clive Township, the CEO of Astral Tech, and this is my trusted inner circle."

A striking woman rose and offered her hand. "I'm Nina Marie Crane, our Chief Operating Officer."

"Wonderful to meet you," Olivia said.

Clive nodded toward a tall thin man with black hair who stood and shook her hand. "And this is our financial voice of reason, Matt Tinley."

"I serve as our Chief Financial Officer," Matt said.

Everyone greeted her warmly, but she felt an undercurrent of tension in the room. It was now her job as their attorney to get this litigation under control and that also meant getting them under control. Half the battle of litigation was controlling your own client before you could even begin to take on the adversary.

"Have a seat and we'll get you up to speed," Clive said.

She sat down in a comfortable dark blue chair at the oblong oak table and pulled out her laptop to take any relevant notes. She opened up her computer, but mainly she wanted to get the lay of the land.

"So the more I can learn about your company and the complaint that Optimism has filed against you the better. One of the first things I'll have to work on is the document collection and fact discovery effort. To be able to do that, I need the necessary background. I'll be happy to go over the discovery process with you, too, at some point so we're all on the same page."

"Where do you want to start?" Nina Marie asked.

"It would be helpful if you gave me a more detailed explanation of your company. I did my own research, but I'd love to hear it from you. Then we can move onto the legal claims brought against you by Optimism."

"Nina Marie is the driving force behind Astral Tech. So I'll let her explain our business," Clive said. "I'm more of the big picture guy and Matt is our number cruncher."

"Sounds good," Olivia said.

Nina Marie smiled. The thin auburn haired woman wore tortoiseshell glasses. Her hair was swept up into a loose bun, and she wore a black blazer with a rose colored blouse. "Astral Tech was my baby, but Clive has the financial backing and business acumen to make it happen."

"I'd like to hear all about it," Olivia said.

"We're a company specializing in bringing New Age theories and ideas into the tech space. We felt like we filled a void in that area. Yes, New Age has been quite popular for years now, but no company has really brought New Age into the current technology arena and made it work for the next generation. Through the Astral Tech app and other electronic means, we're making New Age relevant again. Our target audience is youth and young professionals. We don't even try to reach the baby boomers and beyond because it's a losing battle. They're too traditional, and they're not as tech savvy. We have to target our energy on the demographic that makes the most sense for our product."

"Excuse my ignorance, but you use New Age as a blanket term. I need a bit of education on what exactly you mean in the context of your business."

Nina Marie clasped her hands together in front of her. "Of course. I think a woman like you is in our key demographic. I would love to hear your thoughts on all of this. But to answer your question, New Age is a lot more than incense and meditation, although that is definitely a part of it. New Age is a way of life. A way of spiritually connecting. We care about the whole body—the environment, mysticism, spirituality. And we do that in an innovative way through the Astral Tech app that starts you on your path of self exploration from day one. You have to download it and try it for yourself. It will definitely help you understand our issues in the litigation better."

"Yes, the litigation. I read the complaint on the plane. Optimism's central claim is that Astral Tech actually stole the app from them."

Clive jumped in and leaned forward resting his arms on the table. "It's a totally bogus lawsuit. That's why we're hiring a firm like yours to nip this in the bud. We don't want any copycat litigation. This app was developed totally in house by Astral Tech employees. To say that there is any theft is absolutely false. We certainly didn't steal it. It's just a trumped up charge."

"What about the other claim regarding defamation?"

Clive nodded. "The defamation claim is actually a bit more concerning to me because it's subjective. We won't have a technical expert that can testify about that like we have on the actual theft claim."

She sat up in her seat. "What was said by Astral Tech that they are claiming is defamatory?"

"A few off handed comments about Optimism and their lack of integrity. They claim they're part of the New Age movement, but some of their actions indicate otherwise."

"Could you be more specific?"

"I can elaborate," Nina Marie said. "Optimism isn't really centered on New Age techniques in the same way we are. Their original founder, Earl Ward, was a connoisseur of many New Age techniques, but when he passed away Optimism's purpose shifted a bit under Layton Alito's rule, solidifying their allegiance to the dark arts. Layton is a ruthless leader who doesn't tolerate any type of dissent amongst his ranks."

Olivia felt her eyes widen, but she tried to hide her surprise. "Are you serious?"

"Yes, very," Nina Marie said.

"And Astral Tech isn't like that?" She couldn't help herself. She had to ask. It was better to know.

"We're a big tent. We don't want to alienate anyone who is seeking a spiritual journey," Clive said.

Well, that wasn't exactly a denial. What had she stepped into here? "And why New Age?"

Clive smiled. "Think about this as a lawyer. A businessperson. The world is becoming more and more open minded about spirituality. Which is obviously a good thing. Let everyone do what they want. We're moving away from strict codes of morality to something that fits with the modern person in this country. It's in. It's now. That's why we do it. We're using principles that have been popular for the past few decades and bringing them into the tech arena."

"For some of us, it's more than just about what makes money and make sense," Nina Marie said. "I'm proud to say that I'm a believer. A strong spiritual being. Those things have value. What we're doing matters. We have the ability to revolutionize the way people think about New Age principles."

Olivia could feel Nina Marie's dark eyes on her trying to evaluate whether she was truly friend or foe. A strange uneasiness settled over her. There was more to all of this than Nina Marie was saying. This was much larger than a lawsuit. Spiritual forces were at work here.

Focusing on the task at hand, she stared at her laptop and the page of notes she'd typed while hearing her clients talk. "I'll need to make sure you have a proper litigation hold in place to collect all relevant documents. I'll also want to talk to your IT person on staff right away about preserving all documents. The last thing we want to do is play cute and get sanctioned by the court. If Astral Tech has nothing to hide, then there's no reason to be evasive."

"But that's the thing," Matt said. "We believe we haven't broken any laws, but we also believe in our privacy and that of our customers."

Olivia nodded. "We should be able to petition the court for a protective order for any sensitive information that is turned over in the litigation, including customer lists. That's something we can handle."

Nina Marie stood up from her chair. "Let me take you to the office space we have set up for you while you're working here on this case."

"Thank you." While she was eager to get to work, she wasn't so excited about being alone with Nina Marie. But she followed the woman out of the conference room and down the hall, reminding herself that Nina Marie was still the client.

Nina Marie stopped abruptly about half way down the corridor.

"I know this will sound a bit strange, but I'm getting a really interesting vibe from you."

"Vibe?"

"Yes. Do you have any interest in learning more about New Age spirituality? Anything like that?"

"No. That's not really my thing." She held back her direct answer which would've been totally unprofessional. She didn't feel comfortable in this environment, but she was also torn between her job and her faith. Could she really do both? Would defending a company like Astral Tech really be possible?

Conflicted feelings shot through her. No, she didn't believe in aliens or monsters, but she definitely believed in good and evil. Angels and demons. And this entire situation seemed like a recipe for disaster.

"I'm not giving up on you." Nina Marie reached out and patted her shoulder.

Nina Marie was quite a few inches taller than her, but that wasn't saying much considering she was only five foot three in heels.

"Once you learn more about our product offerings, I think you'll be excited to hear more about what we can do for a strong and smart professional woman like you."

"I appreciate your interest, Nina Marie, but my chief concern and responsibility is the lawsuit. So I think it'd be best if we could concentrate on that."

Nina Marie quirked an eyebrow but didn't immediately respond. Olivia followed her into another conference room, but this one was set up with multiple computer workstations around the large table. The rest of the décor matched the previous room they were in.

"This will be the legal work room for you. You should have plenty of space for everything you need in here."

"This is a great workspace." She looked around the room and was pleased by the size and technical accommodations. "I'm sure I'm going to run into a lot of factual questions as we start preparing for this first phase of litigation. Who is the person at Astral Tech I should go to with questions?"

"That would be me for pretty much anything that is detail oriented about the company or the app. Clive is good on the general business and philosophy but not so much on details. He's also not in the office everyday like I am. Matt can also serve as a resource both on the financial aspects and the spiritual ones."

"Got it." She'd never worked on such a strange case in her seven plus years of practicing law. Thankfully, she was steadfast in her beliefs. She just hoped that nothing in this litigation would require her to do things that went against her faith. Because she'd have to draw that line somewhere. And if it was a choice between her career or her faith, she'd always choose her faith.

———

Grant Baxter reviewed the document requests he had drafted one last time. He enjoyed being on the plaintiff's side of the table— even if it was for an odd client. Some wacky New Age group had retained his small but reputable law firm to sue Astral Tech—an equally wacky company in his opinion.

He didn't have any time for religion whether it be traditional or New Age or whatever. To him it was all just a convenient fiction made up to help people deal with their fears and insecurities. But if this case would help his firm take the next steps to success and keep paying the bills, then he was all for it.

He'd built his law firm, The Baxter Group, from the ground up —something he was very proud of, given all his long hours and sacrifices. Not a thing in his life had been given to him. He'd earned it all the hard way.

He couldn't help but chuckle as he read over the document requests that he had prepared. All the talk of witches and spirituality and the Astral Tech app. He'd never drafted anything like that before. His law school classes and nine years of practice had equipped him with many skills, but working on a case like this was totally foreign to him.

It wasn't like there were witches in a coven out to get him. People were entirely irrational when it came to religion. Luckily for him, he wasn't one of those people. He might be the only sane person in the entire litigation, and he planned to stay that way. One thing he was certain about. A jury was going to eat this stuff up.

"Hey, boss man." Ryan Wilde stood at Grant's door.

"What's going on?" Grant asked.

"I asked around town trying to find info on Astral Tech, but most of my contacts had never heard of them, and the few that had didn't really have anything useful to say except that they're trying to become players in the tech space."

Ryan was only about two years younger than Grant. They'd both worked in a law firm together for years, and Grant was glad that Ryan had joined him at the firm. If all progressed as planned, Grant was going to add Ryan as his partner in the firm.

"If you do hear anything, just let me know."

"Anything else you need from me?"

"Not on this. How are your other cases going?"

"I'm meeting with potential clients this afternoon on a products liability class action. It would be a good case to have."

"Keep me posted."

Ryan nodded. "You got it." Ryan walked out the door and then turned around and laughed. "I have to say, I'm glad that you're working this case and not me. I don't think I'd know how to approach it."

"Just like anything else. It'll be fine."

"If you say so. I hope you don't end up with a hex put on you or something like that."

Grant laughed. "Don't even tell me that you would consider believing in any of this."

Ryan shook his head. "Nah. I'm just messing with you."

Ryan walked out and Grant was anxious to start the discovery process and put pressure on the other side. It was one of those things he loved about being a plaintiff's lawyer. He was in the driver's seat and planned to take an aggressive stance in this case to really turn the heat up on the other side. Going through these steps reminded him how glad he was that he went out and started his own firm. He truly loved his work.

His office phone rang, jerking him back to reality.

"This is Grant Baxter," he said.

"Hello. My name is Olivia Murray from the law firm of Brown, Carter, and Reed. I just wanted to call to introduce myself. We're representing Astral Tech in the suit filed by your client. So I'll be your point of contact for anything related to the case."

Well, well he thought. Astral Tech had gone and hired a high powered law firm based in Washington, DC to defend them. "Perfect timing. I was just getting ready to send out discovery requests for documents. BCR doesn't have a Chicago office, right?"

"No, but I'm actually in town. I'm working at the client's office in Windy Ridge. So you can send any hard copies of anything to the Astral Tech office, and I would appreciate getting everything by email also." She rattled off her email address.

"Of course. And I have the feeling we'll be talking a lot. This litigation is going to be fast tracked if my client has anything to say about it. We're not going to just wait around for years letting things pass us by."

She laughed. "Yes, I know how it is. I'll look forward to your email."

He hung up and leaned back in his chair. Know thy enemy, right? He immediately looked her up on the Internet finding her BCR firm profile. A brunette with big brown eyes smiled back at him. He read her bio. Impressive, double Georgetown girl. Seventh year associate at BCR where she'd spent her entire legal career. That would make her about two years younger than him—but definitely still a seasoned attorney and worthy opponent.

Astral Tech wasn't messing around. That let him know that

they took this litigation seriously. They didn't see this as a nuisance suit. Game on.

———

"Do you think Olivia's ready for this fight?" Micah asked Ben looking directly into his dark eyes.

"It doesn't matter if she's really ready, Micah. It's a battle she has to fight and the time is now. We have no one else. She's the one God has chosen who has to stand up and take this on. She has some idea that she's meant to be here. But it might take her a little time to figure out exactly what she's going to be involved with."

The angels stood behind Olivia watching over her in the conference room. But she hadn't sensed their presence as she continued to type away on her laptop and hum a tune.

"She isn't fully appreciative of how strong she is, but she'll get there," Micah said. He stood tall, his blond hair barely touching his shoulders. The angel warrior was strong but kind—and fiercely protective of Olivia.

Ben nodded. "At least she has the foundation to build upon. A strong faith that has been growing ever since she was a little girl." Ben paused. "Unlike our friend Grant."

"I'm much more worried about him. He has no idea what he's going to be facing, and he doesn't have the skills to defend himself. Nina Marie and her followers are building up strength by the day, and she'll surely want to go after him. We can only do so much to protect Olivia and Grant against the forces of evil running rampant on this earth."

"But we'll do everything we can."

Micah looked at him. "You and me—quite an angel army."

"The best kind."

"Let's pray for her now."

The two laid their hands on her shoulders to help prepare her for the fight to come. A fight unlike anything they'd ever known before.

ALSO BY RACHEL DYLAN

Atlanta Justice Series
DEADLY PROOF
LONE WITNESS
BREACH OF TRUST

READ AN EXCERPT FROM DEADLY PROOF

You can't call that a settlement offer." Kate Sullivan looked directly into the dark eyes of her opposing counsel, who represented a medical device company. Jerry had just made partner and thought he could play hardball, but she wasn't going to let him get the upper hand.

"You and I both know that amount will never cut it. Come back to me when you have a number I can work with." She closed her laptop and shoved it in her bag.

"C'mon, Kate. Fifty grand is a good starting point," Jerry said. "We're done here. Call me when you're actually ready to negotiate." She stood up and walked out of the conference room before Jerry could say anything else. He wasn't taking her client's claims seriously, so she wasn't going to waste any more time playing games. He'd come to his senses soon enough. This case shouldn't go to trial, and he knew it.

Making the quick drive from downtown to Midtown Atlanta, weaving through the usual traffic, she parked in her reserved spot in the garage under a tall office building. The large office tower was home of the world-class plaintiff's firm Warren McGee.

She spent more time at her office than she did at her own home, but that was by choice. Representing innocent victims was her calling.

When she walked out of the elevator and onto the twenty third floor, her assistant, Beth Russo, greeted her warmly.

"How did it go?" Beth asked. Her fifty-five-year-old assistant had been working at the law firm for decades and knew the ins and outs of each case and every schedule. Kate would be lost without her.

"Still no settlement, but they'll cave eventually. They don't actually want to try this case."

"I hope so, because you need to get it off your docket and give your full attention to the Mason Pharmaceutical litigation. You deserve to be running that case."

Kate laughed. "Let me get on the steering committee first, Beth. Then I'll apply for lead counsel."

"Exactly. You're due in court in three hours for the hearing on the steering committee, and you've got calls piled up."

She smiled. "Thanks, Beth. I'll work through them." Calls meant business, and business was what kept her in good standing as a partner at the firm.

In the privacy of her own office, Kate stared out the large window that gave her a fantastic view of Stone Mountain in the distance. She'd earned this corner office by working hard, but she wanted more. Her goal was to be managing partner one day, and this litigation was huge.

Thousands of cases had been filed across the country against Mason Pharmaceutical Corporation, known as MPC. She was responsible for a large chunk of them, representing victims who had taken MPC's migraine drug and had died or been injured. She needed a spot on the exclusive committee of plaintiffs' lawyers that would dictate the entire direction of the case.

Her phone rang, but she let it go, knowing Beth would answer it. She had started flipping through her emails when Beth hurried into her office with a frown pulling at her lips.

"Kate, sorry to bother you, but there's a call I think you have to take."

"Who is it?" Beth's brown eyes narrowed. "She won't give me her name, but she said she has information regarding the MPC case."

Once the litigation hit the news and the firms started advertising to find clients who had taken the dangerous drug, there was a constant stream of inquiries to be fielded. The firm couldn't turn them down without hearing the person out first.

"Why don't you have one of the associates take it?"

Beth shook her head. "She says she'll only talk to you."

Kate was listed as lead counsel on hundreds of the complaints, so it made sense that this person would want to talk to her. "Okay, put her through." She waited for her line to light up red, then picked up the phone. "This is Kate Sullivan."

"I have some critical information for you, but I can't speak over the phone," a woman said, her words rushed and breathless. "Is there a place we can meet?"

Kate needed more before she dropped everything to go on what might be a wild goose chase. "And you are?"

"I don't want to say right now." Her voice was hushed.

"You can come down to my office, and we can talk here."

"No, no. That won't work," the woman said. "It's too risky. Your office is the last place I can be seen."

"Ma'am, as you can imagine, I have a lot on my plate right now. So it would be helpful if I had some idea of what this is all about."

"I have information you're going to need," the caller whispered. "Things related to your case. Things I know because of my job."

That got Kate's attention. "Are you an employee of Mason Pharmaceutical Corporation?"

"I told you, I can't have this conversation over the phone."

Kate's heartbeat sped up at the strain in the woman's voice. "All right. There's a coffee shop in Colony Square on Peachtree and Fourteenth. Can you meet me there?"

"Yes. See you in ten minutes."

Kate hung up, and her mind went into overdrive. If this woman was truly an employee of MPC, then this meeting could be huge. MPC had corporate offices in multiple states, but the company headquarters and largest office was in Atlanta.

It was likely this woman was a disgruntled employee or that she was unstable. But something about her voice tugged at Kate. Her curiosity and desire to be thorough led her to take the meeting.

She made the short walk from her office across the street and down a block to Colony Square, which housed restaurants and shops catering to the Midtown Atlanta community. It was lunchtime, and there were plenty of people out taking breaks in the warm Georgia sunshine. Since it was June, the humidity made the air thick and sticky, but it was better than being locked inside a stuffy office all day.

As Kate stepped into the coffee shop, she looked for someone who could potentially be her tipster. Not seeing anyone promising, she took a seat at the table in the back corner and waited.

After a few minutes, a woman who was probably in her mid-forties took the seat across from her. She had brown hair cut in a no-nonsense bob and wore simple wire-frame glasses that only partially obscured her bloodshot eyes.

"You're Kate Sullivan?" the woman asked in a low voice. Then she turned and looked over her shoulder. Nervous—and paranoid.

"Yes. And you are?"

"Ellie Proctor."

"Nice to meet you, Ellie. Why don't you explain to me what this is all about."

"I'm scared," Ellie said as she clenched her pale hands together in front of her.

"There's nothing to be afraid of. You're safe with me."

"No, you don't understand."

Was this lady a conspiracy theorist? Kate had no idea what she was dealing with. "Just take it one step at a time. Do you work for MPC?"

"Yes."

"And what is your job there?" Kate felt like she was conducting a deposition, trying to get information out of a witness.

"I'm one of the senior R&D scientists." Ellie shivered, but the coffee shop's air conditioning was barely functioning.

Kate pressed on. "What do you work on?"

"A variety of testing and product development for different drugs."

"And you think you know something about Celix? The drug involved in my cases." Ellie nodded. "Yeah. I did my research. I went onto the law firm websites and read all the information about the litigation."

"And what do you think?"

"It's so much bigger than what you and the other lawyers around the country are saying about Celix."

Now Ellie had Kate's undivided attention. "How so?" Celix caused brain tumors, so she wasn't sure how much bigger this could get.

Ellie looked down. Her brown eyes not making contact.

"Listen, Ellie, I can't help you if I don't know what the facts are." She needed to be patient. This woman seemed like she might go off the ledge at any minute.

"You need to dig deeper." Ellie wrapped her arms tightly around herself as she shook. "A lot deeper, but you have to be careful."

"The case is just starting, but I'm always very thorough."

As Ellie's eyes darted back and forth, Kate began to wonder if

Ellie was strung out on something. The red eyes, the shivering, the paranoia. Did this woman even work for MPC?

"The lawsuits say that MPC should have known through its testing that brain tumors were a potential side effect, but . . ."

"What?"

"I've already said too much out in the open like this, but you need to go beyond Celix. This is bigger than Celix. You have to look at other MPC drugs. Get your hands on all of the testing records for Celix and the emails about the test results. I can't provide them to you. My computer has highly restrictive security protocols. I'm hoping you'll be able to get them through your case, but I know some of the documents have already been shredded or deleted. I don't even know what's left on our servers. I think this goes up to the highest levels of the company." Ellie glanced furtively around, then leaned over the table and whispered, "I know it sounds crazy, but I'm taking a risk even coming here to meet you."

Kate looked around, and no one in the coffee shop seemed even remotely interested in what they were talking about. But even given how weird this all seemed, she couldn't just push it under the rug and walk away. "How about we set up a time and place to meet? Your choice. Somewhere you're comfortable talking openly with me, so I can gather more facts."

Ellie let out a long sigh. "Thank you. I think that's for the best. I thought I might be able to talk here, but it just doesn't feel right. Can we meet the day after tomorrow at 7:00 p.m. at the entrance of Piedmont Park?"

"Sure. I'll be there." Ellie reached across the table and gripped Kate's hand.

"Whatever you do, you can't bring my name into this. I'm coming to you because it's the right thing to do. I can't sleep at night with all of this on my conscience." She took a deep breath.

"I'll be discreet." Kate didn't want to jeopardize Ellie's livelihood, but she definitely had to get to the bottom of this.

"I have to get back to work before my lunch break ends."

"Can I get your contact information?"

"Yes. This is my business card. I'll put my personal cell on the back." Ellie took a pen out of her small navy purse and, with a wobbly hand, wrote down her number. Then she scratched through her work contact information. "Please don't ever contact me at work."

"You did the right thing by coming to me, Ellie. I'm going to figure out what's going on here."

ABOUT THE AUTHOR

Rachel Dylan writes legal thrillers and legal romantic suspense. Rachel has practiced law for over a decade including being a litigator at one of the nation's top law firms. She enjoys weaving together legal and suspenseful stories. Rachel writes the Atlanta Justice Series which features strong, female attorneys in Atlanta. *Deadly Proof*, the first book in the Atlanta Justice series, is a CBA bestseller, an FHL Reader's Choice Award winner, a Daphne du Maurier Finalist, and a Holt Medallion Finalist. Rachel lives in Michigan with her husband and five furkids—two dogs and three cats. Rachel loves to connect with readers. You can find Rachel at www.racheldylan.com.

Connect with Rachel:

www.racheldylan.com

Join Rachel's newsletter

@dylan_rachel

www.facebook.com/RachelDylanAuthor

Made in the USA
Columbia, SC
20 November 2018